ONE TOUGH CUSTOMER.

That was Rogerson, or so I was learning. He divided the world coolly into black or white, no grays or middle ground. People were either cool or assholes, situations good or bad. My friends, and my life at school, consistently fell into each of the latter. His friends were older, more interesting, and most importantly, not jocks or cheerleaders. When we did go to parties where I'd see Rina or Kelly Brandt or anyone else from the squad, it was always awkward. They'd want me to stay, pulling up a chair, handing over the quarter so I could take a bounce. But Rogerson was always impatient, finishing whatever business he had and heading straight for the door, making it clear he was ready to go.

NOVELS BY SARAH DESSEN

That Summer

Someone Like You

Keeping the Moon

Dreamland

This Lullaby

The Truth About Forever

dreamland

SARAH DESSEN

An Imprint of Penguin Group (USA) Inc.

SPEAK
Published by Penguin Group
Penguin Group (USA) Inc.,
345 Hudson Street, New York, New York 10014, U.S.A.
Penguin Books Ltd, 80 Strand, London WC2R ORL, England
Penguin Books Australia Ltd, 250 Camberwell Road, Camberwell, Victoria 3124, Australia
Penguin Books Canada Ltd, 10 Alcorn Avenue, Toronto, Ontario, Canada M4V 3B2
Penguin Books (N.Z.) Ltd, 182-190 Wairau Road, Auckland 10, New Zealand

First published in the United States of America by Viking,
a division of Penguin Putnam Books for Young Readers, 2000
Published by Puffin Books, a division of Penguin Putnam Books for Young Readers, 2002
This edition published by Speak, an imprint of Penguin Group (USA) Inc., 2004

15 16 17 18 19 20

THE LIBRARY OF CONGRESS HAS CATALOGED THE VIKING EDITION AS FOLLOWS:
Dessen, Sarah.
Dreamland: a novel / Sarah Dessen.
p. cm.
Summary: After her older sister runs away, sixteen-year-old Caitlin decides
that she needs to make a major change in her own life and begins an abusive
relationship with a boy who is mysterious, brilliant, and dangerous.
ISBN 0-670-89122-3
[1. Dating violence—Fiction. 2. Interpersonal relationships—Fiction. 3. Identity—Fiction.
4. Runaways—Fiction. 5. Sisters—Fiction.] I. Title.
PZ7.D455 Dr 2000 [Fic]—dc21 99-044102

Speak ISBN 0-14-240175-7

Printed in the United States of America

For Bianca, Atiya, Ashley, Hannah,
Gretchen, Leigh, and Charlotte,
who have always told me their stories,
and Jay,
who is still listening to mine

I am grateful to my agent, Leigh Feldman, for seeing me through; Michael and Mariangeles, for support and spirit; and my parents, Alan and Cynthia Dessen, who survived my lost years and, like me, lived to tell. Thank you.

My sister Cass ran away the morning of my sixteenth birthday. She left my present, wrapped and sitting outside my bedroom door, and stuck a note for my parents under the coffeemaker. None of us heard her leave.

I was dreaming when I woke up suddenly to the sound of my mother screaming. I ran to my door, threw it open, and promptly tripped over my gift, whacking my face on a hall light switch. My face was aching as I got to my feet and ran down the hall to the kitchen, where my mother was standing by the coffeemaker with Cass's note in her hand.

"I just don't *understand* this," she was saying shakily to my father, who was standing beside her in his pajamas without his glasses on. The coffeemaker was spitting and gurgling happily behind them, like this was any other morning. "She can't just leave. She *can't.*"

"Let me see the note," my father said calmly, taking it out of her hand. It was on Cass's thick, monogrammed stationery with matching envelopes. I had the same ones, same initials: CO.

Later, when I read it, I saw it was completely concise and to the point. Cass was not the type to waste words.

Mom and Dad,

I want you to know, first, that I'm sorry about this. Someday I hope I'll be able to explain it well enough so that you'll understand.

Please don't worry. I'll be in touch.

I love you both.

Cass

My mother wiped her eyes with the back of her hand and looked at me. "She's gone," she said. "She went to be with *him,* I know it. How can she do this? She's supposed to be at Yale in two weeks."

"Margaret," my father said, squinting at the note. "Calm down."

The "him" was Cass's boyfriend, Adam: He was twenty-one, had a goatee, and lived in New York working on the *Lamont Whipper Show.* It was one of those shock talk shows where people tell their boyfriends they've been sleeping with their best friends and guests routinely include Klansmen and eighty-pound four-year-olds. Adam's job mostly consisted of getting coffee, picking up people at the airport, and pulling guests off each other during the frequent fights that scored the show big ratings. Since she'd come home from the beach three weeks ago—she'd met Adam there—Cass had been glued to the TV each day at 4 P.M., wishing aloud for a good fight just so she could catch a glimpse of him. Usually she did, smiling at the sight of him charging onstage, his face serious, to untangle two scrapping sisters or a couple of rowdy cross-dressers.

My father put the note down on the table and walked to the phone. "I'm calling the police," he said, and my mother burst into tears again, her hands rising to her face. Over her shoulder, through the glass door and over the patio, I could see our neighbors, Boo and Stewart Connell. They were cutting through the tree line that separated our houses for my birthday brunch; Boo had a bouquet of fresh-cut zinnias, bright and colorful, in her hand.

"I just can't believe this," my mother said to me, pulling out a chair and sitting down at the table. She was shaking her head. "What if something happens to her? She's only eighteen."

"Yes, hello, I'm calling to report a missing person," my father said suddenly, in his official Dean of Students voice. "Cassandra O'Koren. Yes. She's my daughter."

I had a sudden memory pop into my head: my mother, standing in the doorway of Cass's and my childhood room, back when we had twin beds and pink wallpaper. She would always kiss us, then stand in the doorway after turning off the light, her shadow stretching down the length of the room between us. She was always the last thing I tried to see before I fell asleep.

"See you in dreamland," she'd whisper, and blow us a kiss before shutting the door quietly behind her. Like dreamland was a real place, tangible, where we would all wander close enough to catch glimpses and brush shoulders. I always went to sleep determined to go there, to find her and Cass, and sometimes I did. But it was never the way I imagined it would be.

Now my mother sat weeping as my father reported Cass's vital statistics—five-four, brown hair, brown eyes, mole on left cheek—and I had the sudden sinking feeling that dreamland might be the only place we'd be seeing her for a while.

I heard a knock and looked up to see Boo and Stewart standing on the patio, waving at us. They'd been our neighbors for as long as I could remember, since before Cass or I was even born. They were former hippies, now New Agers; they believed in massage, fresh-baked homemade bread, and the Dalai Lama. They had absolutely nothing in common with my parents, except proximity, which had led to eighteen years of being neighbors and our best family friends.

"Good morning!" Boo called out to us through the door, holding up the flowers for me to see. "Happy birthday!" She reached down and pushed the door open, then stepped inside with Stewart following. He was carrying a bowl and a plate, each covered with a brightly colored napkin, which he put down on the table in front of my mother.

"We brought blueberry buckwheat pancake mix and sliced mangoes," Stewart said in his soft voice, smiling at me. "Your favorites."

Boo was crossing the room, arms already extended, to pull me close for a tight, long hug. "Happy birthday, Caitlin," she whispered in my ear. She smelled like bread and incense. "This will be your best year yet. I can feel it."

"Don't count on it," I said, and she pulled back and frowned at me, confused, just as my father hung up the phone and cleared his throat.

"Technically," he said, "they can't do anything for twenty-four hours. But they're keeping an eye out for her. We need to call all her friends, right now. Maybe she told someone something."

"What's going on?" Boo asked, and at the table my mother just shook her head. She couldn't even say it. "Margaret? What is it?"

"It's Cassandra," my father told her, his voice flat. "It appears that she's run away." This was my father, always formal: He lived for *supposedlys* and *theoreticallys,* not believing anything without proper proof.

"Oh, my God," Boo said, pulling out a chair and yanking it close to my mother before sitting down. "When did she go?"

"I don't know," my mother said softly, and Boo took one of her hands, rubbing the fingers with her own, as Stewart moved to stand behind her, his hand on her shoulder. They were touchy people, always had been. My father, however, was not, so neither made a move toward him. My mother sniffled. "I don't know anything."

"Caitlin," my father said to me briskly, "get a list together of her friends, anyone she might have talked to. And the number for that Whitter show, or whatever it's called."

"Okay," I said, not bothering to correct him. He nodded before turning his back to my mother and Boo and Stewart to look out across the patio at the few squirrels crowding the bird feeders.

On my way back to my room I picked up my present from where

it was lying in the middle of the hallway. It was wrapped in blue paper, with no card, but I knew it was from Cass. She would never have forgotten my birthday.

I took it into my room and sat down on my bed. In the mirror over my bureau I could see my face was scratched from where I'd hit the light switch, the skin around it a bright pink. No one had even noticed.

I unwrapped Cass's present slowly, folding the paper carefully as I slipped it off. It was a book, and as I turned it over I read the letters on the cover: *Dream Journal.* All around the words were comets and stars, moons and suns, scattered across a light purple background. It was beautiful.

The first page was an introduction about dreams, what they mean, and why we should remember them. This was Cass's thing—she had been big into symbols and signs in the last year. She said you never knew what the world was trying to tell you, that you had to pay attention every second.

As I closed the cover, something caught my eye on one of the first pages. It was an inscription in Cass's loopy script, my name big, the message little.

Caitlin, it said in black ink, *I'll see you there.*

Cass

Chapter One

When I was four and Cass was six, she whacked me across the face with a plastic shovel at our neighborhood park. We were in the sandbox, and it was winter: In the pictures, we're in matching coats and hats and mittens. My mother loved to dress us alike, like twins, since we were only two years apart. We *did* look alike, with the same round face and dark eyes and the same brown hair. But we weren't the same, even then.

The story goes like this: Cass had the shovel and I wanted it. My mother was sitting watching us on a bench with Boo, who had her camera and was snapping pictures. This was at Commons Park, the small grassy area in the center of our neighborhood, Lakeview. Besides the sandboxes it also had a swing set, one of those circular things you push real fast and then jump on—a kind of manual merry-go-round—and enough grass to play baseball or kickball. Cass and I spent most of the afternoons of our childhood at Commons Park, but the shovel incident is what we both always remembered.

Not that we ourselves recalled it that well. We had just heard the story recounted so many times over the years that it was easy to take the details and fold them into our own sparse memories, embellishing here or there to fill in the blanks.

It is said that I reached for the shovel and Cass wouldn't give it to me, so I grabbed her hand and tried to yank it away. A struggle ensued, which must have looked harmless until Cass somehow scraped one hard plastic edge across my temple and it began to bleed.

This moment, *the* moment, we have documented in one of Boo's photos. There is one picture of Cass and me playing happily, another of the struggle over the shovel (I'm wailing, my mouth a perfect O, while Cass looks stubborn and determined, always a fighter), and finally, a shot of her arm extended, the shovel against my face, and a blur in the left corner, which I know is my mother, jumping to her feet and running to the sandbox to pull us apart.

Apparently, there was a lot of blood. My mother ran through the winding sidewalks of Lakeview with me in her arms, shrieking, then took me to the hospital where I received five tiny stitches. Cass got to stay at Boo and Stewart's, eat ice cream, and watch TV until we got home.

The shovel was destroyed. My mother, already a nervous case, wouldn't let us leave the house or play with anything not plush or stuffed for about six months. And I grew up with a scar over my eye, small enough that hardly anyone ever noticed it, except for me. And Cass.

As we grew older, I'd sometimes look up to find her peering very closely at my face, finding the scar with her eyes before reaching up with one hand to trace it with her finger. She always said it made her feel horrible to look at it, even though we both knew it wasn't really her fault. It was just one more thing we had in common, like our faces, our gestures, and our initials.

When Cass was born my mother still wasn't sure what to name her. My mother had suffered terrible morning sickness, and Boo, who had moved in next door during the fourth month or so, spent a lot of time making herbal tea and rubbing my mother's feet, trying to make her force down the occasional saltine cracker. Boo was the one who suggested Cassandra.

"In Greek mythology she was a seer, a prophet," she told my mother, whose tendencies leaned more toward Alice or Mary. "Of course she came to a horrible end, but in Greek mythology, who doesn't? Besides, what more could you want for your daughter than to be able to see her own future?"

So Cassandra it was. By the time I came along, my mom and Boo were best friends. Boo's real name was Katherine, but she hated it, so I was named Caitlin, the Irish version. Cass's name was always cooler, but to be named for Boo was something special, so I never complained. Her name was just one thing I envied about Cass. Even with all our similarities, it was the things we didn't have in common that I was always most aware of.

My sister wasn't a seer or a prophet, at least not at eighteen. What she was, was student body president two years running, star right wing of the girls' soccer team (State Champs her junior and senior year), and Homecoming Queen. She volunteered chopping vegetables at the homeless shelter for soup night every Thursday, had been skydiving twice, and was famous in our high school for staging a sit-in to protest the firing of a popular English teacher for assigning "questionable reading material"—Toni Morrison's *Beloved.* She made the local news for that one, speaking clearly and angrily to a local reporter, her eyes blazing, with half the school framed in the shot cheering behind her. My father, in his recliner, just sat there and grinned.

There were only two times I can remember ever seeing Cass really depressed. One was after the soccer State Championship sophomore year, when she missed the goal that could have won it all. She locked herself in her room for a full day. She never talked about it again, instead just focusing on the next season, when she rectified the loss by scoring the only two goals of the championship game.

The second time was at the end of her junior year, when her first real boyfriend, Jason Packer, dumped her so he could "see other people" and "enjoy his freedom" in his last summer before college. Cass cried for a week straight, sitting on her bed in her bathrobe and staring out the window, refusing to go anywhere.

She drew back from everyone a bit, spending a lot of time next door with Boo where they drank tea, discussed Zen Buddhism, and read dream books together. This was when Cass became so spiritual, scanning the world around her for signs and symbols, sure that there had to be a message for her somewhere.

She got into three out of the four schools she applied to, and ended up choosing Yale. My parents were ecstatic and threw a party to celebrate. We all applauded and cheered as she bent over to slice a big cake that read WATCH OUT YALE: HERE COMES CASS! which my mother had ordered special from a bakery in town.

But Cass wasn't herself. She smiled and accepted all the pats on the back, rolling her eyes now and then at my parents' pride and excitement. But it seemed to me that she was just going through the motions. I wondered if she was looking for a sign, something she couldn't find with us or even at Yale.

She stayed in this funk all the way through graduation. In mid-June she went to stay with her friend Mindy's family at the beach and got a job renting out beach chairs by the boardwalk every day. Three mornings into it she met Adam. He was down at the beach on vacation with some friends from the show, and rented a chair from her. He stayed all day, then asked her out.

I could tell when she called the next morning, her voice so happy and laughing over the line, that our Cass was back. But not, we soon learned, for long.

I don't think any of us knew how much we'd needed Cass until she was gone. All we had was her room, her stories, and the quiet that settled in as we tried in vain to spread ourselves out and fill the space she'd left behind.

Everyone forgot my birthday as our kitchen became mission control, full of ringing phones, loud voices, and panic. My mother refused to leave the phone, positive Cass would call any minute and say it was all a joke, of *course* she was still going to Yale. Meanwhile my mother's friends from the PTA and Junior League circled through the house making fresh pots of coffee every five minutes, wiping the counters down, and clucking their tongues in packs by the back door. My father shut himself in his office to call everyone who'd ever known Cass, hanging up each time to cross another name off the long list in front of him. She was eighteen, so technically she couldn't be listed as a runaway. She was more like a soldier gone AWOL, still owing some service and on the lam.

They'd already tried Adam's apartment in New York, but the number had been disconnected. Then they called the *Lamont Whipper Show,* where they kept getting an answering machine encouraging them to leave their experience with this week's topic—My Twin Dresses Like a Slut and I Can't Stand It!—so that a staffer could get back to them.

"I can't believe she'd do this," my mother kept saying. "Yale. She's supposed to be at *Yale.*" And all the heads around her would nod, or hand her more coffee, or cluck again.

I went into Cass's room and sat on her bed, looking around at how neatly she'd left everything. In a stack by the bureau was everything she and my mother had bought on endless Saturday trips to Wal-Mart for college: pillowcases, a fan, a little plastic basket to hold her shower stuff, hangers, and her new blue comforter, still in its plastic bag. I wondered how long she'd known she wouldn't use any of this stuff—when she'd hatched this plan to be with Adam. She'd fooled us all, every one.

She had come home from the beach tanned, gorgeous, and sloppy in love, and proceeded to spend about an hour each night on the phone long-distance with him, spending every bit of the money she'd made that summer.

"I love you," she'd whisper to him, and I'd blush; she didn't even care that I was there. She'd be lying across the bed, twirling and untwirling the cord around her wrist. "No, I love you more. I do. Adam, I do. Okay. Good night. I love you. What? More than anything. *Anything.* I swear. Okay. I love you too." And when she finally did hang up she'd pull her legs up against her chest, grinning stupidly, and sigh.

"You are *pathetic,*" I told her one night when it was particularly sickening, involving about twenty *I love yous* and four *punkins.*

"Oh, Caitlin," she said, sighing again, rolling over on the bed and sitting up to look at me. "Someday this will happen to you."

"God, I hope not," I said. "If I act like that, be sure to put me out of my misery."

"Oh, really," she said, raising one eyebrow. Then, before I could react, she lunged forward and grabbed me around the waist, pulling me down onto the bed with her. I tried to wriggle away but she was strong, laughing in my ear as we fought. "Give," she said in my ear; she had a lock hold on my waist. "Go on. Say it."

"Okay, okay," I said, laughing. "I give." I could feel her breathing against the back of my neck.

"Caitlin, Caitlin," she said in my ear, one arm still thrown over my shoulder, holding me there. She reached up with her finger and traced the scar over my eyebrow, and I closed my eye, breathing in. Cass always smelled like Ivory soap and fresh air. "You're such a pain in the ass," she whispered to me. "But I love you anyway."

"Likewise," I said.

That had been two weeks earlier. She had to have known even then she was leaving.

I walked to her mirror and looked at all the ribbons and pictures she had taped around it: spelling bees, honor roll, shots from the mall photo booth of her friends making faces and laughing, their arms looped around each other. There were a couple of us, too. One from a Christmas when we were kids, both of us in little red dresses and white tights, holding hands, and one from a summer at the lake where we're sitting at the end of a dock, legs dangling over, in our matching blue polka-dot bathing suits, eating Popsicles.

On the other side of the wall, in my room, I had the same bed, the same bureau set, and the same mirror. But on my mirror, I had one picture of my best friend, Rina, my third-place ribbon from horseback riding, and my certificate from the B honor roll. Most people would have been happy with that. But for me, with Cass always blazing the trail ahead, there was nothing to do but pale in comparison.

Okay, so maybe I *was* jealous, now and then, but I could never have hated Cass. She came to all my competitions, cheering the loudest as I went for the bronze. She was the first one waiting for me when I came off the ice during my only skating competition, after falling on my ass four times in five minutes. She didn't even say anything, just took off her mittens, gave them to me, and helped me back to the dressing rooms where I cried in private as she unlaced my skates, telling knock-knock jokes the whole time.

To be honest, a part of me had been looking forward to Cass going off to Yale at the end of the summer. I thought her leaving might actually give me some growing room, a chance to finally strike out on my own. But this changed everything.

I'd always counted on Cass to lead me. She was out there somewhere, but she'd taken her own route, and for once I couldn't follow. This time, she'd left me to find my own way.

Chapter Two

The next morning when I woke up I realized I hadn't dreamed at all, not even one fleeting image. I took the book Cass gave me out from under my bed, where I'd hidden it, and opened it to the first page. There was a drawing of a full moon, sprinkled with stars, in the corner.

August 18, I wrote at the top of the page. *Nothing last night. And you're still gone.*

I couldn't think of anything else, so I got out of bed, threw on some clothes, and went down the hallway to the kitchen. The door to my parents' room was closed and my father was in his office, on the phone. He had to have talked to a hundred people in the last twenty-four hours.

"I understand that," he was saying, his voice level, but I could tell he was frustrated. "But eighteen or not, we want her home. She's not the kind of girl who does something like this."

The door to his office was half open, and I could see him standing by the window, running his palm over the small bald patch at the back of his head. My father, as the Dean of Students at the university, dealt with problems every day. He was the stand-in parent for thousands of undergraduates, and was quoted each time a fraternity got caught pulling pranks or a beer bash got out of hand. But this was different. This was about us.

I pulled the patio door open and slipped outside, where it was thickly hot and muggy, another August morning. But at least it was quiet.

Next door, I could see Boo and Stewart sitting at their kitchen table, eating breakfast. Boo raised her hand, waved, and then gestured for me to come over, smiling. I took one look back at my own house, where my mother's stress filled the rooms to the ceiling, leaving a stink and heaviness like smoke, and started across the one strip of green grass that separated their backyard from ours.

When I was little and got in trouble and sent to my room, I'd always sit on my bed and wish that Boo and Stewart were my parents. They'd never had kids of their own. My mother said it was because they acted so much like children themselves, but I liked to think it was so they could be there for me, if I ever needed to trade my own family.

The window in my room faced their back sunporch, an all-glass room where Boo kept most of her plants. She was mad for ferns. Stewart's studio—he taught art at the university—was just off that room, in what was supposed to be the living room. They kept their bed in the corner, and they didn't even have any real furniture to speak of; when you were invited over, you sat on big red velvet cushions decorated with sequins that Boo had picked up on a trip to India. This drove my conservative mother crazy, so Boo and Stewart almost always came to our house, where Mom could relax among the safety and comfort of her ottomans and end tables.

But that was what Cass and I loved most about them: their house, their lives, even their names.

"Mr. Connell's my father, and he lives in California," Stewart always said. He was a mild and quiet man, quite brilliant, whose hair was always sticking straight up, like a mad scientist's, and flecked with various colors of paint.

For most of the nights of my life I could hear Stewart coming home late from his university studio, the brakes of his bike—they had an old VW bus, but it broke down constantly—squeaking all the way from the bridge down the street. He'd glide down the slope of their yard, under the clothesline, to the garage. Sometimes he forgot about the clothesline and almost killed himself, flying backward while the bike went on, unmanned, to crash against the garage door. You'd think they would have moved the clothesline after the second time or so. But they didn't.

"It's not the fault of the clothesline," Stewart explained to me one day, rubbing the red, burned spot on his neck. He'd broken his glasses again and had them taped together in the middle. "It's about me respecting it as an obstacle."

Now Boo slid their door open and came out to meet me on their patio. She was in a pair of old overalls, a faded red tank top underneath, and her feet were bare. Her long red hair was piled on top of her head, a few chopsticks stuck in here and there to hold it in place. Inside, Stewart was sitting at the table, eating a big peach and reading a book. He looked up and waved at me; he had juice all over his chin.

"So," Boo said, putting an arm around my shoulder. "How are things on the home front?"

"Awful," I said. "Mom won't stop crying."

She sighed, and we stood there for a few minutes, just looking across their yard. Boo had gone through a Japanese garden stage a few years back, which resulted in a footbridge and a fat, rusted iron Buddha sculpture.

"I just can't believe she didn't tell me anything," I said. "I feel like I should have known something was going on."

Boo sighed, reaching to tuck a piece of hair behind her ear. "I think she probably didn't want to put you in that position," she said, squatting down to pull a dandelion at the edge of the patio, lifting it to her face to breathe in the scent. "It was a big secret to keep."

"I guess." Someone was mowing their lawn a few yards down, the motor humming. "I just thought everything was perfect for her, like it always was. You know?"

Boo nodded, standing up and stretching her back. "Well, that's a lot of pressure. Being perfect. Right?"

I shrugged. "I wouldn't know."

"Me neither," she said with a smile. "But I think it was harder for Cass than we realized, maybe. It's so easy to get caught up in what people expect of you. Sometimes, you can just lose yourself."

She walked to the edge of the patio, bending down to pull another dandelion. I watched her, then said, "Boo?"

"Yes?"

"Did she tell you she was going?"

She stood up slowly. "No," she said, as the lawnmower droned on down the street. "She didn't. But Cass had a hard year, last year. Things weren't always as easy as she made them seem, Caitlin. It's important that you know that."

I watched her pull a few more flowers, adding them to the bunch in her hand, before she came over and squeezed my shoulder. "What a crappy birthday, huh?" she said.

I shrugged. "It doesn't matter. I wouldn't have done anything anyway."

"What about Rina?" she said.

"She's off with her new stepdad," I told her, and she shook her head. "Bermuda this time." My best friend Rina Swain's mom had just gotten remarried again: This was number four. She only married rich, and never for love, which led to Rina living in nicer and nicer houses, going to endless exotic places, and piling up huge therapy bills. Rina had what Boo called Issues, but the guys at school had another name for it.

"Well, come inside," Boo said, pulling the door open and stepping back to let me in first. "Let me make you breakfast and we'll not talk about any of this at all."

I sat down at the table next to Stewart, who had finished his peach and was now sketching on the back of the power bill envelope, while Boo filled a mason jar with water and arranged the dandelions in it. Stewart's canvases, both finished and unfinished, covered the walls and were stacked against any solid surface in the house. Stewart did portraits of strangers: All his work was based on the theory that art was about the unfamiliar.

Stewart might have been unconventional, but his art classes were insanely popular at the university. This was mostly because he didn't believe in grades or criticism, and was a strong proponent of coed massage as a way of getting in touch with your artistic spirit. My father had been quoted about Stewart's teaching practices more than once, and always used words like *unique, free spirit,* and *artistic choice.* Privately, he wished Stewart would wear a tie now and then and stop leading meditation workshops in the quad on big football weekends.

Stewart looked over and smiled at me. "How's it feel to be sixteen?"

"No big difference," I said. With all the confusion, my father had forgotten about taking me to get my driver's license, but everyone had been so crazy I hadn't wanted to ask.

"Oh, now," he said, pushing the envelope away and putting down his pen. "That's the great thing about aging. It just gets better every year."

"Here you go," Boo said, plunking a plate down in front of me: scrambled tofu, Fakin' Bacon, and some pomegranates.

"I remember when I was sixteen," Stewart said, sitting back in his chair. His feet were bare, too, and sprinkled with green paint. "I hitched a ride to San Francisco and had a burrito for the first time. It was incredible."

"Really," I said, picking up the envelope he'd been doodling on. It was just half a face, sketchily drawn. I turned it over and was startled to see something in Cass's writing: her name, doodled in blue, signed with a flourish, as if she'd been sitting in this same chair some other morning, eating scrambled tofu, just like me.

"Just being free, out on the road, the world wide open . . ." He leaned closer to me, but I was still looking at Cass's name, suddenly so sad I felt like I couldn't breathe. It seemed impossible that Cass had been planning to change her life completely while none of us even *noticed;* even when she doodled on that envelope, it could have been on her mind.

". . . anything possible," Stewart was saying. "Anything at all."

I blinked, and swallowed over the lump in my throat. I wanted to keep that envelope and hold it close to me, like it was suddenly all I had left of her, some sort of living part pulsing in my hand.

"Caitlin?" Boo said, coming over and bending down beside me. "What is it?" She leaned down and saw the envelope, catching her breath. "Oh, honey," she said, and even before she wrapped her arms around me I was already leaning in, tucking my head against her shoulder as she held me, as I knew she'd held Cass, in this same chair, at this same table, in this same light, on other mornings, not like this.

When I walked up to our sliding glass door, the phone was ringing. No one seemed to be around, so I picked it up.

"Hello?"

There was a silence, with just a bit of buzzing.

"Hello?"

My father appeared in the doorway, out of breath: He'd been outside, in the garage. "Who is it?"

I shook my head. "I don't—"

He was immediately beside me, pulling the receiver out of my hand. "Cassandra? Is that you?"

"Jack?" my mother said from their bedroom. I could hear her moving, coming closer, and then she appeared in the hallway, clutching a tissue, one hand over her mouth. "I dozed off. Is it—"

"Cassandra, listen to me. You have to come home. We're not mad at you, but you have to *come home.*" His voice was shaking.

"Let me talk to her," my mother said, coming closer, but he shook his head, holding out one hand to keep her there.

"Tell her we love her!" my mother said, and I couldn't stand the way her voice sounded, unsure and wavering. I slipped around them both and into my room, slowly picking up my own phone. On the line, no one was speaking.

"Cassandra," my father said finally. "Talk to me."

Silence. I pictured her standing in a phone booth by a highway, cars whizzing by. A place I'd never seen, a world I didn't know. Then, suddenly, I heard her voice.

"Daddy," she began, and I heard my father take in a breath, quickly, as if he'd been punched in the stomach. "I'm okay. I'm happy. But I'm not coming home."

"Where are you?" he demanded.

"Let me talk to her!" my mother shrieked in the background. She could have gone into my father's office and picked up the extension there, but I knew she wasn't thinking of that, couldn't even move from that spot in the hallway where she was standing. "Cassandra!"

"Don't worry about me," Cass said. "I'm—"

"No," my father said. "You *must* come home."

"This is what I want," she said. "You have to respect that."

"You're only eighteen," my father told her. "This is ridiculous, you can't possibly know—"

"Daddy," she said, and I realized suddenly I was crying, again, the receiver wet against my face. "I'm sorry. I love you. Please tell Mom not to worry."

"No," my father said, firm. "We are not—"

"Caitlin?" she said suddenly. "I know you're there. I can hear you."

"What is she saying?" my mother kept asking, now close to the receiver. "Where is she?"

"Margaret, just hold on," my father told her.

"Yes," I whispered back to Cass. "I'm here."

"Don't cry, okay?" she said. The line crackled, and I thought of her tackling me that night, her breath against my neck, laughing in my ear. "I love you. I'm sorry about your birthday."

"It's nothing," I said.

There was a voice outside her end, a yell, and another buzz on the line. "Is that him?" my father demanded. "Is he there?"

"I have to go," she said. "Please don't worry, okay?"

"Dammit, Cassandra," my father said. "Don't you hang up this phone!"

"Good-bye," she said softly, as my father's voice dropped away. "Good-bye."

"Cassandra!" my mother wailed into the phone, all the anger and fear of the last twenty-four hours bursting across the line. "Please—"

Click. And she was gone.

Chapter Three

By the time I started school two days later, we hadn't heard from Cass again. The first call had come from somewhere in New Jersey, but beyond that there was a whole world that could have swallowed her up.

I still didn't have anything I thought worthy of being entered in my journal. I was waiting for something that was meaningful, real, a night when I saw Cass and she spoke to me. But instead my dreams were as dull as my everyday life, consisting mostly of me walking around the mall or school, looking for some undetermined thing that I could never find, while faces blurred in front of me. I woke up tired and frustrated, and felt like I never got any real sleep at all.

My mother kept Cass's bedroom door shut, with all of her Yale stuff piled up on the bed, waiting for her. I was the only one who ever went in there, and when I did the air always smelled stale and strange, pent up like the sorrow my mother carried in her shoulders, her heart, and her face.

She was taking it the hardest. My mother had spent the last eighteen years just as involved in Cass's activities as Cass herself was. She sewed sequin after sequin on ballet costumes, made Rice Krispies Treats by the panful for soccer team bake sales, and chaperoned Debate Club bus trips. She knew Cass's playing stats, SAT scores, and GPA by heart. She'd been prepared to be just as involved long-distance. A copy of Cass's Yale schedule was already taped to our refrigerator, my mother a member of the Parents' Organization, plane tickets prebought for Parents' Weekend in October. But now, in claiming her own life, Cass had taken part of my mother's as well.

I got my license, finally, and without comment was given the keys to Cass's car. It was due to be mine anyway, since she couldn't have taken it to Yale, but it still felt strange. I put all her tapes and the Mardi Gras beads she'd hung on the rearview mirror into a box and stuck it in the corner of the garage, under a patio chair and some flowerpots. It seemed like I couldn't do anything without thinking about her: The scar over my eye was always the first thing I noticed in the mirror's reflection now.

As for my father, he threw himself into his work. With a new semester, he was now busy with a class of incoming freshmen, a set of demonstrations over a controversial speaker, and a group of football players who had started a brawl at a local dance bar. He couldn't "fix" the problem of Cass running away, but through work he could still do his daily miracles, smoothing tensions and reassuring nervous administrators.

Whenever I see my father in my mind, he is wearing a tie. They were the only gifts Cass and I ever gave him for his birthday, Christmas, and Father's Day, year after year. In all, he owned hundreds by now, the collection carefully hung and organized in his closet by color and degree of loudness. (During our grade school years, we were enamored of polka dots and big stripes.) It had become somewhat of a family joke, at this point, and we'd taken to wrapping them in strangely shaped boxes and tubes, even folded up tiny in a jewelry box—just to make things more interesting. But he wore them, proudly, each day to work, and prided himself on remembering not only the giver and the occasion, but the year as well. If my mother was the emotion of our family, he was the fact-keeper. He remembered everything.

"Caitlin, Christmas, 1988," he'd say, smoothing his hand proudly over a tie I myself didn't even recognize. "You had the chicken pox."

The other thing my father loved—besides ties, and us—was sports. Whenever the university basketball or football team played, Cass and I would find our way into the living room and plant ourselves on the floor at his feet to watch and scream and trash the refs together. It was the only time we got to see him lose his cool, get so emotional and ecstatic, and we loved it. The rest of the time, he was like the player with nerves of steel, the only person you want to get the ball to when it's a tie game with only seven seconds left. He'd never let you down.

But now, Cass had done something to him: an intentional foul, illegal movement, the biggest of penalties. I'd been there the day Yale called to check on whether Cass was still coming, and saw my father's face as he explained, no, not this semester. Then he sat back down in his chair to watch baseball while I went to her room and sat on her bed, breathing in that pent-up air, and pictured that world, too, going on without her.

I'd been back in school about a week when my best friend, Rina, finally convinced me to try out for cheerleading. She argued that it was one of the *few* things Cass had never done, and therefore I was pretty much required to do it. I wasn't so sure about this.

"She never did it for a *reason,*" I told her as we walked to the gym for tryouts after school. Getting adjusted to school after a long, lazy summer had been tough, not to mention the occasional whispers or stares from people who knew about Cass running away. She'd been well-known at school, and it was great end-of-summer gossip, earning me a newfound notoriety that made me very uncomfortable.

"And what reason was that?" Rina asked me.

"Because she was an athlete," I said. I was realizing that more and more I was referring to Cass in the past tense, as if she was dead and not just gone. "Not a Barbie doll."

"Cheerleading is a sport," Rina said firmly. "And besides, you get to go to all the good parties."

I sighed, shaking my head. Rina and I were mismatched as friends, but somehow we'd stuck together since seventh grade, when she moved to town with her mom from Boca Raton to live with Stepdad Number Two, the dry-cleaning king, across the street from us. All the girls at school hated her immediately because she was flat-out gorgeous, even then: tall, with a perfect figure, strawberry-blond curls, huge blue eyes, and full lips in a heart-shaped face. Her arrival at Jackson Middle preceded the breakup of two well-established couples, as well as marking the beginnings of a reputation built more on speculation and wishful thinking than truth, which had followed her since.

But I knew Rina. I knew she only chased boys because her father, who hosted a cartoon and kids' show in Boca called *Harvey's Heroes*, had refused to acknowledge her as his daughter, even after a blood test proved otherwise. She once told me that as a kid she watched his show every day, and that he was great with the children in the audience, so funny and silly, pulling rabbits out of hats or telling stupid jokes.

"He just seemed like he'd be the perfect dad, you know?" she said. "And all I could think was that he hated me. But I still watched, every day. I don't even know why."

Rina's mom, Lisa—also tall, blond, and gorgeous—kept remarrying, and Rina got trips, clothes, jewelry, and big rooms in nice houses with her own TV and phone. The love she wanted she'd learned to look for elsewhere, with mixed results.

At the beginning of ninth grade, Lisa had an affair with her boss and moved Rina across town, divorcing Number Two to live with the man who would soon become Number Three. My mother breathed a sigh of relief, thinking now I could find a "nicer" girl to be best friends with. But I knew Rina, like me, didn't make friends very easily. And she was good to me: strong, fun, and fiercely loyal. And if I didn't have many other friends because of her—most girls were intimidated by her looks, or thought she was too pushy, or just flat-out feared for their boyfriends—it never bothered me. I never missed having a wide, thick circle of girlfriends: Rina was more than enough. We were comfortable with each other's flaws and weaknesses, so we stuck together and kept to ourselves. And once my mother realized that I wasn't going to start wearing tight skirts and dating half the basketball team—so Rina-esque—she relaxed and got used to her as well. She always liked to see Rina as needing *structure* (it was all those divorces), so she took to inviting her to dinners and holidays and on our yearly beach trip, folding her into our extended family.

Now, as we walked into the gym, a pack of girls by the bleachers turned to look at us, narrowing their eyes, mouths already whispering. This was the standard reaction to Rina, anywhere we went, from Wal-Mart to the movies, from both strangers and schoolmates. It always bothered me—I was protective of her—but she didn't even seem to notice anymore.

"I don't want to do this," I complained, even as she was writing both our names down at the sign-up table, which was manned by Chelsea Robbins, head cheerleader, runner-up to Cass for Homecoming Queen the year before.

"Sure you do," Rina said easily, flashing her million-dollar smile at Chelsea, who smiled back just as fake, tossing her blond ponytail. "It'll be fun."

"So Caitlin," Chelsea asked me, "how are you doing?"

I looked at her. Her head was cocked to the side, her face serious. "Fine," I said.

She nodded, sympathetic, and dipped her blond head and her voice a little lower before adding, "I can't believe it about Cass. I mean, she never struck me as that type."

I had a sudden flash of Chelsea standing on the Homecoming Float, in her runner-up sash, waving with a perky smile that couldn't completely hide the fact that she was bitter she'd been beaten. "What type is that?" I asked her.

Her big blue eyes widened. "Well, I mean, I just think . . . she was going to Yale and all. She like, totally, flaked out, right?"

"Come on, Caitlin," Rina said, locking her fingers around my wrist.

What I was feeling was new for me, a bubbling up of anger, mixed with so many images from the last two weeks: my mother weeping; my father running his hand over his head, closing his eyes; Cass's name doodled on the back of that envelope; her inscription to me in blue ink: *See you there.*

Rina yanked me by the arm, hard, and began to pull me away.

"Good luck," Chelsea yelled after us, and I tried to turn back but Rina held me tight. Someone was blowing a whistle: Tryouts were starting.

"Caitlin," Rina said in a low voice. "I like a good fight as well as the next person, but—"

"Did you hear what she was saying?"

"She's a bitch," Rina said flatly, plopping down on the bleachers and crossing her legs. Two heavyset girls sitting farther down looked over, their eyes traveling up and down Rina from her face to her toes. She ignored them. "We knew that already, right? But starting something now would blow our chances at cheerleading, and we don't want to do that, do we?"

"Yes," I said.

She sighed, reaching up to fluff her curls. "Do this for me, okay? I promise you'll thank me later. Trust me."

I looked at her. Those two little words had gotten me into more trouble than I cared to remember.

"Okay, fine," she said quickly. "Do what Cass would do, then."

"And what's that?" I said.

She shook her head. "You don't know?"

From the middle of the gym floor, Chelsea Robbins began clapping her hands. "Okay, ladies, it's time to get started! We're going to show you a basic routine to learn for first cuts. Let's go!"

Rina turned and smiled at me. "Kick their butts," she said, standing up. "That's what Cass would do."

At least two hundred girls were milling around the gym floor, stretching and talking. I was sure they all wanted this more than I did. But still.

"Kick their butts," I repeated, as if it would be that simple, watching as Chelsea Robbins cartwheeled down the gym, showing off her bounce and pep. "Okay."

When I brought my cheerleading uniform home three days later, I saw Boo coming but didn't move fast enough. She intercepted me on the front porch, leaving from a visit to my mother.

"Hel-lo!" she said cheerfully. "I have been working on your mother for the last hour to join this pottery class with me. You know, something to get her out of the house. But she's so stubborn."

The uniform was folded over my arm, and I tried to shift it behind me. "That's great," I said.

"Well, she's not firm on it yet," she said, craning her neck as I slipped the uniform around my back. "What's that?"

"I don't think . . ." I said, but it was too late; she had it now, pulling it around me to hold up in front of her.

"Oh," she gasped, one hand moving to cover her mouth. I felt my face burn, ashamed, as deep red as the raised JHS on the sweater. As far as Boo was concerned, I might as well have joined the Klan. "Oh, goodness."

"I know what you're going to say," I began. "But—"

"No, no," she said quickly, handing it back to me. "That's great. Good for you."

"It was Rina's idea," I said, feeling so lame I could hardly stand it. Boo, a professor of women's studies, had fundamental problems with pageants, the beauty industry and, of course, cheerleading. I knew this.

"It's okay," she said to me calmly, smiling now. "Whatever makes you happy."

"It's not making me happy," I explained hastily. "It just kind of happened."

And it had. One minute I'd been hating every second, the next so fired up no one could stop me. I'd had my requisite one year of gymnastics; I could do handsprings and cartwheels. But in the process of showing them—and channeling Cass to kick their butts—I'd gotten picked for the squad. The rest was just a blur of the squad hugging me and pom-poms rustling in my face. Rina had made it too, mostly because half the judges were football players.

"I understand," Boo said, pulling back and holding me at arm's length. "These things sometimes do that. They just—" and she looked at my uniform again, brushing her hand over the sweater—"happen."

And then, before I could say anything, she squeezed my arm and went down the stairs, her clogs thunking across the walk and into the grass.

When I went into my room, I held the uniform up against me, trying to picture myself cartwheeling across the football field. It was hard.

There was a knock at the door. "Caitlin?" my mother called out. "Are you in there?"

"Yeah," I said. "Come on in."

She opened the door and stuck her head in. She'd put on fresh lipstick and a squirt of Joy perfume, which I could smell, just as she did every day before my father was due home. She looked nice, but her face had that hollow look it had taken on since Cass left, like she was just a shell of her former self, functioning and talking but hardly alive. "How was school?"

"Fine." I turned around, still holding up the uniform against me. "I made the cheerleading squad."

"Really?" Her face brightened and she stepped into my room, clasping her hands in front of her. "Oh, Caitlin, that's great! Why didn't you *tell* me you were going out for the team?"

"It just kind of happened," I said.

She walked right past where I was sitting to the chair where my uniform was, picking it up and holding it in front of her. "Well, look at *that!*" she said excitedly. "It's just gorgeous. Now, you can't just leave this here, it needs to be hung up. And this sweater looks like a good dry cleaning couldn't hurt it."

"Oh," I said. "Okay." I hadn't seen her so excited about anything since Cass left.

"Now, did they tell you what kind of shoes you need? And what's the practice schedule like?" She walked to my closet and hung up the uniform, smoothing the skirt with her hand as she did so. "I can't believe they only give you one; we'll have to really keep it clean if you have a lot of games." I could see her mind already working over this problem as she examined the fabric of the skirt, turning it in her hand.

"There's a meeting tomorrow," I said. I was starting to feel a little strange about this, now. "I think they tell me everything then. All we got today was a game schedule," I added, pulling it out of my pocket. She was standing in front of me immediately, hand out, ready to take it.

She unfolded the paper, then scanned it quickly. "My," she said, "you *are* going to be busy. But we'll work around it. We always have before, right?"

"Um, right," I said. This *we* thing was kind of strange, considering I'd never been involved in any school teams, so far. It was like she'd forgotten I was even there.

She was already on her way out the door, the schedule in her hand. "I'm going to stick this on the fridge right now, so we'll know when you need to be where. And tomorrow night, after they tell you what you need, we'll go to the mall. Okay? Unless they have to special-order things from a catalog, in which case maybe I should just go ahead and write you a check to take with you . . ."

"I don't know," I said quietly.

"Well, I'll just send a blank one with you and that way if they are ordering you can go ahead and do it right away. You don't want to wait too long. Unless they all order in a group together . . . ?"

"I don't know," I said again. My stomach was starting to hurt.

"Well, we'll figure it out later," she said, beaming and waving the paper at me before she disappeared down the hall. I knew she was pulling the Scotch tape out of the drawer by the stove, centering the paper on the fridge in the exact same spot where Cass's soccer/student government/Debate Club/Yale schedule had always been.

The only reason I'd even tried out was to do something different from Cass. But here, in the end, I was following her again.

I looked out my window to Boo and Stewart's. They were cooking dinner. Stewart was peeling carrots and talking, while Boo stirred something on the stove with a long wooden spoon, a glass of wine in her other hand. And I wished again that I was their daughter, just once, sitting in that kitchen eating spicy greens, peeling carrots, and just being me.

One time, when I was about eight or nine, Boo was watching me at her house. I had my Barbie bedroom/carrying case and was dressing my Barbie for a big date with Ken, who was half-naked on the floor waiting for me to find his blue velour pants.

"So what's your doll's name?" Boo asked me.

"Barbie," I said. "All their names are Barbie."

"I see," she said. "Well, I'd think that would get boring, everyone having the same name."

I thought about this, then said, "Okay, then her name is Sabrina."

"Well, that's a very nice name," Boo said. I remember she was baking bread, kneading the dough between her thick fingers. "What does she do?"

"Do?" I said.

"Yes." She flipped the dough over and started in on it from the other side. "What does she do?"

"She goes out with Ken," I said.

"And what else?"

"She goes to parties," I said slowly. "And shopping."

"Oh," Boo said, nodding. "She can't work?"

"She doesn't have to work," I said.

"Why not?"

"Because she's *Barbie.*"

"I hate to tell you, Caitlin, but somebody has to make payments on that town house and the Corvette," Boo said cheerfully. "Unless Barbie has a lot of family money."

I considered this while I put on Ken's pants.

Boo started pushing the dough into a pan, smoothing it with her hand over the top. "You know what I think, Caitlin?" Her voice was soft and nice, the way she always spoke to me.

"What?"

"I think your Barbie can go shopping, and go out with Ken, and also have a productive and satisfying career of her own." She opened the oven and slid in the bread pan, adjusting its position on the rack.

"But what can she do?" My mother didn't work and spent her time cleaning the house and going to PTA. I couldn't imagine Barbie, whose most casual outfit had sequins and go-go boots, doing such things.

Boo came over and plopped right down beside me. I always remember her being on my level; she'd sit on the edge of the sandbox, or lie across her bed with me and Cass as we listened to the radio.

"Well," she said thoughtfully, picking up Ken and examining his perfect physique. "What do you want to do when you grow up?"

I remember this moment so well; I can still see Boo sitting there on the floor, cross-legged, holding my Ken and watching my face as she tried to make me see that between my mother's PTA and Boo's strange ways there was a middle ground that began here with my Barbie, Sabrina, and led right to me.

"Well," I said abruptly, "I want to be in advertising." I have no idea where this came from.

"Advertising," Boo repeated, nodding. "Okay. Advertising it is. So Sabrina has to go to work every day, coming up with ideas for commercials and things like that."

"She works in an office," I went on. "Sometimes she has to work late."

"Sure she does," Boo said. "It's hard to get ahead. Even if you're Barbie."

"Because she wants to get promoted," I added. "So she can pay off the town house. And the Corvette."

"Very responsible of her," Boo said.

"Can she be divorced?" I asked. "And famous for her commercials and ideas?"

"She can be anything," Boo told me, and this is what I remember most, her freckled face so solemn, as if she knew she was the first to tell me. "And so can you."

So now I found myself a cheerleader, using pom-poms and pyramids to forge my way into new and unbroken territory. I wondered again what Cass would think of me: would she be disappointed, like Boo, or ecstatic, like my mother. If I knew my sister, she'd be a little of both.

Every year for as long as I could remember, my family and Boo and Stewart have had an end-of-summer cookout to celebrate Labor Day. This year, with Cass gone, I wondered if we'd stick with tradition or just let it go. It was hard to say. In the end, it was my mother who made the call.

"Well," she said to Boo the weekend before, over coffee, "I suppose Cassandra would be gone anyway. Freshman orientation started on the third."

As she said this, she glanced over to the fridge, where the Yale calendar still hung next to Cass's junior prom picture and the grocery list. It was the one reminder of Cass's thwarted college plans that she hadn't taken down yet.

"Exactly," Boo said, taking another grape out of the bowl in front of her and tossing it into her mouth. "Besides, it's bad luck to mess with tradition. And I have a wonderful new recipe for eggplant pasta salad that will knock your socks off."

My mother smiled at this. "I suppose I'll make my ambrosia salad," she said, stirring her coffee with a clink of her spoon. "And Jack can handle the steaks, like always."

"Stewart will make his famous tempeh fajitas," Boo added. "What about you, Caitlin? What can you make for us?"

I thought about this: My biggest traditional contribution was usually lighting the grill. Cass had been famous for her chocolate-chip cheesecake. It was the only thing she *could* make, and it was always a huge production, involving her taking over the entire kitchen. She'd bang pans, mumbling and cursing to herself, before finally emerging with a somewhat lopsided, always delicious dessert. As a vegetarian dish, it was loved all around, unless Stewart was in a vegan cycle, which just meant more for the rest of us. The image of Cass in the kitchen with her face smeared with flour, using a spatula to shoo us all out of the kitchen as we tried to help her, always symbolized—more than the pool closing, cooler nights, and homework—the end of summer to me.

In the end, I made coleslaw; it was, after all, a summer dish. My mother turned on the bug light, Boo brought a huge bouquet of the last of her zinnias and cosmos, and my father flipped the steaks on the patio and drank beer with Stewart, who had pre-cooked his fajitas to avoid any meat-tempeh interaction.

My mother and Boo took their wineglasses and went for a stroll in the yard, already discussing fall bulbs, while I went inside and turned on the football game for my father, who could half-watch it while keeping an eye on his steaks. The bugs were out in force, and since Stewart had a conscientious objection to the bug light, he winced, as if in pain himself, each time it claimed another victim.

"Well, I hear we have quite a team this year," said Stewart, trying to make conversation. He knew nothing about sports and had lost our respect years ago by asking how many points a basket counted for while watching the second half of an NCAA Final Four Game.

"Quarterback's good," my father said, poking at a steak with a fork. "But the defensive line needs help. A good rushing team and we're in trouble."

"Ah," Stewart said, nodding. A bug flew into the light—BZZZT!—and he sighed. "Right."

"What's that score say, Caitlin?" my father asked me, squinting through the patio door.

"I'll go check," I said, picking up my Coke and going inside. "Ten–seventeen. Nebraska's up."

"Good," my father said, flipping another steak.

I was standing in front of the TV, watching the offense get organized, when Stewart said, in a lower voice, "Is there any news about Cassandra?"

I glanced outside at my father, who didn't even flinch at the sound of her name. We'd all been acting like things were fine. It was just another Labor Day, I was already back at school, Cass was at Yale—I mean, there was her schedule up on the fridge.

"No," my father said in his press-conference, news-sound-bite voice. "Nothing new."

Stewart nodded, rubbing his hand over his chin. "I know this probably doesn't help," he said. Stewart, who prided himself on Being Fully in Touch with His Emotions, was the complete polar opposite of my stoic father. "But you know, I took Boo away from her family when she was eighteen. We were just kids, of course, and it was stupid, and it took years for her parents to forgive me."

My father flipped another steak, then pushed down on it, hard, with the spatula. A bug flew into the bug light, dying a loud, noisy death.

"But I took good care of her," Stewart went on. "And I know that Adam is doing the same for Cassandra. She's such a smart girl. She wouldn't be with anyone who'd do anything less."

My father, with those nerves of steel, didn't react to this except by one, solid nod. Outside, I could hear my mother laughing, her and Boo's voices getting closer.

"Well," my father said, glancing in again at the game as a quarterback ran down the field, dodging and twisting, ducking and rushing, all the way to the end zone. "I hope you're right."

They were quiet after that, with just the sizzle of the steaks and the bug light buzzing every few minutes. It was getting dark outside, and the food was almost ready. So I went into the kitchen, watched the sun set, and ate ambrosia salad with my fingers at the end of this, another summer.

Chapter Four

My making cheerleader changed my mother's life. She showed up at all our early exhibitions and games, wearing one of many Jackson High School sweatshirts and pins, clapping and cheering so loudly I could always hear her over anyone else. She organized our bake sales and car washes, packed snack bags full of apples and Rice Krispies Treats for away trips, and had my uniform dry-cleaned and pressed promptly after each game. She had finally found something to concentrate on that was familiar and busy in the strange silence of Cass being gone. She was almost happy. And that should have been enough for me to keep at it.

But the truth was, I hated cheerleading. Whatever zest and pep the other girls had that made them cartwheel, high kick, and smile constantly was missing in me, like a genetic or chemical malfunction. I felt like an impostor, and it showed.

Because I was the lightest of all the girls, it was decided early on that I would be the one at the top of the pyramid formation we did in our big cheers. This also led to me being hated with a passion by Eliza Drake, who because of the birth control pill had put on about fifteen pounds over the summer—mostly in her hips and butt—and was subsequently bumped to a lower, supporting position. She could have been on top, for all I cared. I was scared of heights, and climbing up all those backs to be lifted to stand, with someone grasping the backs of my knees, made my head spin. All I could think about was toppling down, falling head over feet to crash on the gym floor just as the marching band trampled over me playing "Louie Louie."

When I was up there, wobbly and light-headed, I always thought the same thing: *After this game, I quit.* But then I'd look out in the stands and see my mother beaming up at me, waving and wearing the same proud smile my father had the night Cass kicked the winning goal, bowed her head to accept her Homecoming Queen crown, or stood up for human rights on local TV. In all my life, going for the bronze, I'd never gotten a look like that before, and I knew if I quit, it would break her heart. It was like I'd somehow thrown her a lifeline, without even meaning to, and to let go right now meant she'd fall back into missing Cass and just drown.

But I was not my mother's only new hobby.

"What is *this?*" Rina whispered to me one afternoon when we stopped by my house after school en route to a game. I'd forgotten my cheerleading sweater again, just as I was always forgetting something crucial—regulation socks, matching ponytail holders, pom-poms. I was learning this sport had too many accessories for my taste: It was like *being* Barbie.

The *this* Rina was referring to was my mother's new Victorian decorating scheme, which consisted mostly of wreaths, sprigs of dried flowers hanging from the walls, and various knicknacks—thimbles, tiny tea sets, families of glass swans—cluttered on every flat surface. The worst, however, were the Victorian-era dolls she kept ordering from QVC, all of them with porcelain white skin and spooky eyes. They came with their own stands and were suddenly just *everywhere:* in the living room by the magazine rack, on the credenza, with a pack of swans, and even in the guest room, where they were lined up across the bureau, staring blankly at the closet. Sometimes when I couldn't sleep I'd think of them there, just staring in the dark, and shudder all the way down to my toes.

"I told you," I said to Rina, "my mother's going through some kind of weird adapting phase." She was out, for once, probably buying more ceramic plaques shaped like apples and houses to hang on the walls.

"What?" Rina said.

I shook my head. "I don't know." I opened my bedroom door to see a Victorian-style teddy bear sitting on my bed. He was wearing spectacles, a bow tie, and a period vest. Another QVC special.

"Man," Rina said in a low voice, walking over and picking it up. "Get out the Prozac."

"Shut up," I said, grabbing my sweater off the chair. "Let's just go."

There really was no stopping my mother. Boo had tried, convincing her to take that pottery class at the Community Arts Center on Tuesday nights. The teacher was a woman artist with dreadlocks and a tattoo, and my mother reported to us in a worried tone that she did not shave her legs or underarms. This did not, however, seem to hinder her ability to teach my mother how to make lopsided bowls, ashtrays glazed with smeared reds and greens, and a ribbed tall vase for me that leaned like the Tower of Pisa.

I truly believed that my mother thought she could replace Cass if she filled the house with enough clutter. But no matter what she brought in there was still something missing, which led to more swans, dolls, sprigs, tea sets, ashtrays. My father sighed when he saw the UPS truck pulling away, frowned over the credit card bill, and when my mother was out or not looking, turned the dolls in the living room to face the wall.

"There's something unsettling about all this *staring*," he explained sheepishly when I caught him one night, crouched by the magazine basket, furtively rearranging the dolls. He looked embarrassed to be even holding one in his arms, the School Marm, her book and slate stuck to her hands with heavy-duty wire.

"I know," I said. But by breakfast the next morning she, the mother with two children, and the baby in the christening dress were all turned back the right way, as if they'd done it themselves during the night.

My father missed Cass, too, but his loss was more subtle. Things kept coming from Yale: Obviously we were still on the mailing list, so the parents' newsletter and fund-raising requests arrived with regularity. My mother left them on the table by the door without comment and I'd figured my father was throwing them away, until I went into his office one day to look for a pencil sharpener and found them all neatly stacked in a drawer, envelopes not even opened.

The truth was, I was trying not to look too hard at anything. Not at myself, the swans, my mother mouthing the cheers along with me, the crooked ashtrays, the tired look on my father's face when another Yale bulletin came in the mail. It was easier to just float along as if sleeping that whole first part of the year, going through the motions and staring like one of those ghostly dolls, waiting for something to wake me up.

It was a game night in October, right around Halloween. We were playing our biggest rival, Central High, at home, and the crowd was huge. We'd been working on a big halftime number for a couple of weeks that involved not only a pyramid but some heavy-duty dancing, a can-can line, and a row of subsequent backflips. This was a Very Big Deal, at least for everyone else.

We were up at the half, and the squad had gone back to the dressing rooms to change into our purple-sequined tops, which my mother, of course, had helped to design and sew. Everyone was nervous as we stood waiting to run out onto the field from the opening under the bleachers. I was cold and convinced that I would blow my backflip as I'd done in practice just the day before, when I landed with a resounding *whump* on my back, knocking the wind out of myself. I just lay there, feeling oozy and strange as I stared up at the rows of retired basketball jerseys, fluttering from the ceiling overhead.

"You'll be fine," Rina said to me now, grasping my hand and squeezing it. Rina, of course, loved cheerleading. She was a natural. We had still been in pre-season when she started dating the quarterback, and she was the clear crowd favorite, eliciting cheers—mostly male—just for walking out onto the field. Eliza Drake hated her, too.

The band started playing "My Girl," the squad theme song, and I knew Boo was in the stands, her face twisting, disgusted. The girls in front of me began psyching up, jumping up and down and shaking their pom-poms, as we all started running down the slope to pop out onto the field to the cheers of the crowd. There was a pack of people that was especially into the cheerleaders—mostly guys, girls who hadn't made the squad, and parents—who were sitting right at the overhang where we came out, and as we ran forward they chanted each of our names.

"Eliza!" they yelled, and Eliza Drake did an impromptu handspring, showing off.

"Meredith!"

"Angela!"

"Rina!" And the crowd went wild, screaming and cheering, as Rina turned around and waved one pom-pom, smiling at her public.

I was the last one out.

The music was loud as the cold air hit me, and I was already thinking of my backflip when I heard someone over my head yell, *"Cass!"*

I stopped dead in my tracks, causing Caroline Miter, the mascot, to crash right into me. I don't know if everyone was yelling my sister's name: The one voice was the only one I could hear. And for one fleeting, crazy second I thought she must be there, somewhere close, in the places I'd always searched for her in my dreams.

"Cass!" the voice yelled again, and I looked up to see a man pumping his fist. He was talking to *me*. His breath was coming out in small white puffs. *"Cass!"*

"Come on," Caroline said to me, her voice muffled under her tiger head as she yanked me by my sleeve out onto the field. "Hurry!"

I scrambled behind her into formation, but I couldn't stop looking at that guy as he yelled my sister's name at me again and again. I was barely aware of the dance routine as I did it, everything in slow motion as the girls squatted and built the pyramid and I climbed up. When I stood, knees wobbling, the crowd was a blur of noise and color in front of me. It was so cold as I reached up to touch the scar over my eye, tracing its length and feeling my pulse there. I tilted my head back and looked up at the stars; I could still hear Cass's name in my head, and suddenly I felt wide awake.

The world is speaking to you every day, she'd said to me so many times. *You just don't always know how to listen.*

I was listening, then. I could hear everything.

"Cass!" The guy was still shouting, or maybe he wasn't and I was only dreaming, really dreaming now. I closed my eyes. *"Cass!"*

And that is the last thing I remember before falling.

It is nothing short of a miracle that Eliza Drake happened to look up and see me begin to fall backward. Regardless of her feelings for me, she jerked out from under Lindsay White, who fell and broke her nose, to stagger backward and catch me. Those new fifteen pounds in her butt and hips most likely saved my life.

When I opened my eyes, my ears were ringing and the first thing I saw was a circle of cheerleaders standing around me in purple sequins, pom-poms limp at their sides. I wondered for a second if I'd died and gone to hell.

"Caitlin?" I turned my head to see a man in a paramedic outfit. "Can you hear me?"

"Yes," I said, and sat up, slowly. I found out later I'd been lucky enough to fall square on Eliza, who suffered only a bad hip bruise and scraped elbows from catching me. I'd escaped pretty much unscathed, other than some scratches, a bad scrape on my arm, and a cut on my knee that didn't even require stitches. My mother, who herself had almost passed out after seeing me fall, kept telling everyone it was nothing short of a miracle.

When Eliza, Lindsay, and I all finally stood up to walk to the ambulance to get bandaged up, the crowd stood and gave us a standing O. We went on to win the game big, but my topple made everything else anticlimactic.

"It's a miracle," my mother said to me again as we stood watching the ambulance drive off, a new white bandage wrapped around my knee. I'd already thanked Eliza Drake, who was now somewhat of a hero and suddenly popular, and apologized to Lindsay, who was forced to wear nose splints for two months and subsequently kiss her teen modeling career good-bye. My temporary pyramid insanity, clearly, had serious and far-flung ramifications. "Can you imagine how bad it could have been? What if you'd been seriously injured?"

"I know," I said.

"You're just so lucky," she said again, squeezing my arm. "And next game, you'll be right back out there."

But something had changed in me, even if I didn't know what it was just yet. All I could think was that I felt alive for the first time since my birthday. From wherever she was, Cass had finally spoken to me, reaching out from dreamland to where I stood in this waking world, half-asleep and wobbly, under those bright, bright stars.

My mother had wanted me to come right home, sure I had a concussion or at least some broken limb the paramedics had missed, but my father let me go to the team party over her objections. On the way, me, Rina, and another cheerleader named Kelly Brandt stopped at the car wash to vacuum out Kelly's Camaro. The car was trashed; the night before her boyfriend, a tailback named Chad, had gotten sick in the backseat. She'd done the best she could with towels and Lysol spray, but at the car wash we had to get down to business.

"This is so disgusting," Kelly said between clenched teeth, wiping the seat with the towel. As she did so she sprayed a cloud of Lysol around her head, to balance out the smell. Kelly was a nice girl, kind of a mother hen, and had taken me and Rina on to show us the ropes since she had a year over us and therefore some kind of squad seniority.

She looked out at me and Rina where we were sitting by the vacuum station, smoking cigarettes. I didn't usually, but after the game everyone had been pressing around me, talking about my fall, and I needed something to calm me down. I still felt strange, as if everything was crackling and alive all around me. Kelly said, "I can't believe you're not even helping me."

"Chad's your boyfriend," Rina pointed out. "If he was mine, I'd be on puke patrol."

"Funny," Kelly growled. She hit the Lysol again, the smell wafting out into the cold air. We were all still in our cheerleading uniforms and the cut on my leg was throbbing a bit under my bandage. The car wash was deserted.

"You know he's just going to do it again," Rina said to Kelly, blowing out a huge cloud of smoke. She tossed her hair, drawing out one curl to inspect the ends. "I don't even see why you're bothering."

"Because it stinks," Kelly snapped. "And he's not going to do it again."

"Whatever," Rina said. She was in a hurry to get to the party and Bill Skerrit, the quarterback, a short little guy, all pointy and pockmarked, but whenever I asked her what she saw in him she just smiled and shook her head.

"You'll see someday," she'd say, and I'd look at Bill again and wonder what she meant. She'd spent all week pushing me together in the courtyard and on the bus with Mike Evans, a running back who was tall and a little dopey with pretty blue eyes. We were meeting him and Bill at the party and I was under stern instructions to accept his letter jacket—which would signify that we were now *officially* dating after the past couple of weeks of flirting—if it was offered to me.

There was another spurt of Lysol from inside the car and Kelly said, "Hey, Caitlin, grab that dollar out of the ashtray and go get some quarters, okay?"

"Okay." I hopped down and reached into the car for the money, then walked down past the washing bays to the change machine. There were no other cars except a BMW convertible, at the very end. It was black and parked crooked, with the top down.

I put the dollar in the machine and four quarters clanked out into my hand. As I turned around to walk back, my breath clouding out around my face in the cold, I got my first look at Rogerson Biscoe.

He was standing next to the black BMW, arms crossed, looking down at the car. He was in a short-sleeved shirt with a kind of tribal print, and old khaki pants with worn cuffs. His hair was brown, a mass of curls thick enough that they were almost like dreadlocks, and he had a dark, kind of olive complexion. He wore a leather cord necklace around his neck and penny loafers with no socks on his feet. He didn't look like Bill Skerrit or the rest of the guys I knew. He didn't look like anybody.

As I passed he looked up and watched me, staring.

"Hey," he called out just as I passed out of sight. Around the corner Rina was talking, her voice high and light, and I could smell Lysol.

I took a few steps back and suddenly he was *right there;* he'd moved to catch up with me. Up close I could see his eyes were a deep green. I realized I was staring but somehow I couldn't stop.

"You got change for a ten?" he said suddenly, holding up a bill folded between two fingers.

"Uh, no," I said. "I don't think so."

He smiled, then looked me up and down. Suddenly I knew I looked idiotic in my cheerleading uniform, not to mention the sequined top: I felt bright and tacky enough to explode. "Nice outfit," he said. I couldn't tell if he was joking.

"Oh," I said, looking down. "Yeah, well."

He glanced at the bandage on my upper arm, then asked, "What happened to you there?"

"Caitlin!" I heard Kelly shout. "Where are you?"

"I'm coming," I called back, then said to him, "I fell off a pyramid earlier tonight."

"Ouch," he said, and before I could even move he reached out and touched my bandage, running a finger across it. Then he looked up at me and said, "You okay?"

"I . . . I don't know," I said. This was strangely true at that moment.

"Caitlin, we're going to miss the whole party—" I heard Rina saying suddenly behind me, her voice growing louder as she impatiently rounded the corner, her cheerleading sneakers squeaking against the pavement. I turned around and she stopped suddenly, staring.

"I'm coming," I said quickly. I glanced back at the strange guy in front of me and he was smiling, his green eyes almost glittering.

"Okay," she said just as fast, and I heard her backing away around the corner.

"I should go," I said, but it was like someone else was talking. My head felt fuzzy and strange, and I wondered if maybe I *had* whacked it on the way down.

"Sure," he said nodding. "See ya around, Caitlin." And he raised his chin, backing up, keeping his eyes on me.

I stood there, my breath clouding out around my face, as a police car raced by on the road facing us, the siren screaming.

"Wait," I said, and he stopped. His hands were in his pockets. "You didn't tell me your name."

"Rogerson," he said, and then he turned his back and walked away, leaving me to stand there and watch him go.

When I came back around the corner Rina and Kelly were both right there waiting for me, identical in their letter jackets, stomping their feet to keep warm. I walked straight to the car and climbed into the backseat while they tumbled in behind me, already asking questions.

"Who was that?" Rina said. The smell of Lysol, pungent, was

hanging all around us in a big cloud. "I *know* he doesn't go to Jackson. I would remember him."

"I didn't even get to look at him," Kelly complained.

"Too bad for you. He is *hot,*" Rina told her, and there was that smile again, sly and clever.

"His name's Rogerson," I said. Just saying it felt weird, like I suddenly knew him or something.

"Rogerson," Rina repeated, trying it out. "That's sexy."

"You think *everything's* sexy," Kelly said in a flat voice. To me she added, "Do you have my quarters?"

I was surprised to find that I did: They were clutched in my hand. She held out her palm and I dropped them into it, one by one. She said, "I guess I'll just skip the vacuum."

"Please do," Rina said, settling into her seat and crossing her legs. She flipped down the vanity mirror and checked her face. "We're late as it is."

Kelly started the engine and pulled around the vacuum station, rolling down her window. As we cut through one of the bays to turn back to the road, we passed him again, standing by his car, hosing it down, the water steaming in the cold. I took it all in again: the curly dreadlocked hair, the bright printed shirt, the cord around his neck. Here I was, on the way to a party where, if everything went according to Rina's well-laid plans, I could go home with Mike Evans's letter jacket, all mine. But now, something was different.

"Is that him?" Kelly asked, whispering. We were all staring as we passed him, slowly, like tourists at a wildlife park watching elephants from the safety of their station wagon. He lifted his head, seeing us, and looked right back, still hosing off his car.

"Yep," Rina said. "Isn't he something?"

"He looks like a drug dealer," Kelly said. She was kind of uptight, the mother of the cheerleading squad. Any man not wearing a letter jacket was *dangerous,* in her opinion.

"He's got that wild look," Rina said in a low voice.

"Yes, he does," Kelly agreed, like it was a bad thing. Then she said, "Does it still smell back there, Caitlin?"

Rogerson was still watching us, as if the sight of a carful of girls ogling him did not faze him in the least. I wanted to think he was only looking at me, but I couldn't be sure.

"No," I answered her softly, as we rounded the bays and pulled onto the road. Then I turned in my seat and watched this Rogerson disappear, car length by car length, out of sight.

"Looks like we didn't miss much," Rina said as we came into the party. Most of the football team was in the dining room, bouncing quarters off what looked like an antique table. In the living room Melissa Cooper, school slut, was already making out with Donald Teller, who'd thrown the winning pass that night. Everyone was looking at me, patting me on the back as I passed, and making jokes about my fall. I felt prickly and strange, and each hand that touched me seemed heavy and hot against my skin.

"Chad!" I heard Kelly yell from behind me, and then she was off like a shot down the hallway to the kitchen. Chad was sitting on the floor, up against the refrigerator, a beer clutched in his hands. He looked like he was asleep. She knelt down beside him and made sure he was breathing, then pulled him to his feet. Kelly was what I later learned was called *co-dependent.*

"There's Mike," Rina whispered, poking me in the side. I looked over to the dining room, where Mike was sitting and watching us. He waved, smiling, in his letter jacket. Mike was a nice guy but very, very *bland.* Like a big saltine cracker.

"Come on," Rina said, taking my hand and pulling me behind her into the dining room, where Bill Skerrit was at the head of the table.

"There you are!" he said, and she immediately sat down in his lap and took a swig of his beer, while his hands moved easily around her waist.

"Give me that quarter," she called out, wriggling in his lap. Mike, on the end, slid it across to her.

"That's my girl," Bill said.

"Caitlin," Rina said in a low voice, and when I looked at her she cocked her head very obviously toward Mike. "Go on."

And so I did, working my way around the table, squeezing past chairs and bodies to sit in the chair next to him.

"Hi," I said.

"Hi." He smiled and lay his hand loosely along the back of my chair. This was all arranged. I had learned there was no room for chaos theory or chance in the carefully choreographed world of jock love.

I sat there with Mike, but I still felt strange. Like every inch of me was alert, on guard, ready for what might happen next.

By the time Rogerson appeared in the open doorway of the dining room it was like I'd been waiting for him, wasn't even really surprised to see him standing there in the next room, hands in his pockets. I had this crazy thought that he'd come for me.

"Hey, Bill," one of the running backs, Jeremy Light, called out. "Someone here to see you."

Bill Skerrit turned around, with Rina still in his lap. "Oh, hey, man. Hold on."

We were all looking at Rogerson. And as he scanned the room, all of Jackson High's best and brightest, he saw me.

"Who is that?" Mike Evans asked me, and without even really realizing it, I pulled out from under his arm, one quick movement, costing him all the progress he'd slowly attained in the last thirty minutes.

"I don't know," I said. "Excuse me." And I stood up and squeezed back around the table, then pushed my way into the kitchen. It was littered with beer cans and empty Bud twelve-packs. There was a small, scared-looking dog on a blue blanket in the corner who looked up, distressed, upon seeing me.

I walked across the kitchen toward the bathroom, and as I passed the hallway that led to the front door I saw Bill Skerrit, quarterback, handing a few folded bills over to Rogerson, who handed him something back in return. Then they just stood there, by the door, talking, before Bill turned back to the dining room. Rogerson put the money in his pocket and turned to the door, pushing it open.

"Caitlin?" I looked at the door to the dining room and saw Mike Evans standing there, beer in hand. "What's wrong?"

"Nothing," I said quickly, and as I spoke Rogerson turned back from the open door, seeing me. "I was, um, cold."

"Cold?" Mike looked around the room, as if he might see something to corroborate this, like icicles or penguins.

"Yeah," I said. I glanced back at Rogerson. "The door's open."

"Oh." We faced off across the shiny tiled floor as the tiny dog made a squeaking noise and lay back down, closing its eyes. "Well," Mike said, "you can have this."

And with that, he slid off his letter jacket, holding it out to me like an offering. And I stood there, frozen. From the open front door, Rogerson was watching me.

I looked over at him. "Hey," he mouthed soundlessly, smiling that wicked smile again. "Come on."

Mike was still holding the jacket out to me, and now he started to come closer. This was a Big Deal. It meant we were together, that I was his girl, and would lead to Homecoming Dances and proms and a hundred Saturday nights, a big class ring on a chain around my neck. I knew this. I'd seen Cass do it all before.

"Here," he said, holding the jacket up so that I could slide right in. He shook it a little bit, encouraging me, and then said, "Go ahead."

I glanced back at Rogerson. He lifted his chin at me, smiling. It was a gesture I would associate with him for the rest of my life. And I saw myself, then, setting out across uncharted territory, places Cass had never been or seen or even heard of. My world was suddenly wide and limitless, as vast as the sky and stars I'd been dazzled by earlier, and it all started there with the door he was holding open for me.

"I'm sorry," I said to Mike Evans and his jacket as I walked down the hallway to where Rogerson was standing, ready to help me along as I stepped past him and into the night.

As I walked down the front walk with Rogerson, across the yard to his car, I had no idea what I was doing. I knew that back inside the house Rina was probably mad at me for thwarting her plans, and Mike Evans had most likely already put his jacket back on and reported to everyone that in my fall I'd whacked my head and was now, clearly, insane.

"So," Rogerson said to me. He seemed to be laughing at me, or so I thought, and suddenly I felt completely idiotic. He leaned against his car and said, "What now?"

I stood there in the cold, in my little skirt, my hair pulled back in matching school-color barrettes. And I thought of Rina, the only woman I knew who always told men exactly what she wanted.

So I tossed my head the way she did and said, "Give me a ride home?"

"Okay," he said. And he got in the car and unlocked my door. He didn't know who I was. He didn't know about Cass or anything about my entire life up to that very second. I could have been anybody, and it made everything possible.

"Where we going?" he asked me as he started the car. As he reached to shift into reverse, his hand brushed against my knee and, instead of pulling away, I moved closer.

"Lakeview," I said, and he nodded, reaching forward to turn up the stereo. We didn't talk the whole way there.

He parked a ways down from my house and cut the engine, then turned and looked at me.

"So," he said evenly. "You regret that yet?"

"Regret what?" I said.

"Leaving back there," he said. "Looked like somebody had plans for you."

I thought of Mike Evans, holding out his jacket, and the blandness of his face, plain plain plain.

"He had plans," I said. "But they weren't really about me."

He nodded, looking down to run his finger along the bottom arc of the steering wheel. "I knew you were trouble," he said in a low voice. "Could tell just by looking at you."

"Me?" I said. "Look who's talking."

He raised his eyebrows. "What's that supposed to mean?"

"Oh, you know," I said. "You've got that whole thing going . . . the car, the hair."

"The hair?" he said, reaching up to touch one dreadlock. "What about it?"

"Oh, come on," I said. "You know."

He shook his head, smiling. "Whatever," he said. "Whatever you say."

I got the feeling he was waiting for me to leave: Of course he was.

I was just some dinky cheerleader, entertaining for a minute or two, but now he was ready to move on to other things. But I didn't want to leave, just yet. It was like being in a long, dark corridor and having someone crack a door, just for a second, and let a slant of light peek through. For one instant, I could have been anyone else.

But now, sitting in front of my neighbor's house, with all the landmarks—fire hydrants, streetlights, sidewalk pavement I'd played a million hopscotch games across—I was quickly becoming just me again, plain and simple.

He was leaning back in his seat, eyes on the dim green glow of the dashboard. Waiting, I knew, for me to leave. I had my hand on the door handle, ready to slip out, when he said, "Caitlin?"

I turned to look back at him: his green eyes, wild hair, so foreign and strange, a million miles from Mike Evans and the defensive line. And I could understand why Cass had rolled around the bed, so giddy and stupid, saying good night a hundred different ways just to keep that voice there, one more second.

"Yes?" I said, and before the word even fully left my mouth he was leaning forward, one hand rising to brush back my hair, and kissing me.

We made out for thirty minutes in front of the Richmonds' mailbox, parked behind their blue Astrovan. There was something especially wicked about this setting. I realized as he struggled to unhook my bra that I didn't even know his whole name and this, suddenly, seemed wrong.

"What's your last name?" I said, coming up for air somewhere near his left ear.

"Biscoe," he said, still working the clasp.

"Oh," I said.

Just then a shadow passed over the car, and we both froze. It was

Mr. Carnaby, from down the street, with his so-old-it-was-almost-dead Irish setter, out for a late night walk. They were about to go right by us.

Rogerson reached down next to my seat, grabbed the reclining lever, and in a split second we dropped quickly together out of sight, *whump*. I looked up into his face, those green eyes, and felt something all the way down to my toes.

"Rogerson Biscoe," he said, right into my ear, and then I went under again.

At some point I saw on the little digital clock on the dash that it was past midnight, my curfew. "I have to go," I said, buttoning my shirt so fast I forgot to put back on my bra, which I stuck in the pocket of my cheerleader jacket. One tumble off the pyramid and look how far I'd fallen.

"Go where?" he said. His lips were right on my cheek, salty and cool.

"Home." I brushed my fingers through my hair. "I have to be in by midnight."

"It's only five after," he said.

"I know. I'm late."

He leaned in and kissed me again, a good long one, then kept his hand on my knee as he drove up the street, turned around at the pool, and cut back toward my house.

He slowed down in front of my house, idling the engine.

"Well," I said. "I'm going now."

"So you said," he replied.

I opened my door and got out, noticing the light next to my father's chair, by the window, was still on.

"Bye," I said, walking around the front of the car, wondering if I'd ever see him again or if he just cruised the county, seducing cheerleaders on some eternal quest, obsessed with letter sweaters and pompoms.

It was a full moon as I walked up my front steps, bra in my pocket. In less than seven hours my entire life had shifted and changed, starting with that man yelling Cass's name and ending here, as I listened to Rogerson Biscoe start his car and rumble slowly down the street. It was like it had all happened to someone else, but each thing, each kiss and thought, were strangely mine. He beeped the horn, once, and I turned back to watch as he hit the gas, taillights growing dimmer as he picked up speed over the bridge, to the highway.

Once inside, I washed my face, put on my pajamas, and crawled into bed, reaching under the mattress to pull out the dream journal. I flipped to the first page again, where I'd only written that one sentence, and looked at the blank lines ahead of me.

I wrote as if Cass would someday read it, telling her everything that had happened, from start to finish. Her name, my fall, Rogerson, the full moon, and what I'd done. When I was finished, I'd filled up four pages, my hand cramping as I shut the book and slid it back under my mattress, holding all my secrets in.

I turned out my light and just lay there, seeing Rogerson's glittering green eyes in my head. For once, I didn't think about dreamland and finding Cass there. And as I drifted off, I heard Stewart's bike brakes squealing as they came closer, and knew without looking that he was drifting down the slope of the yard, faster and faster, before ducking the clothesline one more time to ease into home, safe.

Chapter Five

Rogerson didn't get in touch with me the next day, or the day after, or even the day after that. The first two days I sulked, eating multiple Clark bars and lying on my bed studying the ceiling. I'd felt so different in just the short time I'd spent with him, like I'd finally stepped out of not only Cass's shadow but my own as well. It was a letdown to just be the old me again.

By day three, however, something else happened to make me forget about him, at least temporarily.

It was after school, one day when I didn't have practice, and I was sitting in the living room with the TV on, half watching it while half reading the two chapters I'd been assigned for Social Studies. I was flipping between a movie, an after-school special about the perils of steroid use, and MTV, when I somehow landed on the *Lamont Whipper Show.* The topic was "You're Too Fat to Be All That!" and at some point one woman began yelling, every other word bleeped out but just barely. I looked up at the noise, ready to change back to the steroid show, and saw my sister.

She was standing off to the side, by the edge of the audience, holding a clipboard up against her chest, a pen tucked behind her ear. The *Lamont Whipper Show* was famously low-budget, and you often could see different staff members standing around, watching and conferring—it added to the real TV, no-holds-barred image. Now the woman onstage, who was short and redheaded, was jabbing a finger in her sister's face, telling her off, and in the background Cass was watching intently, reaching back at one point to brush her hair away from her face.

I jumped out of my chair, sending my book flying, and leaned in closer to the TV, just so I could see her. She looked the same, although her hair might have been shorter. Her nails were painted and she was wearing a black turtleneck she'd borrowed from my closet and never returned. It was funny how I'd forgotten about that, until now.

"Caitlin?" I heard my mother from behind me: She was coming up the hallway. "Can you turn that down, please? All that yelling—"

And then she just stopped, in mid-sentence, and as I turned around I saw her hand fly to her mouth, her face shocked.

"Oh, my God," she said in a low voice, coming closer and leaning into the TV, where we could still see Cass standing there, now jotting something on her clipboard and nodding as a big guy in headphones said something in her ear.

On-screen, the woman's sister was yelling, "If you'd treated him better he wouldn't have *come* looking for anything from me!" This was rebutted by a long series of beeps, punctuated only by the audience making *oooohhhhh* noises.

"It's her," my mother said, and on-screen my sister smiled, laughing at something the guy next to her said, and hugged the clipboard back up to her chest. "Look at her. It's Cassandra."

"I know," I said.

"Look at that," she said softly, kneeling down in front of the TV, her face just inches from it. Cass brushed her hair out of her face again, twisting one strand around a finger, and my mother's face crumpled.

"Oh, my God," she said, and as I watched she reached out one hand and pressed it against the TV screen, running her own finger across Cass's face. Cass, unaware, half-smiled.

"Mom," I said, and I was almost sorry now she'd seen it, she looked so pathetic crouched there, reaching out, with one of those hollow-eyed dolls—the Sunday School Teacher, apple and Bible in hand—watching from beside the magazine rack.

Just then the sisters disappeared from the screen, as did Cass, replaced by Lamont Whipper's big face. "Coming up next: Judy and Tamara's older sister, who has a secret about one of their husbands to share with them—and with us! Stay tuned!"

A Doublemint commercial came on but my mother remained crouched there, hand on the screen, as if she could still see Cass in front of her, close enough to touch.

"She's okay," she said softly. I wasn't even sure she was talking to me. "She's alive."

"Of course she is," I said. "She's fine."

She let her hand drop then, and sat back on her heels, wiping at her eyes. "I just am so glad . . . she's okay. She's okay."

We sat there and watched the rest of the show, catching glimpses of Cass again and again, but never for as long. The third sister confessed to affairs with both husbands, which resulted in a full-out brawl during which we got to see Adam, who bounded onstage to break things up. My mother seemed horrified by this kind of behavior that went against everything she believed in—but she kept her eyes glued to the set. I had a feeling the *Lamont Whipper Show* would now become regular viewing in our house.

When my father came home, she told him everything. He nodded, looking tired, then went to his study and shut the door. My mother watched him go, then walked to the kitchen and picked up the phone, drawing out the list of numbers they'd called that first day Cass was gone and finding the one for the show.

"Yes, I watched your program today," she said in her best Junior League voice when someone answered, "and . . . and what? Oh, yes, it was very good. Entertaining. But I'm trying to reach one of your staff members, and I was wondering . . . oh, I understand. Of course. But could you give her a message, please? It's kind of important."

My father came out of his study, took off his reading glasses, and tucked them in his front pocket. I thought about all those Yale bulletins stuck in his study drawer, and how he must feel to know Cass was working at a trash talk show, lining up angry confrontations and shocking confessions.

"Her name is Cassandra O'Koren," my mother said, and now her voice didn't sound so strong. My father turned and watched her as she spoke, and I realized I was holding my breath. All I could see was my mother in front of the TV, one hand reaching out to touch Cass's face, any way—the only way—she could. "And please just tell her, would you, that her family loves and misses her, very much. Thank you."

After my first night with him, I expected Rogerson to show up at another game, or a party, or even just drive past my house slowly enough to draw me to the window or outside. He didn't. First, I was surprised, then sad, then really, really pissed off. Rina said these phases were normal, even documented. She shared endless Clark bars with me, seeing me through what she called The Cycle of Recovery. I had just cleared Letting Go and Moving On when I saw him again.

The cheerleading squad was at the Senior Center for an event called Senior Days, which consisted of different community groups performing and teaching everything from ballroom dancing to lanyard making. We were on hand to do one of our dance routines, as well as fill in the gaps while other groups moved on and off the stage. It was ten in the morning and we'd had a big game the night before. I had a sore back from adjusting to my new position at the midpoint in the pyramid, Rina had a hangover, and Kelly Brandt and Chad had broken up—again—about seven hours earlier. Clearly, we were not at our best.

"I think they hate us," Rina whispered to me as we did our shimmy-shake number to "My Girl," with rows and rows of elderly people sitting in folding chairs in front of us. They were watching in a polite, if somewhat bored fashion: Some had their hands over their ears to block out our music. Kelly was sniffling, wiping her eyes during her handspring run, and Melinda Trudale had somehow missed our dance coach's advice to "tone things down a bit" and was doing her normal gyrating and hip-snapping right up front, much to the horror of a frail woman with an oxygen tank in the front row who was trying to knit some booties.

"I don't care," I said to Rina, and this pretty much summed up everything I'd been feeling in the last week. I'd begun to wonder if I really had dreamed everything that had happened with Rogerson. That whole Friday before seemed unreal now. And it *could* have been, except for the fallout I was suffering for rejecting Mike Evans. Rina had only been upset with me for about five minutes, but Mike had been alternately glaring or sulking at me all week. Not that I cared that much, being that I was doing much of the same, feeling cheap and lost and unable to forget kissing Rogerson for all that time in his car, even as I tried to.

We finished our number and got a pattering of polite applause as we ran off the stage, yelling and high-kicking. A man with a beard, barefoot and carrying a pillow, took the stage after us.

I could see Stewart and Boo in the back of the room. They were teaching an art workshop involving fruit and personal experience in another part of the building. My mother was there too, with the Junior League, assembling snacks and punch in the back kitchen. She'd been so preoccupied catching every airing of the *Lamont Whipper Show*—which was on daily at eleven, three, and ten at night on various channels—she hadn't even noticed anything different about me this last week. She'd only seen Cass on one more show, but still she sat through all the catfights and cussing, waiting for another glimpse.

"Hello, everyone," the man with the beard and pillow said softly into the microphone. "My name is Wade, and I want everyone to take a deep, cleansing breath, because for the next half hour, we're all going to get a little closer to ourselves."

After Melinda, the knitting woman in the front row had obviously had enough of anyone getting close to themselves. She picked up her bag and her booties, and wheeled her oxygen tank right on out of there.

Wade, at the microphone, didn't seem to notice. "I'm an artist, a writer, a dancer, and a survivor, and I want to show you even the smallest movement can spur happiness and healing."

"Oh, Jesus," Rina said in a flat voice, reaching up to adjust her bra strap. "I'm going outside for a cigarette."

"I'm right behind you," Eliza Drake said, pulling her pack out of her purse.

"You coming?" Rina asked me.

"In a minute," I said. Onstage, Wade had taken his pillow and sat down, folding his legs in the position I recognized from Boo's biweekly garden meditation. The crowd was thinning out, slowly, chairs rattling as people headed back to the snack area, where I could see my mother pouring punch into little blue cups.

"Now, the first thing I want everyone to do," Wade was saying into the microphone, "is to take a breath and hold your arms over your head, like this."

I watched as a few senior citizens followed his lead: Boo and Stewart's arms shot straight up, and they both had their eyes closed. Beyond the huge windows on the other side of the room I could see Rina and Eliza sitting by the fountain outside, smoking, tapping their ash into the water behind them.

I went back to the punch area, where my mother was handing out cups and cookies.

"Hi, honey," she said to me. Her face was flushed and she was smiling. My mother liked nothing more than a nice project to lose herself in. She'd been baking cookies and brownies all week for Senior Days, as well as coordinating thirty other Junior Leaguers for everything from decorations to scheduling. "Do me a favor?" she asked me.

"Sure," I said, as an elderly woman with a walker bumped me out of the way to grab a cookie.

"Go back in the kitchen and bring out another tray of these, would you? We've got some kids helping out back there. They can show you where they are."

"Okay."

"Wonderful," she said, already having moved on to a group of older men who were struggling to open a container of juice. "Let me get that for you . . . here you go! And help yourself to a cookie. We've got chocolate chip, lemon drop, pecan . . ."

As I walked through the open kitchen door, I saw the room was empty, save for a guy stacking cookies onto a big platter on the far countertop. The room was very bright, with fluorescent lights and clean, white floors and walls, and I found myself squinting as I crossed over to where he was standing. Outside, in the main room, I could still hear Wade talking; he was saying something about freedom of movement.

"Excuse me," I said, and I remember thinking there was something about this person that was familiar, even before he turned around, "I'm supposed to—"

It was Rogerson. He wore jeans and a white T-shirt, his hair pulled back at his neck, and seeing him in such bright light was startling, and made him suddenly real. He didn't seem surprised to see me at all, just leveling me with a look and smiling slightly.

Outside, Wade was directing everyone to breathe and do a personal movement, something spontaneous. "You just might surprise yourself," he said.

Rogerson put a cookie on the tray. "Supposed to what?" he said, and there was that look again, half mocking me, and I felt woozy under all those lights, like I might fall down.

"Get those," I said, pointing to the tray, which he picked up and handed to me. I turned around and started for the door, feeling him watching me as I walked away.

"Remember to breathe," Wade was saying from the stage, his voice low and soothing.

I turned around and Rogerson was still there. He raised his eyebrows.

"So," I said, "were you, like, not even going to *call* me?"

He looked surprised. "I didn't know your last name."

"You know where I live," I said.

"Yeah," he said, sticking his hands in his pockets. He ducked his head and a few dreadlocks slipped and fell over his forehead. Then he looked up and said, "I was working on that."

"Really."

"Yep," he said, leaning back against the counter. There was something about the way he moved, slowly and deliberately, that drove me crazy. "Really."

I just shook my head and walked back out to the punch table, where my mother, exasperated, yanked the tray out of my hand, knocking a few pecan cookies to the floor. "Well, it's about time," she said as she put it on the table, and hands immediately began grabbing.

But I was already turning back to the kitchen, walking through to find Rogerson standing just where I'd left him, as if he'd known I'd be back and was waiting for me.

"Let it go," Wade was saying, and I could still see him in my head, fingers touching, as I walked across that bright kitchen. "Open up your mind and find yourself there."

I stood in front of Rogerson and looked into his green eyes. He smiled at me.

"I can't believe you," I said to him.

"It's the hair," he explained.

I shook my head. "What are you doing here, anyway?"

He slid his hands around my waist, his fingers sliding up to touch my back just where I'd hurt it in pyramid duty the night before. "It's a long story," he said. "You really want to hear it?"

And I didn't at that moment, not really. Onstage behind me Wade was still talking, reminding me to breathe, breathe, open up and be free, and all the other nonsense words, so it was his voice I heard, and none of the others in my own head, as Rogerson leaned in and kissed me and I let go, closing my eyes and breathing all the way.

Chapter Six

"Caitlin," my mother said that night, as I waited for Rogerson to pick me up. "I'm just not sure about this."

I was standing at the top of the stairs, looking out the front window from which I could see the stoplight that led into Lakeview. With the leaves off the trees, I could see its colors clearly, and each time it turned green I held my breath and waited for him to slide into sight on the other side of our glass storm door.

My father, in his chair, put down the paper and looked at me. "About what?" he said.

My mother walked across the room and adjusted her newest Victorian doll, the Shopkeeper, a short, portly man carrying what looked like a sack of flour. "Caitlin met this boy today," she began, smoothing her fingers over the doll's shiny balding head, "and now she's going out with him."

The light changed again, this time to red. I looked at my watch: quarter of seven. He'd said seven, but I'd been ready since five-thirty.

"Who is he?" my father asked.

"Rogerson Biscoe's son," she said, dropping her hand from the Shopkeeper and reaching to move the milk pitcher in the tiny tea set sitting on the end table.

"The one that was the standout point guard, or the other one?" my father said.

I watched as the light dropped from red to green again.

"The other one," my mother said quietly.

"Oh," my father replied.

I didn't even bother to turn around and defend him, or me. When my mother had seen me in the kitchen with Rogerson, she asked me how I knew him and I said from school. It turned out his "long story" for being at Senior Days started with some kind of misdemeanor and ended with community service, which led to lemon cookies and punch and me. Obviously Kelly Brandt's hunch about Rogerson had been correct.

My parents also knew his parents: His mother was Bobbi Biscoe, a local realtor with big blond hair whose face appeared, it seemed, on practically every residential For Sale sign in town. She was always giving the thumbs-up, her head cocked confidently to one side. She was also in Junior League. Rogerson Senior was the head of a local pharmaceutical corporation and golfed at the same country club as my father. And older brother Peyton, after leading Perkins Day to the state championships the year before, was in his freshman year at the university. Normally, this would have been enough for them to approve of anyone. But Rogerson apparently had a lot of "long stories," some of which he'd shared with me when he drove me home from the Senior Center that afternoon.

He said, when I asked, that he went to Perkins Day, the elite prep school on the other side of town, where he was a fifth-year senior; he'd "taken some time off," apparently because of "some problems with administration." He didn't elaborate.

His family lived in the Arbors, a development of luxury homes based around a golf course: Their house was on the edge of the ninth hole. Rogerson lived in the pool house, where he could come and go as he liked. He was back in school, working part-time at a garage that fixed foreign cars, and working off his community service volunteering at the Senior Center on snack detail. Sure, he may have "had some problems," but he seemed to be on the right track now. I wasn't worried, even if my mother was.

Now she walked across the room, brow furrowed, and moved the County Squire doll closer to the magazine rack. "I just think . . ." she began in her light, passive-aggressive way, then trailed off, waiting for someone to take the bait.

"What?" my father said, folding the paper and laying it on the end table beside him.

"You had a very long day today," she said to me, still bustling around. "I'm worried you might be tired."

"I'm not," I said. "I'm fine."

"You have that big game on Monday afternoon," she added, reaching to smooth the skirt of the Ladies' Choir Soloist, whose mouth was posed in a wide, creepy kind of O, mid-note. "Not to mention Homecoming on Friday. I wouldn't be surprised if you had some extra practices this week."

"Mom, it's only Saturday," I said, as the light dropped to green again, through the trees.

"Well, I'm just saying," she said, glancing at my father before crossing the room to sit on the couch, her hand already reaching out to slide a row of glass thimbles there a bit to the right, "that I don't think this is a good idea." The last two words she said in a clipped, even voice, her eyes on my father, waiting for his response.

Bingo. He looked up, at her, then at me. "Caitlin," he said, as the light turned red again. "Maybe this isn't the best night for you to go out."

"It's Saturday night," I protested, turning away from the light to look at him. "Dad, come on. I did school stuff all day. It's the weekend."

"You have a math test on Monday, too," my mother added in a

low voice, picking up one of the thimbles and examining it. I felt an itchy uncomfortableness climb up the back of my neck, hating that she was this involved in my life, knowing my cheerleading schedule, my classes, my every move, as if we were somehow one person. This was the way she'd been with Cass, so proudly taping every schedule to the fridge. I'd always thought Cass liked it: I'd almost envied her. Now, I wasn't so sure.

My father picked his paper up again, unfolding it to the sports page. "Be home by curfew," he said, into a picture of the university football coach lifting his hands in victory. "And study tomorrow. Right?"

My mother, on the couch, turned and looked out the window, but she couldn't see the stoplight, turning from yellow to red again.

"Right," I said. "Okay."

Rogerson showed up exactly at seven, pulling to a stop at the end of our walkway. Our hall clock was chiming as I stepped outside. I didn't look back to see if my mother was watching as I started down the walk: I wanted this to be all mine, not part of any schedule or plan she could claim as her own. I wondered if Cass had felt the same way when she'd slipped out the door on that August morning and started toward a car idling there, waiting, for her.

"Hi," I said as I got into the car, shutting the door behind me.

"Hey," Rogerson said. Then he put the car in gear, turned around in the McLeans' driveway, and headed to the highway and the light I'd been watching all night. It was solid green as we coasted under it, and I looked over at Rogerson, wondering what he thought of me. He was in a brown sweater, jeans, and old scuffed loafers, a cigarette poking out of one side of his mouth. He didn't talk to me, and I couldn't think of a single thing to start a conversation that wouldn't sound even stupider if I said it aloud.

After a few minutes he said he had an "errand to run" and had to "drop by some place for a second." This someplace turned out to be a huge house in the Arbors, at the end of a cul-de-sac. There were about fifty cars parked along the street, but Rogerson pulled right up in the driveway.

"Come on," he said, getting out of the car, and I followed him. I didn't know what exactly I'd been expecting. Nothing had been normal about our relationship so far, so it wasn't like I'd been looking forward to a movie, pizza, and sipping one Coke with two straws, like I'd be doing with Mike Evans. Still, I had expected *something*. I just didn't know what it was.

When I stepped inside the house, I knew I'd walked into a Perkins Day party. Everyone looked like they'd just that instant jumped out of a J. Crew catalog, all crewnecks and cashmere and straight, white teeth.

"This way," Rogerson said, leading me past a trickling indoor fountain by the front door. He seemed to know his way around, and as we passed a group of girls sitting drinking wine coolers by the fountain, they all stared at me, with the same kind of slit-eyed look I always saw women give Rina. That was new.

"Hey, Rogerson," some girl said as we passed, and Rogerson nodded his head but didn't say hello.

"Who was that?" I asked, just to say something, as we walked through the living room where the carpet felt thick and spongy beneath my feet. There was a loud quarters game going in the next room at the dining room table, which was long, seating at least twenty people. I watched as a quarter bounced down its length, missing the glass by a mile, and everyone booed.

"Nobody," he said, walking up to a closed door off the living room and knocking twice before pushing it open. It was a study, with deep wood walls and red carpet, a huge desk sitting in front of several built-in shelves, each of which was crowded with trophies, framed pictures, and diplomas. There was a tall blond guy sitting at the desk, a lighter in his hand, about to light a bowl. A girl with red curly hair wearing ripped jeans and a Perkins Day sweatshirt was sitting on the desk blotter, smoking a cigarette, a huge cut-glass ashtray balanced on one leg.

"Rogerson," the blond guy said, setting the bowl down beside one of those miniature Zen gardens with the rocks and sand, and standing up. "Been waiting on you."

"Yeah, well," Rogerson said. "I'm here now."

"Good," the guy said. He had that classic All-American look, blond, blue-eyed, tall, creamy skin. "What you got for me?"

Rogerson reached into his pocket and pulled out a bag of pot, then held it up and shook it, evening out its contents. I don't know why this surprised me, but it did: He was serving cookies at Senior Days for "something," but I'd imagined parking tickets or ten miles over the speed limit. He put the bag on the desk and slid it across to the blond guy, who picked it up and examined it, flicking the small green buds with his finger through the plastic.

"How much?" he said.

"Seventy-five," Rogerson told him. "And a pinch for me."

The guy nodded. "Okay," he said. Then he looked at the redheaded girl, who stubbed out her cigarette in the ashtray and hopped off the desk, reaching into her back pocket for a wad of money, which she handed to him. He counted a few bills off, folded them, and slid them across the desk to Rogerson, who counted them quickly himself before sliding them into his own pocket.

The guy sat back down, opened the Baggie, and started to pack the bowl.

The redheaded girl looked at me, smiled, and said, "I'm Lauren."

"Caitlin," I said. "Hi."

"Rogerson's *so* polite," she said sarcastically, reaching out to poke him with her finger. As I looked more closely at the pictures on the shelves I could see she was in several of them: one in a soccer uniform with a ball in her lap, another in a long white dress, sitting on a green stretch of grass, her arms full of roses. "Isn't he?"

"Sorry," Rogerson said. "This is Caitlin. Caitlin, Lauren and Walter."

"Hi," Walter said to me, and I realized suddenly I recognized him from the Perkins football team, which had creamed us three weeks earlier at home.

Lauren lit another cigarette, blowing smoke toward the picture of her holding the roses, while Walter packed the bowl and handed it to Rogerson, a lighter balanced on top of it. He took a hit and handed it to me.

"No, thanks," I said.

"You sure?" he asked.

"Yeah."

He shrugged. "She's a cheerleader," he explained to Lauren as he handed her the bowl. She took a big hit and promptly started coughing, her face turning red. "She's got a reputation to protect."

"And she's going out with you?" Lauren said, between hacks.

"I know," Rogerson said. "Must be the hair."

"Must be," Lauren said, picking up her pack of cigarettes and shaking one out into her hand. "'Cause we *know* it's not your charm."

"Ha," Rogerson said, his expression flat.

"Ha, ha," she said, and smiled at me. I smiled back, still not quite sure I was in on the joke.

Later, after we'd left and gotten back into the car, I said, "So Walter plays for the football team, right? How long have you known him?"

He looked at me and half-smiled, then reached to shake a cigarette out of the pack wedged under the visor. "You know," he said thoughtfully, "you ask a lot of questions."

"I do not," I said indignantly. I didn't even know why he bothered to ask me out. It was like I wasn't even there. "You, like, haven't even *talked* to me since you picked me up."

"Talked?" he said. The lighter popped out with a click and he reached forward to grab it.

"Yes."

He pressed the lighter to the cigarette. "Okay, then. What do you want to talk about?"

"I . . . I don't know," I said. "I mean it's not like I want sparkling conversation. . . ."

He raised his eyebrows at me, replacing the lighter. There was something so striking about him. Even the smallest gesture or expression seemed important.

"But," I added, getting back to the point, "I just wondered why you asked me out tonight, if you didn't really want me here. That's all."

He thought about this. "You want to know why I asked you out?"

"Well," I said, rethinking that. Now I wasn't so sure I wanted the answer to that particular question. "Not necessarily."

He put out the cigarette in the ashtray, then turned a bit so he was facing me. "Do you want me to take you home?"

I looked back at the house. It was huge, the windows all lit up, shapes and bodies moving back and forth across the yellow light inside. Every other Saturday night I'd been at a party just like this with

Rina, in another part of town, playing quarters and waiting for something to happen.

"No," I said. "I'm fine."

"All right then," he said easily, starting up the engine. "I've gotta go by one more place, but that's it. Okay?"

"Yeah," I said. "Okay." And he put his hand on my leg, his fingers spread across my knee, as he put the car in gear and drove us away.

The next place was a trailer, out in the country. We crossed over Topper Lake, past the radio towers and several cow pastures before finally turning onto a dirt road so riddled with potholes we slowed to a crawl navigating them.

"Lost my tailpipe here last spring," Rogerson explained as we bumped along. "Real pain in the ass."

I nodded as we crested a huge crater, my head rising up to whack the ceiling so hard it brought tears to my eyes. Finally we pulled into a short dirt driveway, parking right outside a white double-wide with a rusted swing set and a warped baby pool in the yard.

"You better stay here," he said to me as I reached to open my door. "I'll be just a second, okay?"

"Okay," I said, glancing around me. I could see only woods, a huge crescent moon overhead, and another trailer—this one yellow, and more rusted—through a few scrubby pines to my left.

The trailer door opened as Rogerson walked up the steps, revealing a stocky blond woman with a baby on her hip. She had her hair pulled up on top of her head, Pebbles Flintstone–style, and was wearing a faded Gucci T-shirt and jeans. The baby reached out for Rogerson as he stepped inside and she shifted him to her other hip, his pacifier falling out of his mouth and down the steps in the process.

She didn't notice, and he was still reaching for it, his face twisted in a cry, as she let the door fall shut.

I sat there in the car for eighteen and a half minutes. I knew this because the glowing blue clock on the dash was right in front of me, and I felt like I was watching my life tick away, minute by minute, in a place where I could stay forever and no one could ever find me. I was so fixated on this that I jumped, my heart racing, when Rogerson tapped on the windshield in front of my face.

"Sorry about that," he said as he got inside. "Got held up."

"It's okay," I said, "but I think I want to go—"

And then he leaned over and kissed me, hard, his hand reaching behind my neck and holding me there, his mouth smoky and sweet. I kissed him back with that huge moon shining down on us, and thought the whole time of that clock, still counting down, minute by minute, hour by hour, forever.

We ended up back in the Arbors, cutting through side streets and past the country club to pull up in front of another house, where cars were also lining the street. Rogerson parked behind a silver Lexus, then reached under his seat and fiddled around for something, his brow furrowed, until he found it.

"Bingo," he said in a low voice, and as he opened his clenched fist I saw a ceramic bowl in his palm. He reached into his pocket and pulled out a small Baggie, packing the bowl quickly, then handed it to me.

"Oh, no thanks," I said. "Reputation and all that."

"It's your choice," he said, shrugging. "But if I were you, I'd take a hit. You're gonna need it."

"For what?" I said.

"Just trust me." He reached in his pocket for a lighter and a flame jumped up between us, illuminating both our faces in a warm, yellow light. "Okay?"

I'd been taught since sixth grade about Peer Pressure and Bad Influences and Just Saying No. But for all he knew, I could be the kind of girl that smoked. I could be anything.

I lit the bowl and took a big drag, feeling the smoke tangle in my throat, making me cough hard, fast. Tears came to my eyes as I handed it back to him, already feeling something change in me, as if I was slowly falling into warm water, one inch at a time.

When we finished the bowl, Rogerson tapped it out, stuck it back under the seat, and leaned forward to kiss me again. It felt good, and I could have stayed there doing that forever, I was sure, but he pulled away and smiled at me.

"Ready?" he said.

"Sure," I replied, not even knowing what I was getting into.

"Then look right here," he said, holding up a finger, and when I did he squirted something in my mouth that tasted strange and fresh, surprising me so much it made me gag, then start coughing again.

"Whoa," he said, pounding me on the back. "Watch out there. Sorry about that."

"What is that?" I said, still coughing.

"Breath spray," he said, shooting two quick squirts into his own mouth. "Breakfast of champions."

"Next time," I told him, still coughing, "warn me."

"Gotcha," he said. "Let's go."

We got out of the car and started up the driveway, walking around three Mercedes and a Jaguar on the way. As we walked Rogerson was making fast business of tucking in his shirt and smoothing back his hair. This struck me as funny, for some reason.

"What are you doing?" I asked him. Everything seemed kind of fuzzy and mild, as if I was actually standing off to the side watching but not really involved.

"It's the hair," he said seriously, pulling it back at the base of his neck and fastening it with something. "It scares them."

I laughed out loud and it sounded strange, fast and sharp: *Ha!* "Scares who?" I said.

And at that moment he reached out and grabbed my hand, squeezing it just as above us, up the rolling curve of the thick green lawn, the huge front door opened and I saw Bobbi Biscoe, star of a million For Sale signs, standing there. Up close, I could see she had the same dark coloring as Rogerson—I found out later that she was Greek—and the same thick, curly hair.

"Rogerson Biscoe!" she called out. She was smiling but her voice sounded angry, irritated, and the contrast was strange. Rogerson pulled me close to him, locking his fingers tighter into mine. "Where have you *been?*"

"Mom," Rogerson said.

"You were supposed to be here to meet and greet," she scolded him between clenched teeth—still smiling—as we got closer. She was in a short black cocktail dress and heels and in person she looked older than her picture. There was a half ring of pink lipstick on the mouth of the glass in her hand, which she took another big gulp of as she narrowed her eyes at Rogerson. "Your father is *not* pleased, and for once I do not feel like sticking up for you when—"

"Mom," Rogerson said again, calmly, "this is Caitlin O'Koren."

She looked at me quickly, as if she hadn't even noticed I was standing there, then made no secret of looking up and down once, as if sizing me up.

"Is Margaret O'Koren your mother?" she asked me, and I swallowed hard, aware of how dry my mouth was.

"Yes," I said, standing up straighter. "She is."

She nodded, finishing off her drink and reaching around her back to stick it on a small table behind her, then took her fingers and fluffed a small piece of hair over her forehead, drawing it out. "Well, come in, then," she said to Rogerson in a tired voice, pushing the door the rest of the way open. "He's in there."

The house was enormous, the entryway opening up into a huge room with high cathedral ceilings, where the voices of the fifty or so people chatting and eating canapés rose up and mingled overhead into one musical sort of buzz. There was a thick pack of people straight ahead of us, all centered around an older man with ruddy skin who was holding a drink and appeared to be telling a joke that hadn't yet reached the punch line.

"I'll be right back," Rogerson said into my ear, then let go of my hand and started down the stairs, leaving me there. There was a sudden loud burst of laughter as the joke finished, and then his mother appeared at my elbow.

"Caitlin, honey, come help check on the spinach phyllo," she said smoothly, hooking her arm in mine and walking me down a short hallway to the kitchen, where a group of people in white shirts and black ties were all bustling around arranging fruit and cheese on various platters. Everything seemed to be going in fast forward, while I felt like I was hardly moving, my feet and head heavy and thick. "What can I get you to drink?"

"Um," I said. My tongue was sticking to my lips but I wasn't ready to risk having to do anything with my hands, so I said, "I'm fine."

"Well," she said, lowering her voice as if speaking to me confidentially, "*I* need another." She walked to a counter, bypassing two caterers arguing over clam strips, and picked up a bottle of wine, pouring herself a big glass. "Ingrid, sweetheart, what's happening with the phyllo?"

"It's coming, ma'am," a short woman in jeans, by the oven, said, twisting a dishtowel in her hand. "Just a minute or two."

"Marvelous," Mrs. Biscoe said dryly, taking a sip of her drink. "It's to die for, that phyllo," she said to me. Under the bright lights of the kitchen I could see the tiny imperfections of her face: small lines by her eyes, the uneven slope of her nose. These things were fascinating, and I found myself completely unable to stop staring at them. "Costs an arm and a leg, but what are you going to do?"

I nodded, having lost track of the conversation. Where was Rogerson? He'd dumped me, stoned, with, of all people, his *mother.* This had to be some kind of cruel test. He was probably already long gone, laughing hysterically about me with his real friends while I tried somehow to find my way home.

"So," Mrs. Biscoe said, fluffing that same piece of hair again as she jerked me out of this paranoid reverie, "how did you meet our Rogerson?"

There was a sudden crash in the corner of the kitchen as something was dropped, and someone cursed. Mrs. Biscoe turned around, looked over as if mildly interested, and shook her head.

"At a party," I stammered. "We met at a party."

"Oh, yes," she said absently, as if she wasn't really listening, still looking at something over my head. "He likes those."

The door opened behind me, letting out two caterers and in Rogerson, finally, who looked across the room at me and smiled. I had this wild thought that he was the only one in all this chaos who was just like me, and that was comforting and profound all at once.

"Hey," he said as he came closer, reaching to grab something off a passing tray and pop it in his mouth. "Doing okay?"

"Rogerson, darling," Mrs. Biscoe said, reaching over to smooth her hand over his hair. "Did you apologize to your father?"

"Yep," he said, still chewing. "Man, those triangle things are good, Mom."

She looked at me. "Phyllo," she explained, as if proving a point, before letting her hand drop onto his shoulder.

"Oh," I said. "Right."

"We're gonna go out back, okay?" Rogerson said, as his mother took another sip of wine, distracted. The kitchen was so noisy, full of voices and clanging, oven doors slamming shut, but she didn't seem to hear any of it.

"Yes, okay," she said, snapping to and standing up straighter to fluff that one bit of her bangs again. "But stay close. Right?"

"Right," Rogerson said, reaching for my hand and winding his tightly around it before leading me through a group of caterers to a door across the room. When I looked back I could see Mrs. Biscoe standing in front of the swinging kitchen door, framed for a second against the movement and color of the party. The door swung out behind her and for a moment it was like everything froze and she was just there, suspended. Then the door started to swing back and she stepped through, disappearing like a dove in a magician's handkerchief.

Rogerson took me back to the pool house, where he lived. His room was probably the neatest I'd ever seen in my life. It looked like you could run a white-gloved fingertip over any surface and never find one fleck of dust, with everything having a place and an order, from the CDs stacked alphabetically on the shelves over his bed to the way the towels were folded in the bathroom. It was the kind of place where you were conscious not to disrupt the neat vacuum lines on the carpet or the perfectly plumped pillows—sitting at exactly forty-five-degree angles—on the couch.

I would have assumed it was a maid's doing, but the first thing Rogerson did when we walked in was bend down to fix the base of a coatrack by the door so that its stand fit squarely in the middle of a tile there. This was all his.

I went to use the bathroom—marveling at the shiny chrome sink and fixtures, the sharp cleanliness of the mirror—and when I came out someone was knocking at the door.

"Hold on," Rogerson said, starting back across the room, but the door was already opening and Rogerson's father—the older man I'd seen at the center of the party, telling jokes—came in. He was wearing a golf sweater with a little gold insignia on it and dress pants and loafers. He couldn't see me.

"I told you to be here at seven o'clock," he said to Rogerson, crossing the room with smooth strides. His face was pinkly red, flushed.

Rogerson glanced at me, quickly, and the look on his face—strange and unsteady—made me step back instinctively into the darkness of the bathroom, my hand resting on the cool countertop there. "Dad," he said. "I—"

"Look at me when I'm talking to you!" Mr. Biscoe said, and right as he crossed my line of vision, his face now beet-red, he suddenly reached out and hit Rogerson, hard, across the temple. Rogerson's neck snapped back reflexively, and he lifted a hand to shield himself. "When I say you are to be somewhere, you are *there*. Understood?"

Rogerson, hand over his face, nodded. I felt my stomach turning. I wasn't even sure I was breathing.

"Are we clear?" Mr. Biscoe bellowed. I could see one vein, taut, sticking up in his neck. "Look at me."

"Yes," Rogerson said, and his father reached over, irritated, and snatched his hand away from his face, gripping his wrist. "Yes. I understand."

"Good," his father said. "Then we're clear." He dropped Rogerson's wrist, then reached up to hook a finger around his own collar, adjusting it, before turning back toward the door. I kept my eyes on the tiled bathroom floor, studying the colors: black and white, over and over, like a chessboard.

I stayed still until I heard the door slam, and Rogerson stumbled backward to the bed, sitting down and spreading his fingers over the side of his face. I walked out of the bathroom and went to sit beside him, but he wouldn't look at me.

"Rogerson," I said, turning to face him. "Let me see."

"Don't touch me," he said in a low voice. "I'm fine."

His eyes were so dark, the place where he'd been hit flushed and red. "Please," I said. "Come on."

"Don't," he said, but when I reached over and put my hand over his he didn't shake me off. "Don't touch me."

"Rogerson," I said, slowly pulling his hand away. I could feel his pulse beating at his temple under my forefinger, the skin red and hot there.

"Don't touch me," he said, so softly this time, and I took my finger and traced his eyebrow where he'd taken the brunt of the hit, the same way Cass had done to me so many times, her face changing as she saw again what she'd done. "Don't."

"Shh," I said.

"Don't touch me," he whispered. "Don't."

But he was already leaning in, as my own hand worked to cover the hurt, his eyes closing as his forehead hit my chest and my finger traced the spot again and again that I knew so well.

Rogerson

Chapter Seven

I never told anyone what happened at Rogerson's. But from then on, we were together.

We didn't talk about it: It was just understood. In that one moment I'd seen some part of him that he kept hidden from the rest of the world—behind his cool face, his bored manner, his hair. I'd edged in past it all, and now I found my own place there.

The next Monday, after cheerleading practice, I walked outside to find Rogerson parked in front of the gym. He was leaning against his car, smoking a cigarette, waiting for me. I hadn't asked him to pick me up. But there he was.

"Oh, my God," Kelly Brandt said as we came to the main doors. She and Chad had made up and exchanged "friendship rings." She kept flashing hers around, wanting everyone to ask about it. "What is *he* doing here?"

"I told you Caitlin had a big weekend," Rina said slyly, poking me in the side. I'd told only her about our date, and as much as she might have wanted us to both date football players, she loved the idea of me with Rogerson. It was just forbidden and wild enough to appeal to her.

"That was him you were talking about?" Kelly said incredulously. Outside, Rogerson flicked his cigarette and turned around, leaning his head back to look up at the gray November sky. "I mean, Caitlin, he's . . ."

"He's what?" Rina said, as a pack of soccer players crossed between us and Rogerson, jogging. They were all blond or dark-haired, tall and athletic, moving in perfect synchronicity. When Rogerson came back into view he was watching them pass, his hair blowing in the wind, an expression I couldn't make out on his face. "*Tell* us what he is, Kelly."

"Well," Kelly said, lowering her voice and brushing her hair back with her friendship ring hand, "I've just heard some stories, that's all. He's been in trouble, you know. Like with the *police*. I mean, I have this friend at Perkins Day, and she said . . ."

But I wasn't even listening, already pushing through the doors into the cold air. Rogerson stood up from where he was leaning when he saw me. He had told me himself about his "long stories," and I didn't care. I myself had no stories of my own yet, but I was ready. More than ready.

That first week, whenever I thought about him, I remembered brushing my finger over his eyebrow, tracing the hurt, trying to give back what his father had taken away. Now I'd take that bit of Rogerson and hold it close to me. That fall, as I struggled to leave Cass's shadow behind once and for all, he was just what I needed.

From that day on, Rogerson was suddenly just *there*. He drove me home every day. He came over from Perkins at lunch to take me out and called me every night—usually more than once—and then again before I went to bed. On Fridays he came to my games, home or away, and stood off to the side of the bleachers, watching me cartwheel and cheer while he leaned against the fence, smoking cigarettes and waiting for me.

We never really went on "dates," exactly: With Rogerson, it was all about being in motion. Going from party to party, place to place. Sometimes I stayed in the car, but more often now I came in and was introduced. To the college guys in the dorm room with the huge Bob Marley poster and the couch that smelled like rancid beer. To the woman who lived in that trailer and her little boy, Bennett, who sat quietly on the floor, playing with a plastic phone as she weighed bags of pot on a digital scale. And to so many others, whose faces and names I would never remember. They blurred together, weekend after weekend, as Rogerson made his rounds.

Sometimes I missed the whole movie-restaurant-mini-golf-basketball-game kind of dating lifestyle. But this was just how it was with Rogerson. He had a lot of nervous energy, business to attend to, and frankly I couldn't really picture him standing in front of a windmill at Jungle Golf, lining up his shot. That was more of a Mike Evans thing, and I'd made my choice there. So I was happy to be with Rogerson, in transit, always with a bit of a buzz and his hand on my knee. It was just fine.

"So what do you guys *do,* anyway?" Rina always asked me. Her quarterback was a date kind of guy—they were always going out to dinner, or to the movies, or double-dating with other couples. I couldn't see Rogerson doing that, either.

"I don't know," I told her. "We just hang out."

That was the only way I could describe it. Most of the time spent with Rogerson was in the car, him driving and me in the passenger seat, his fingers spread across my knee. He'd take me to McDonald's and buy me chocolate shakes, which he already knew were my favorite, or drive us out to Topper Lake, where we'd take the car onto the flats and listen to the radio. The only time we ever argued was about music.

Rogerson liked classic rock. Pink Floyd, his favorite, depressed the hell out of me. So whenever he left me alone in the car, engine running, I'd change the station to G103, cranking it up to fill the air around me with bouncy pop tunes, the kind that get stuck in your head all day and all night long, like a soundtrack in your dreams. Rogerson would come out of the Quik Zip, or down the stairs of someone's apartment, and head for the car. I'd watch his expression change as he got closer, hearing the strains of one of my baby-baby-oh-please-baby songs.

"Oh, my God," he said to me once as he flopped into the driver's seat, pulling the door shut behind him. "What is this shit?"

"Number one in the country," I told him smugly, even as he reached forward, hitting one of the preset buttons. Suddenly we were surrounded by the sound of funereal gonging, interwoven with some woman moaning.

"See," he said, pointing to the radio, "now *that's* music."

"No," I told him, hitting another preset—the one I'd changed a few days earlier, when he'd been busy pumping gas—"this is."

But it wasn't. Instead, it was some woman singing about dandruff control.

"Nice," he said, snapping his fingers as if it was just so catchy. "Better than most of the stuff you listen to."

"Shut up," I said, rolling my eyes.

"I don't even know why you like that," he said, cranking the engine.

"I don't even know why I like *you,*" I replied, as the dandruff song finally ended.

"Yes, you do," he said, turning his head to back us out of the parking lot.

"I do?"

"Yeah." He smiled at me. "It's the hair."

And then he changed the station again.

My mother tut-tutted, worrying about me being out too much, until my father reminded her that Cass, too, had dated and managed to juggle her various responsibilities. Still, whenever the phone rang past nine, I'd watch a ripple pass over my mother's face, or hear her sigh just loudly enough so we could all hear it.

Within a week I'd stopped riding home with the team and squad, leaving instead in the BMW with him. We'd pull up beside the bus at a stoplight and I'd see everyone grouped in the back, laughing and talking, and know that Rina was probably on someone's lap, that Kelly and Chad were making out, and that Coach Harrock was half-heartedly telling everyone to quiet down, please, and reflect on the game. Rina would always look out and wave, smiling, but the rest of the girls and the team just looked down at us, lips moving and brows instantly furrowing as they discussed me.

"God, they're all staring," I said to Rogerson the first time it happened. "I don't even want to know what they're saying."

"Why do you care?" he said, switching gears with a squeal—he drove like a crazy person—as we moved up the smooth orange of the bus. "They're a bunch of idiots. I don't know why you'd want to hang out with them anyway."

That was Rogerson, or so I was learning. He divided the world coolly into black or white, no grays or middle ground. People were either cool or assholes, situations good or bad. My friends, and my life at school, consistently fell into each of the latter. His friends were older, more interesting, and, most importantly, not jocks or cheerleaders. When we did go to parties where I'd see Rina or Kelly Brandt or anyone else from the squad, it was always awkward. They'd want me to stay, pulling up a chair, handing over the quarter so I could take a bounce. But Rogerson was always impatient, finishing whatever business he had and heading straight to the door, making it clear he was ready to go.

Now, as we passed them, I looked up at the bus windows, seeing the faces I'd spent the last few months with: Kelly, Mike Evans, Melinda, the offensive line. And they all looked right back at me, still staring, as if we were some strange culture to be studied and discussed.

Whenever Rogerson trashed them I didn't know what to say. I wasn't even sure why I'd hung out with them. It had just sort of *happened,* like everything else in my life. Now, with him, I felt finally like I was making my own choices, living wide awake after being in a dreamworld so long.

I kept my eyes on the faces in the windows of the bus, staring back hard as Rogerson hit the gas, shifting gears again, and we were gone, leaving them to be just a bright orange speck in the sideview mirror, falling farther and farther behind me.

I got home after practice one unseasonably warm afternoon in mid-November to find our back glass patio door open and my mother and Boo sitting outside in lawn chairs. The garden plot in the side yard had been turned over, and a few packages of flower bulbs lay nearby, some open, a trowel abandoned at the foot of my mother's chair. From the kitchen I could see the TV was on in the living room, low volume: Lamont Whipper came on at six sharp. The warm air was blowing through the back door, stirring the stale air of our house with the smell of a misplaced spring. Outside, however, it was already starting to get dark, the sky streaked with deep pinks and grays.

"Oh, Boo, you're awful," my mother was saying, her voice drifting into the kitchen. The chairs were arranged so their backs were to me, just the top of their heads—my mother's, carefully coiffed and in a bun, Boo's, wild red with a couple of chopsticks poking out at strange angles—peeking over and visible from where I was standing by the counter.

"You mastered pottery," Boo said. "I think coed massage is the next logical step."

"Boo, really," my mother said. "What would Jack say?"

Boo considered this, then chuckled. "Okay, so massage is out. For now. How about . . . introduction to aromatherapy?"

"What's that?"

"Using scents to calm and ease," Boo explained, flipping the page. "But it can get kind of smelly and boring. How about cake decorating?"

"Too fattening," my mother said, and Boo clucked her tongue, agreeing.

"Well, are you specifically interested in anything?" Boo asked her.

"I don't know," my mother said. "Cassandra and I had always talked about taking a photography class. She said my family pictures were so bad, since I always cut off people's heads. We were going to do it over the summer, but then she went to the beach, and was so busy there, and then . . ."

Then her voice just dropped off, suddenly, and I could hear Boo turning pages, smoothly, one right after another. Neither one of them said anything as I crossed the kitchen to the fridge, opened it, then shut it again.

"I've written her five times now," my mother said suddenly, and as I turned to look out at them again I saw it was getting dark more quickly now, harder to make out their shapes against the sunset. "I never know what to say. It's so hard to put it into words."

"She'll write when she's ready," Boo said, turning another page. I was sure she couldn't even see the words in front of her, now.

"I still can't believe she could have been unhappy. I mean, when we went to buy those pillow shams for Yale, she was so excited. Just as excited as me. I *know* she was."

There was something so lonely in her voice, something that made me look back out at her suddenly. But it was so dark I couldn't even make her out, and this made me sadder still.

"I don't think it was about you," Boo said softly, and I could tell by her tone that she'd said it before, often, in just the same way.

"Then what could it have been, that she couldn't tell me? What?"

"I don't know, Margaret," Boo said. "I just don't know."

And there it was. Even with the dolls, and the crooked pottery vases, even with my cheerleading and bake sales and fretting over my relationship with Rogerson, my mother still couldn't fill the space left behind by my older, more dynamic, more everything, sister. We might have felt like things were going on, seasons changing, months passing. But we would have been wrong.

The door slammed downstairs, announcing my father's arrival. "Hello," he called out, as he always did, and I heard him stop to flip through the mail on the sideboard as he hung up his coat.

"Oh, that's Jack," my mother said, and suddenly she was walking through the patio door, squinting in the sudden light, one hand reaching back to smooth her hair. She seemed startled when she saw me. "Oh! Caitlin, honey, how long have you been home?"

"I just got here," I said.

Boo walked up and stood in the doorway, tucking her catalog under one arm. When she smiled at me, her eyes crinkled in the corners, freckles folding in on each other. "Hey, beautiful," she said. "Want to take a photography class with us?"

My mother was crossing the room from the fridge now, opening the oven to slide in a casserole. I could hear my father coming up the stairs, his footsteps heavy.

"Sure," I said.

"Caitlin, I don't know," my mother said, shutting the oven. "You're so busy with practice and school, I'm not sure it would be best."

"I'm not that busy," I said. I'd only been trying to help. "But, whatever. If you don't want—"

"No, I'm just saying," my mother said quickly, setting the oven timer with a few jabs of her finger. "I just thought that maybe—"

"Then it's settled," Boo said over both of us, reaching up to adjust one of her chopsticks, jabbing it on the other side of her head. "Photography it is. Just us girls."

"Well," my mother said, crossing the kitchen to pull a bag of rolls out of the fridge. "I guess if it's on the weekends . . ."

"No arguments," Boo said. "Classes begin in two weeks. Saturdays at noon. Okay?"

My mother glanced at the clock—it was almost six—and then into the living room, where the talk show before *Lamont Whipper* was rolling credits up the screen. "Well, okay," she said. "I really should—"

"Go," Boo told her. "I'll come by tomorrow."

"See you then," my mother said, waving over her shoulder as she walked out of the kitchen to the TV, as the *Lamont Whipper* theme music came on. Boo looked at me and smiled again, cocking her head to the side as if she'd known I'd been standing there, listening to them all along.

"You holding up okay?" she said suddenly, and the last of the sunset was so pink behind her. I remembered how I'd wished all those nights in my room that *she* was my mother as I watched Stewart glide down the slope of their lawn, bike chains rattling, under the moonlight. Sometimes it seemed like she was the only one who even noticed I was alive.

"Sure," I said, unable to stop myself from turning to see my own real mother pull a chair closer to the television, leaning in for the slightest glimpse of the one face she would recognize, the only one she wanted to see. "I'm fine."

It was about a week later that I was stuck in practice for an extra twenty minutes while Chelsea Robbins drilled us, again and again, on a new dance routine she'd come up with during a bout of inspiration at a Baptist Youth retreat. It involved a lot of backflips, a pyramid, and a complicated formation that was supposed to result in us all lying down in various positions to form a tiger (our mascot) but instead ended up looking like some variation of a sloth without a head.

"This is ridiculous," Rina—who was making up part of the mouth—said after our fifth try. "All anyone is going to be doing is trying to look up our skirts anyway. It's humiliating."

"Ladies!" Chelsea yelled at Melinda Trudale and me. We were supposed to be forming the tiger's chest but our legs were too short. Above us, we could hear rain pounding on the roof: It was pouring. "Extend! You have to extend!"

"Screw extending," Melinda said under her breath. "It's six-friggin'-o'clock. I'm going home."

"One more run-through," Chelsea said, reaching over to rewind the music—our school fight song, set to a disco beat—again. But, led by Melinda, everyone was now getting up, grumbling and shaking the floor dust out of their sweatpants and T-shirts, and heading for their backpacks and the parking lot. "Fine, fine," Chelsea said in a clipped tone, grabbing the tape player and yanking the cord out of the wall.

"We'll start fresh tomorrow. And think formation, please. Think teamwork!"

"Think therapy," Rina said, nudging me with her elbow as she passed, on her way to meet Bill Skeritt, who was standing by the doorway waiting for her. "See you later, okay?" she said as he looped his arm around her waist, leaning to kiss her neck. She laughed, pushing him off, while her fingers looped around his wrist, at the same time pulling him closer.

"See you," I said. Everyone was filing out of the gym, talking and complaining about Chelsea, while I bent down to grab my books and jacket. The rain was still coming down, beating hard overhead. When I stood up, Mike Evans was right behind me.

"Hey, Caitlin," he said. He was wearing his letter jacket and his hair was damp, curling slightly over his collar.

"Hi." I slung my backpack over my shoulder, glancing at the doors that led to the outer building. I was hoping for Rina, or Melinda Trudale, or even Chelsea Robbins and her boom box, anyone to stop this inevitable discussion I was about to have with saltine-esque Mike Evans, whom I hadn't been really face-to-face with since the night I rejected both him and his letter jacket and ran off with Rogerson, never looking back.

But the hallway, and the gym, were empty. It was just us.

"So," he said, sticking his hands in his pockets, "how've you been?"

"Um, good," I said, taking a step closer to the door and glancing—hint, hint—at my watch. "I really should—"

"So what happened that night, at the party?" he asked me suddenly, and I felt so uncomfortable I just looked at my shoes, the shiny wooden gym floor beneath them. "I mean, I thought you liked me. Rina said you did."

"Mike," I said.

"And then you leave with that *guy.*" The way he said it Rogerson could have been some infectious disease involving pus, boils, and graphic bodily functions. "I mean, what was that all about?"

Before, I might have tried to squirm out of it. But my obligation to Mike Evans had been small at best.

"It's not really your business," I said, affecting my best Cass coolness. "And it's late. I really have to go—"

"You should know what people are saying about you," he blurted out quickly as I turned away from him. "I mean, someone should *tell* you."

"What who is saying about me?" I said. The rain was letting up some, but I could still hear it, plinking overhead.

"Everyone," he said. "The team, the rest of the cheerleaders."

Like these were important people, the *most* important people, and their opinions should be of utmost importance to me. And for one split second, standing under that roof with the rain banging overhead, I knew why Cass had left, could almost have been her, in that instant. Maybe she got tired of her strings being pulled, too.

"I don't care what people are saying," I said slowly, turning my face up to look Mike square in the eye.

"This Rogerson," he said, and it was strange to hear him say his name. "He's been in a lot of trouble, Caitlin. I've heard stories. I mean, he's not your type."

"You don't even know him," I said, suddenly defensive of Rogerson, seeing him holding his face the night of his parents' party, how dark his eyes were. "You don't even know *me.*"

"Oh, come on," he said, smiling. "Of course I do."

But he didn't. He knew Cass, and Rina. But Mike Evans had never said more than ten words to me before that night we were supposed to suddenly become a couple. He was just a stupid jock who wanted a cheerleader—not me. Not even close.

"I'm leaving," I said, brushing past him.

"Wait," he said, reaching out and grabbing me by the arm. I looked down at his fingers, spread over the fabric of my shirt, and then up at his face. "Listen to me. I'm just trying—"

"Let go," I said, trying to pull away.

"Just hold on." He gripped me harder, his fingers pulling at the fabric. "Listen." The rain was hitting hard now, so loud I almost didn't hear the door banging open in front of me.

Rogerson was standing there. His hair was wet, dripping down onto the shiny wooden floor, and his jeans and jacket were both damp and dark, as dark as his eyes.

Mike dropped his hand, quickly.

"Caitlin," Rogerson said. I could barely hear him above the rain. But even as he spoke, he wasn't looking at me; his eyes were on Mike. "What's going on?"

"Hey, man," Mike Evans said, too loudly, as he put another arm's length between us, "we're just talking here. That's all."

Rogerson looked at me, to confirm this, and I wondered, suddenly, just what would happen if I didn't agree. I felt strangely flattered, protected, as I walked over to stand beside my boyfriend, who kept his eyes solid on Mike Evans, even as I wrapped my fingers around his.

"Come on," I said. "I'm late already."

Rogerson looked like he wasn't quite sure about this, even as I smoothed my hand over his damp shoulder, his wet hair brushing against my skin. "It's nothing."

He left with me, then. And Mike Evans was brave enough to wait until we were out of sight before he called out, "Think about what I said, Caitlin. Okay?" his voice bouncing down the empty school corridors.

Rogerson and I were standing at the front doors. I could barely see the car through the rain, falling thick and fast, in sheets.

"What did he say?" Rogerson asked me, taking one last glance back as if still contemplating finishing what Mike had started.

"Nothing important," I said. Then he pushed the door open and I pulled my jacket over my head, the rain already whistling in my ears, as we started to make a run for it together.

Cass's first real boyfriend, Jason Packer—the boy who had broken her heart—was part of our family for the two years they dated. He came for Thanksgiving dinner, exchanged Christmas gifts with my family, and helped my father install the track lighting in our upstairs hallway. He was accepted to the point that we gave up maintaining what my mother called "company behavior." It was like we were all dating Jason Packer, and when he dumped Cass, each of us took it a little personally.

I didn't expect things to be this way with Rogerson.

We'd been together about three weeks when I finally had to bring him inside for a Formal Introduction. After her initial hesitation—and once I'd proven I wasn't blowing off everything else to be with him—my mother surprised me by asking about Rogerson occasionally, the way she did about cheerleading or school, although more out of duty than of real interest. My father was doing his part from the comfort of his chair: he'd reach over and flip on the front porch light when Rogerson and I had been parked for more than twenty minutes, reminding me that I was due inside.

This was strange to me. I had expected my parents to be even more vigilant about my relationship with Rogerson because of Cass running away. After all, they'd already lost one daughter to a boy they didn't know.

Maybe it was because they knew what his father did, who his brother was, had seen his mother's face on For Sale signs staked into a million lawns, and this made him safer, somehow. The other option—that somehow, losing me would be less of a loss, never as hard as the one already suffered—was something I pushed out of my head each time it rose up, nagging.

It was a Friday night, during my parents' and Boo and Stewart's weekly Trivial Pursuit war. I was standing in the bathroom, putting on lipstick, when my mother called out, "Caitlin, honey, when Rogerson comes, ask him to say hello, won't you?"

I blinked at my reflection, then cut off the light and stepped out into the hallway. My parents, Boo, and Stewart were in their customary Friday night places, sitting around the dining room table, with the Trivial Pursuit board spread out in the middle. My father was studying a card in his hand, his eyes narrowed; Stewart sat beside him, chewing, a bag of dried figs on the table next to him. My mother and Boo were at the other end of the table, stirring their tea with their heads bowed, discussing strategy.

"Why?" I said, and my mother looked up at me, eyebrows raised.

"Well, you've certainly been spending a lot of time together," she replied. "We should at least meet the boy face-to-face. Don't you think, Jack?"

My father glanced over at me, smiling mildly. "Sure," he said. "Bring him in."

Introducing Rogerson was one thing. Doing it during the Friday Night war was another altogether.

It had been going on for at least five years, ever since Boo had given my father a Trivial Pursuit game for a birthday present. The first game had begun innocently enough, played over coffee and cookies—my mother and Boo versus Stewart and my father. But over time and many games, things were said. Assumptions made. Challenges extended. It was as if they were drunk on trivia, and every Friday was a bender.

"I don't know," I said to my mother as Rogerson's car slid into sight by our mailbox. "We kind of have plans. . . ."

"It will only take a second," she said cheerfully, letting her spoon clink against the edge of her mug. "Come on, Caitlin."

Outside, Rogerson was waiting. I could see him illuminated in the green dashboard lights, leaning forward, looking in at me. I glanced back at the table. So far, the game had been pretty docile, save for a short disagreement over the capital of Indonesia.

"Bring him in," my father said, pushing the dice over to my mother, who handed them to Boo—the lucky roller. "We should know who you're spending all your time with."

"It won't be that bad," Boo said, the dice clinking off her rings as she shook them up in her hand. "We'll be on our best behavior, we promise."

I shut the door behind me and headed down the walk to Rogerson's car. He sat there, waiting for me to get in, and when I didn't, he rolled the window down and leaned over, looking up at me.

"What's the problem?" he said.

"They want to meet you."

He blinked. "They?"

I gestured back toward the house. "It'll only take a second."

He sat there, considering this, then cut off the engine. "All right," he said, opening his door and getting out. He was wearing jeans and

Doc Martens, a bowling shirt with the name *Tony* written in script over the pocket, and a leather jacket, his hair loose and wilder than usual. "Wait," he said as we started up the walk. He stopped, reaching into his pocket with one hand while collecting his dreads at his neck, then snapping the rubber band he'd fished out around them.

"Good plan," I said. "We'll wait until next time to spring the hair on them."

"Usually a good idea," he said.

The first thing I heard when we stepped inside was my mother's voice, loud and argumentative.

"It's Tokyo, it has to be Tokyo," she was snapping at Boo as we came up the stairs.

"Need to give us an answer," my father said in a level voice, his eyes on the tiny hourglass—stolen from our Pictionary game, in an effort to make Boo and my mother respond within a set time limit—as the sand slipped through.

"Don't rush me!" my mother shrieked. "You always do that. You know it makes me crazy, and you do it anyway. It's like some kind of psychological warfare."

"Margaret," my father said, "either you know the answer or you don't."

"Mom?" I said.

"Just a second," she said. "First city in the world to have population of one million . . . first city . . ."

"New York," Boo said. "I have this strong aural feeling it's New York."

"No, no," my mother replied, frustrated. "It's . . . it's . . ."

"And time is . . . up," my father said, holding up the hourglass for proof. "Stewart, roll the dice."

"Mother of pearl!" my mother said angrily, and Stewart laughed. She never actually cussed, but her variations were just as good.

"Take it easy," Boo said. "We'll get them next time."

"It had to be New York," my mother protested. "Why didn't we just say New York?"

"I have no idea," Boo said darkly, and they both fell silent, not talking to each other, while Stewart rolled the dice.

I decided to just bite the bullet while the frenzy had died down. "Mom? Dad? This is Rogerson Biscoe."

Now they were all looking at us, or more specifically, at Rogerson. I watched as they took in his dark, olive skin, his deep green eyes, the bowling shirt. And, of course, the hair.

Boo, as always, was the first to speak. "Hello, Rogerson," Boo said. "I'm Boo Connell."

"Stewart," Stewart chimed in, waving.

"Hi," Rogerson said.

My mother gave him a polite smile as she extended her hand. "Hello, Rogerson," she said, as he shook it. "Do you, by chance, happen to know the first city to have a population of one million?"

"Margaret, honestly," my father said. "Your turn is over."

"Only because you flustered me!" she shot back, reaching to stir her coffee.

"Um," Rogerson said. "It's London. Right?"

My mother studied his face, then looked at my father, who flipped the card over and glanced at it. "He's right," he said.

"My goodness! London!" she said, slapping her hand on the table and making all the glasses jump. "Of course. London!"

"Pull up a chair for the boy!" Boo said, yanking one over beside her. "I am claiming him for our cause. Have a seat, Rogerson."

"No, no," my father protested, already reaching for the top of the box, where the rules were. He lived for the rules, knew them by heart, and referred to them constantly during the game. "It specifically says that no team shall have more than—"

"We need to go," I said loudly over them. "Really."

"Roll the dice, roll the dice!" my mother said to my father. Boo had already pulled Rogerson down in the chair beside her and handed him some dried figs, which he was holding, politely, but not eating. He looked up at me, half-smiling, and I just wanted to die of embarrassment.

"Okay," Boo said, patting Rogerson on the arm as she drew out a card. "Stewart and Jack. This was thought in ancient times to be solidified sunshine or petrified tears of the gods. Go!" And my mother turned the hourglass and slammed it on the table.

My father, brow furrowed, and Stewart, chewing thoughtfully on a fig, considered this.

"Need to give us an answer," my mother said, needling my father. "Hurry now."

"I don't know," my father said, shooting her a look. "Solidified sunshine or tears of the gods . . . so it has to be some kind of natural resource. . . ."

"Running out of time," my mother said, and my father looked at Stewart, who just shook his head, spitting out a bit of fig into a napkin. When the hourglass was empty, my mother clucked her tongue, sliding the dice back to her side of the board.

"Okay, then, Rogerson," Boo said, hiding the card in her hand. "What do you think?"

Rogerson looked at me, and I rolled my eyes. "Amber," he said. "Fossilized resin. Right?"

Boo nodded, and my mother's eyes widened, looking up at me, impressed, as if I'd created him myself from scrap. "My goodness, Rogerson," she said.

"You are brilliant," Boo said, squeezing his arm. "A boy genius! How do you know so much?"

"We really have to go," I said again.

"I don't know," Rogerson said. "Just watch a lot of *Jeopardy,* I guess."

"Roll the dice, Margaret," my father said, standing up. "Rogerson, it was good to meet you."

"You too, sir," Rogerson said, shaking his hand. Next he offered it to Stewart, who instead stood up and hugged him while my father looked embarrassed.

"You kids have fun," Boo said, squeezing my arm as we finally began to head to the door.

"Don't stay out too late," my mother added.

Outside, Rogerson pulled the rubber band out as we walked to the car, shaking his head to let his hair get loose.

"I'm sorry," I blurted out as soon as the door swung shut behind us. "They just . . . they get crazy when they play that game. It's like a drug or something."

"It's all right," he said, and from the house, behind us, I heard someone yelling, then a chorus of boos.

We got into the car and he started the engine, flicking on the lights as he put the car in gear. The radio blasted on as well—Led Zeppelin. I reached forward and changed the station and he rolled his eyes at me.

"So," I said. "How *do* you know all that stuff?"

"You heard them," he said, flicking down his visor to let a pack of cigarettes fall into his lap. "I'm brilliant."

"No kidding," I said, sliding closer to him. "What else don't I know about you?"

He shook his head, punching in the car lighter with one hand. "You'll find out soon enough," he said. "I got a million of 'em."

"Oh, that's right," I said. "You're a complex man of mystery."

He shrugged. "It comes with the hair. You know."

"Yeah," I said, reaching over to smooth my hand over his face—my new mysterious, brilliant boyfriend. "I know."

When Rogerson and I weren't in the car we were at his pool house, shoes off, making out on his perfectly made bed. Maybe because I was forging my own, new, non-Cass way, things had been moving fast with us from the start. Up until then, my experience with guys had been limited to a couple of boyfriends. One, Anthony Wayan, I'd met at camp. We'd been hot and heavy for three weeks, but once he went back home to Maine things just died out, typical summer romance. Then, sophomore year, I'd dated a junior named Emmet Peck who I sat next to in Ecology class. We were together a full four months, and he'd wanted me to sleep with him. But as much as I liked him, something always stopped me—he was a nice guy, yet ultimately forgettable. And I wanted my first time to be with someone I would always remember.

I already felt that way about Rogerson. But I still wanted to take my time, not have it happen in some mad rush or on a random Tuesday afternoon. He seemed to understand this, and when I told him to stop—and even for me, it was *always* hard—he complied, the only protest a little bit of grumbling into my neck as his hands moved back up into the safe zone. But each time it got harder, and I knew I couldn't wait too long.

I was beginning to understand that small smile Rina gave me whenever I asked her what she saw in Bill Skerrit.

Rogerson seemed to almost *like* the fact that I was inexperienced, not just about sex, but most things. He enjoyed carting me around in my cheerleading outfit while he took bong hits or talked business with people who eyed me strangely, as if I was a cartoon, not quite real. This was the same reason, I was sure, that he'd been interested in me the first night we'd met. It was a fair trade. With Rogerson, I was someone else. Not Cass. Not even me. I took his wildness from him and tried to fold it into myself, filling up the empty spaces all those second-place finishes had left behind.

There were so many things I already loved about him. The smell of his skin, always slightly musky and sweet. His hair, wild and dreadlocked, thick under my hands as I combed my fingers through it. The way he pressed his hand into the small of my back whenever I walked into any place ahead of him. He was so attentive, with one eye on me regardless of what else he was doing. Even with his back turned, he always seemed to know exactly where I was.

Of course, there were the drugs. Rogerson operated a brisk business selling pot and other various illegals to the kids at Perkins Day and Jackson. Because of this and other distractions, added to the fact that he never seemed to mention school, I was surprised at the pool house one day, when he was on the phone, to find poking out of his backpack not only a calculus midterm (on which he scored a 98) but an English paper entitled "Storms and Sacrifice: Weather and Emotion in King Lear" for which he'd gotten an A–. Obviously Trivial Pursuit was not his only strength. Rogerson was what his guidance counselor called "driven but misdirected" (from a letter home I found under my seat in the car, crumpled and bent). He was a perfectionist, whether it came to measuring out a perfect quarter-ounce or knowing the complete French conditional tense.

I, however, was struggling to keep my grades up, since I was suddenly spending so many weeknights (when my parents assumed I was doing cheerleading squad activities) with him. My mother, now distracted with Cass's *Lamont Whipper* sightings, had eased off on her own involvement in my cheerleading: something that almost would have bothered me, had I really taken the time to think about it. It was so easy, again, for Cass to take center stage.

But it made lying that much easier. It became a given that I rode around with him for all his errands almost every night. It was like he just *needed* me there, even if I was sitting in the car chewing my pencil and working trigonometry proofs while he talked business and divided up bags inside various houses. If I did want to go home early or spend an evening at home, he'd always drive by my house at least once, slowing down and just idling, engine rumbling, until I went outside to talk to him.

"Just come here for a second," he'd say, rolling down his window and cutting off the engine as I came down the walk. "I'll even let you listen to that stupid music you like so much."

"Rogerson," I'd tell him, "I told you I have *got* to study. You don't understand."

"I do, too," he'd say, opening the car door and holding out his hand. Even if it was dark I could tell when his eyes were sleepy, half-stoned, which always made him mushier than normal. "One second. I just want to talk."

"Yeah, right," I'd say.

"I'm serious." And then he'd smile at me, strict honest face. "You trust me, right?"

This was his line. It was what always led to me giving in, regardless of the issue, and coming two or three steps closer to give him my hand.

Which would, of course, lead to him pulling me inside the car and kissing me, which always made me somehow forget about studying the dates for the Italian Renaissance, or the periodic table, or *Macbeth,* entirely.

There were some nights, though, when something was wrong. He wouldn't talk and just wanted to lean into me, putting his head on my chest while I ran my fingers through his hair until he fell asleep. I always wondered if his dad had hurt him again. But like most things with Rogerson, I was usually given half the puzzle or just one clue, never enough to piece together the full story.

This is what I did know. That he was quiet and never spoke without thinking. That he drove like a maniac. That the only time I saw the small simmering of temper behind his cool demeanor was when someone was late or not where they said they'd be. That he liked his brother, tolerated his mother, and never mentioned his father at all. And that whenever I pressed him for details about any of these things, he would sidestep me so gracefully that I could never find a polite way to ask again.

Still, there was something so strange and tender about those nights when I just sat with him in the car, my arms around him, wondering what had happened at home that brought him here, needing me so much. It reminded me of how I'd felt when Cass and I shared our room, the peace of mind that comes from knowing someone is so close while you sleep that the worst of the monsters and nightmares can't get to you.

Rogerson and I would stay that way until my father flicked on the outside light, bright and yellow and startling in my eyes. Then I'd wake him up, kiss him good night, and he'd drive off, drowsy, while I went back to my own bed feeling warm and content. I'd close my eyes, alone in my room, remembering him breathing and wonder who he saw, or found, in dreamland.

Rogerson's depth of knowledge continually surprised me. It seemed like there was literally *nothing* he didn't know.

One day, he was changing the oil in his car and I was sitting on a lawn chair in his garage, doing my homework. The Biscoe garage was jam-packed with stuff. His mother was apparently addicted to shopping, and there were boxes upon boxes, unopened, of laundry detergent, Tupperware, canned goods. In the back, where Mr. Biscoe kept his fishing supplies, was a graveyard of barely used exercise equipment, including a treadmill, a bike, and some strange contraption that looked like skis attached to a trampoline. Whenever Rogerson worked on his car I could spend hours just walking around, poking behind boxes, excavating things.

But today I was trying to cram American history, as well as complaining out loud about my teacher, Mr. Alores, who gave trivia quizzes each Friday for extra credit. He didn't teach the material on them; you either knew it or you didn't, and lately I'd been falling into the latter category.

"I mean, it's so ridiculous," I said to Rogerson, or rather to Rogerson's legs, which was all I could see of him poking out from under the car. "How am I supposed to know this crap?"

"It can't be that hard," he said.

"Yeah, right. Okay." I pulled out my last quiz—I'd gotten a zero—and unfolded it. "Here. Number 4. The *Victoria* was the name of the first ship to what?"

"Hand me that wrench by your foot," he said, and I kicked it under the car to him. "Thanks. Circumnavigate the globe."

"Do what?" I said.

"The *Victoria.* It was the first ship to circumnavigate the globe. Magellan. Returned 1522. Right?"

I glanced down at my sheet, where Mr. Alores had written the correct answer in his clear, block-style printing. "Yeah. That's right."

Something clanked, hard, under the car. "Shit," he said. "Damn screw's practically rusted on."

I glanced back down at my quiz. "Rogerson."

"Yeah."

"Who was the first person to climb Mount Everest?"

"Sir Edmund Hillary. 1953." He pushed out from under the car and stood up, walking over to his toolbox.

"The Ojibwa Indians are better known as what?"

He picked up a screwdriver, examined it, and dropped it back in the box. "Chippewa," he said.

I could not believe this. "The cluster of stars called Pleiades can be found in which constellation?"

He crouched down, sliding back under the car. "The Seven Sisters," he said.

I looked down at my sheet.

"Taurus," he added, his voice muffled. "Also known as."

Right again. I put the sheet down. "Rogerson. How in the world do you know all this stuff?" I walked over and knelt down on the floor, peering under the car while he drained the oil into a pan resting on his stomach. "It's, like, amazing."

"I don't know," he said.

"Come on. Nobody just *knows* stuff like the thyroid is located behind the breastbone. It's insane."

"Thymus," he said.

"What?"

"The thymus is behind the breastbone," he explained, shifting the oil pan. "Not the thyroid."

"Whatever," I said. "You're like a genius or something."

He smiled at this. "Nah. I was just really into history and science as a kid. And my grandfather was a trivia addict. He bought me books for practically every birthday and then tested me." He shrugged. "It's no big deal."

But it was. There were moments—when *Jeopardy* came on, in the car during radio trivia challenges, or for practically any question I couldn't answer in any subject—that Rogerson simply amazed me. I started to seek out facts, just to stump him, but it never worked. He was that sharp.

"In physics," I sprung on him as we sat in the Taco Bell drive-through, "what does the capital letter W stand for?"

"Energy," he said, handing me my burrito.

Sitting in front of my parents' house as he kissed me good night: "Which two planets are almost identical in size?"

"Duh," he said, smoothing my hair back, "Venus and Earth."

"Rogerson," I asked him sweetly as we sat watching a video in the pool house, "where would I find the pelagic zone?"

"In the open sea," he said. "Now shut up and eat your Junior Mints."

Rogerson, for the most part, didn't like any of my cheerleading friends. Rina was the only one he could tolerate, and her just barely. He said she was too loud, but he liked her spunk nonetheless. Since she was still hot and heavy with her quarterback, not to mention a developing situation with a college-boy shoe salesman she'd met at the mall, I didn't see much of her other than at practice. When I wasn't there, I was with Rogerson and his friends.

We'd been together about a month when he took me one Sunday afternoon to an old farmhouse out in the country. It was yellow, and kind of ramshackle charming, with a big yard and a dopey looking yellow Lab, curled up in the late winter sunshine, that yawned, uninterested, as we walked up the steps. There were two cars—a yellow VW bug and a pickup truck—parked in the driveway, and when Rogerson knocked on the heavy wooden door I could hear the TV on inside.

"Come in," a voice called out, and as I stepped in behind Rogerson I saw it belonged to a girl with long, straight blond hair who was sitting on a big couch in front of the TV, her feet tucked up under her. The room was small, with bright white walls, sunshine slanting in through a window with a bunch of plants crowded on the sill. The coffee table was an old trunk, covered with magazines and packs of cigarettes, some bracelets and a flurry of envelopes. There was a fishbowl on top of the TV with one bright orange goldfish in it, circling.

The girl on the couch was smoking a cigarette and watching the Home Shopping Network, which I recognized instantly from my mother's newfound doll addiction. The jewelry segment was on, with some woman talking up a cubic zirconia bracelet she had draped over her fingers, modeling it this way and that.

"Hey," Rogerson said to the girl, who looked up and smiled at him. She had a pretty face and cat-shaped eyes.

"Hey yourself," she said, reaching over to lift a stack of magazines off the couch beside her. "Have a seat. Dave's in the kitchen making lunch."

"Is that Rogerson?" a guy's voice yelled from the next room.

"Yeah," Rogerson said.

"Get in here, man. I need to talk to you."

Rogerson stood up, squeezing my shoulder, and walked to a swinging door, leaning into it to push it open. I caught a glimpse of a guy in his early twenties, in cutoffs and a long flannel shirt, barefoot, standing over a frying pan. On the wall behind him there was a huge velvet Elvis, hanging by a row of cabinets. When the guy saw me he lifted his spatula, smiling, and waved at me before the door swung shut again.

"That's Dave," the girl beside me said. "He's making Hamburger Helper. I'm Corinna."

"Caitlin," I said, and she nodded, smiling at me. "Rogerson has problems with introductions."

"No big deal. We're definitely not formal here," she said, flicking her wrist absently, clattering the thin silver bangles she wore there. Then she reached forward to stub out her cigarette in an ashtray shaped like Texas, picking up the remote with her other hand to flip channels. She cruised by MTV, a political news show, and two old movies before finally landing on an infomercial about acne medicine, where they were interviewing a kid with horrible skin, all red and splotchy and riddled with bumps like the surface of the moon.

"Oh, man," she said, reaching over the arm of the couch, feeling around for something, and coming up with a blue ceramic bowl and a bag of pot. "That poor *kid*. Look at that. Like high school isn't bad enough, you know?" She opened the bag and quickly packed the bowl, pressing down on it with her index finger. "I had acne in high school, but it wasn't that bad, thank God. And I still couldn't get a date. But you probably don't have that problem, right?" She fumbled around on the coffee table, moving a *TV Guide* and two emery boards to unearth a lighter. "I mean, you have *great* skin."

"Oh, well," I said, watching as she lit the bowl, drew in a deep breath, and held it a second before slowly letting out a long stream of smoke. "Not really."

"Oh, you do, though. It's all genes. Does your mom have good skin?"

It was strange to think of my mother, here, but her face popped into my head instantly, smiling, lipstick perfect. "Yeah, she does."

"See?" She tapped the bowl with the lighter. "Genes." And then she handed it to me.

Up until that point, I'd only smoked a few times: with Rina, experimenting; at one or two parties with the more rebellious of the jocks; and the night I'd seen Rogerson's dad hit him. I'd never cared one way or the other for it, but being in that little farmhouse, on a sunny afternoon, sitting in the corner of that big comfortable couch talking to Corinna, it just seemed *right,* or as right as anything technically wrong could be.

"Thanks," I said, taking it, lighting the lighter and drawing in a big hit of smoke, which immediately set me to coughing like crazy. The next one went down easier. And by the third, I felt like an old pro.

Afterward, Corinna lit a cigarette and offered me one, too, which I took, lighting it and smoking like I'd been doing it all my life. We sat there together, smoking and watching the acne doctors work their magic. By now they'd moved onto a cheerleader with bug eyes and skin so bad it seemed like she was wearing a big red mask.

"I admire her so much," Corinna said, picking up the ashtray and moving it onto the couch between us. "I mean, being a cheerleader and getting up in front of people with that face. She must really have some self-esteem, you know?"

"I know," I agreed, tapping my ash and pulling my legs up underneath me, like Corinna. "Plus cheerleading is so awful anyway."

She looked at me, tucking a few blond strands behind her ear, her bracelets tinkling against each other, like music. "You think so? I always wanted to be a cheerleader. And a prom queen. And I was, like, neither. Not even close."

"I'm a cheerleader," I said, taking another drag off my cigarette. "And I hate it." And there it was, the truth, popping out when I least expected it: I *did* hate cheerleading, always had. And this girl, this stranger, was the only one I'd ever told.

"Wow," she said, laughing, "that was, like, so *direct*. I love that."

I laughed, too: It seemed funny to me now, almost hysterical in fact. My head felt fuzzy and relaxed and the fish on top of the TV just kept swimming, around and around, and Corinna flipped her long blond hair, smiling that cat-smile. Something smelled good from the kitchen and it was a lazy Sunday and everything was okay, suddenly—as okay as things had been since Cass left and the summer ended—even if just for an instant.

We sat there, watching the infomercial and talking, for what seemed like a long time. Corinna told me she worked at Applebee's, waiting tables, producing her ASK ME ABOUT SOUP 'N' SKILLETS! button from under a couch cushion. She and Dave had been together since high school—they'd gone to Jackson, too, graduating five years earlier—and sometime soon, they were planning to move to California.

"Palm trees, movie stars," Corinna said with a smile. She was so nice, I felt like I knew her already. She reminded me of Cass that way, the kind of person you felt friendly with at first sight. "I can't wait to get the hell out of this place."

A few minutes later, as they were showing the After pictures of both acne victims, the kitchen door swung open and Dave and Rogerson came in. I'd forgotten, temporarily, that they were even in the house. Dave was carrying the frying pan, Rogerson a stack of plates.

"Dinner is served," Dave said, kissing Corinna on the top of the head as he sat down beside her.

"It's lunchtime," she told him.

"Lunch then. Whatever. Anytime is a good time for Hamburger

Helper à la Dave," he said, passing his hand over the frying pan with an exaggerated flourish.

"Which means," Corinna explained to me, "that we didn't have money for hamburger this week so it's just noodles."

"Better for you anyway," I said. "A diet heavy in meat causes heart disease and high blood pressure."

Dave raised his eyebrows at me and smiled. He had short brown hair and bright blue eyes and looked, strangely, a little bit like Mike Evans. "I like this girl," he said to Rogerson, handing me a plate and a fork.

"That's Caitlin," Corinna said, digging into the pile of noodles on her plate. "She's a rebel cheerleader."

"Ah," Dave said. "My favorite kind."

"Mine, too," Rogerson said, sliding his arm around my waist and forgoing the food as I leaned back against him, eating my Hamburger Helper—which was, quite honestly, one of the best meals I'd ever eaten.

"Oh, Jesus, Corinna," Dave said as he looked at the TV, where they were showing the Before picture of the cheerleader again. "Why do you always have to watch this crap?"

"Hush," Corinna said. "Eat your food."

"She's obsessed," Dave told us. "This acne commercial, it's on every single time I come home. I don't *get* it."

Corinna smiled at him, reaching to smooth one hand over his face. Her bracelets fell down her arm, one by one. "Just one more time," she said, putting her now empty plate on the coffee table. "I just love to see a happy ending."

So we all sat there, silent, our eyes fixed on the pock-faced cheerleader, watching the Before and After as the acne medicine worked miracles, smoothing over bumps, wiping away scars, changing her face, her future, her life.

Chapter Eight

As December began, when I wasn't in photography class with my mother and Boo, continuing my rapid falling out of favor with the cheerleading squad, or listening to Rina wail about her love life, I was at Corinna's. It was the only place I felt like I got some peace of mind, and I found myself drawn there whenever things got crazy. I'd creep up the front steps and knock softly, always worried I was interrupting something, and she'd yell out for me to come in. When I pushed the door open I usually found her sitting on the couch with a cigarette in one hand and the remote in the other, smiling as if she'd been waiting for me to show up all along. We'd sit on the couch, smoking, and watch soap operas, eating frozen burritos and talking while the world outside went on without me.

I'd discovered that Corinna and I had a lot in common. Besides the fact that we'd both gone to Jackson—she was three years ahead of Cass—her mother and mine were each Junior Leaguers, and she'd grown up in Crestwood, a subdivision on the other side of the highway from mine. She said she'd been a geek her freshman year, doing time in student council and dance committees, until she met Dave, who was two years older. She fell in love with him and became, in her own words, a "burnout," spending more time in the parking lot than in class. In her yearbook, which she kept on the coffee table, there was a picture of her sitting on the hood of someone's car in cutoff jeans and a tie-dyed T-shirt, barefoot and wearing sunglasses. She was laughing, beautiful, even then.

For graduation, she'd gotten a tiny green vine tattooed around her left ankle, and Dave had given her the first of the thin, shiny silver bracelets she wore on her left wrist. He had continued to give her one for every Christmas, birthday, and Valentine's Day since. They clinked against each other whenever she walked, or gestured excitedly, or reached to brush her hair out of her face—Dave said it was her theme music.

But what I liked most about Corinna was that she liked *me*. She was pretty, smart, and funny but I didn't feel like I faded out when I was with her, like I always had with Rina and Cass. I loved her easygoing manner, hanging on every one of her horror stories about waitressing at Applebee's and her own wild high school years. She seemed to have the perfect life to me: independent, fun job, living with a man who loved her in their tiny, funky farmhouse. I could see me and Rogerson like that, someday. Us against the world. It was the way I imagined Cass living in New York with Adam, starting over all on her own. Being with Corinna always made me miss Cass a little less.

She didn't talk to or see her family much, even though they lived right in town. One afternoon we went to the grocery store and bumped into her mother, leading to a strange, awkward exchange in the frozen food aisle that made me so uncomfortable I slipped off to the produce section. Her mom looked a lot like mine, with the blond bob, khaki skirt, conservative V-neck sweater, and pearl earrings. She was buying salad dressing and scallops, and when she asked Corinna about Dave her nose wrinkled just slightly, as if she'd gotten a sudden whiff of something rotten.

Afterwards, riding home, Corinna chain-smoked cigarettes, hardly talking except in small argumentative spurts, as if her mother was still there, arguing back.

"They never even *tried* to like him," she said, hitting the gas to pass a slow-moving school bus. "They hated him on sight. But it was never really about him. They had already decided they wanted me to be chaste, go to college, and be a lawyer. It was always about what *they* wanted." Then she hit the volume on the radio, cranking it up to drown herself out.

We drove on, and a second later she reached forward, turning the sound down again. "I mean," she added angrily, "they'd already, like, decided exactly what I was supposed to do, and be, for God's sake. I never even had a say in *anything*."

I nodded as she twisted the volume up, the speakers rattling around us. We drove on, whisking past the dairy farm at the top of the road, the smell of cows and manure wafting in through the open window.

"And now," she said, reaching impatiently to cut off the radio altogether as we bumped down the dirt road to her house, "they're so *disappointed* in me. Like I've let them down by not doing everything they planned. I can see it in their faces. Like waiting tables is so awful. I'm not costing them anything, for God's sake. I mean, I can't even afford to go to the dentist, but do I ask them for help?"

"No," I said as she yanked the wheel and we sputtered to a stop behind Dave's truck.

"No," she repeated. "Exactly. I don't." She got out of the car, grabbed her one bag of groceries, and slammed the door. I followed her up the steps into the house, where Dave was sitting on the couch in jeans and a Spam T-shirt, an open bag of Fritos on his lap.

"Hey there," he said cheerfully as she brushed past him into the kitchen, the door swinging shut behind her. I could hear her bracelets clanking as she moved around, putting things away, cabinet doors banging shut, one by one. Dave, with one Frito halfway to his mouth, raised his eyebrows.

"We saw her mom at the store," I explained.

"Oh," he said, popping it into his mouth. "How'd that go?"

"Shit!" Corinna said loudly, as something crashed and broke in the kitchen. "Goddammit."

"Not so good," I told him.

He sighed, standing up. "Here," he said, handing off the Fritos to me. "I'm going in."

I watched as he pushed the kitchen door open. It started to swing shut behind him before catching on the stubborn piece of kitchen tile that poked up at the edge of the threshold. He walked over to where Corinna was standing, crying, holding a piece of broken plate in her hand.

"This fell," she said, holding it up as proof. "I didn't drop it."

"I know," he said, taking it out of her hand and putting it on the counter. "It's okay."

She wiped at her eyes, impatiently. Then she said, "I hate that I let her do this to me. It's so dysfunctional."

"It's not your fault," Dave said as Corinna closed her eyes, leaning her face against his chest, and I felt bad for watching, turning my attention to the *Brady Bunch* rerun on the TV.

I wondered again if this was what Cass's life was like with Adam in New York. I hoped so. Even if she was struggling and living off Ramen-noodle soup, it seemed perfect to be in this kind of love.

Corinna was still crying, even as Dave kissed her forehead and smiled, taking one of her hands and twirling her around the small, paint-peeling kitchen. "Stop," she said, half-laughing as he dipped her over the garbage can. "David, honestly."

He was humming something, a song I didn't know, as he twirled her out, then pulled her back, scooping an arm around her waist, and led her into an exaggerated tango, both of them stepping expertly over the dog bowl.

"You're crazy," she said, but now she was smiling.

Outside the window over my shoulder it was winter, flat and gray. But in the kitchen, under the warm bulb light, they were still dancing, laughing, twirling across the tiny floor while those silver bracelets jingled, making music all their own.

My mother was still buying dolls and glued to the *Lamont Whipper Show* daily, where she caught glimpses of Cass every once in a while. Adam, however, she saw every day, since at least one fistfight or hair pulling incident occurred on each show. He was always bounding onstage, grabbing wives off their cheating husbands or separating angry drag queens while the crowd roared in the background.

She was also writing Cass each week, and although she hadn't heard back yet, there'd been four hang-ups so far on our phone, all coming during the official O'Koren dinnertime: six to six-thirty. My mother would throw down her napkin and run to grab the phone, then stand there saying hello again and again, her fingers gripping white around the receiver, before finally replacing it and walking slowly back to the table. She'd sit down, not saying anything, while my father and I watched her, the only sound the scraping of forks against plates.

"Margaret," my father would say, finally. "It's probably just some long-distance company—"

"She almost said something that time," my mother would blurt out. "I could hear her breathing. She *wants* to talk to me. I can feel it."

This was probably true. Cass had always been easily homesick. Even when we went to camp as teenagers she'd bawled at the bus station. I knew the only reason she hadn't gotten in touch so far was just because she was afraid my parents would somehow force her to come home. Even as I imagined her making Hamburger Helper without the hamburger with Adam in New York, being madly in love, I knew my sister, and I was sure she missed us.

On Saturday afternoons, I went to the Arts Center with my mother and Boo for photography class. I'd regretted agreeing to it almost instantly—mostly because between cheering and school I didn't see Rogerson as much as I wanted, to begin with—but in time I found that I actually liked the class. The instructor was a young, energetic photographer named Matthew, who sported a scraggly goatee, as well as a seemingly endless number of tattered wool sweaters. He gestured excitedly, eyes sparkling, as he guided us through the first few discussions on light, focus, perspective, and setting. Then he just set us loose in different places—Topper Lake, the old graveyard, the supermarket—encouraging us to "create our own personal vision" of each.

At the supermarket, for instance, my mother spent the full hour in the floral section, trying to get the perfect shot of the rows of cut flower bins, while Boo went for the abstract, selecting a round, bright, yellow squash and arranging it on the meat counter, right next to a freshly cut set of bloody steaks. "Contrast," Matthew proclaimed excitedly, as she circled the meat with her camera, getting it from every angle. "Make us think about your meaning!"

I myself was sorely lacking for inspiration. I contemplated the rows of milk bottles—white, smooth, cold—but moved on when I saw two people from our class already there, taking identical pictures from the same angle. Should I do the bored lobsters in their tank? Seek deep introspection in the cheese aisle? I was beginning to lose hope.

"Five minutes, people!" Matthew called out as he passed me. "We'll regroup by customer service, okay?"

Five minutes. I was getting desperate and had decided to go back to the milk when I walked past the frozen foods. It was empty except for an elderly woman with her cart, who was pulling a door open to get out a frozen dinner. She was small and frail, with skin almost translucent and made whiter by the bright fluorescent lights overhead. I started up the aisle toward her, popping the lens cap off my camera, already lifting it to my eye and adjusting the zoom so that her profile took up the entire frame. Then she leaned in, reaching forward, and as her breath came out in a sudden, small white puff, she closed her eyes, reacting to the cold. I snapped the picture, catching her in that one instant with a simple click.

The next week, when we did our developing, I stood and watched as her image emerged in front of me: distinct, perfect, in all that cool white. Matthew held it up for the class to see and congratulated me on my "sense of face." For me, it was the first thing I'd done in a long time that I was truly proud of, so much so that I hung it on my mirror, replacing my second-place ribbons and B honor roll certificates.

But even as I was doing well in photography, things were going from bad to worse in my cheerleading career. Choosing Rogerson over Mike Evans had been the beginning of the end, but now I was so busy with him that I just didn't have the energy for pyramids and dance routines anymore. This was added to the fact that Corinna's was about a mile from school, so I often headed there for the half hour between last period and practice. Corinna was usually in her Applebee's uniform, lazily putting on her makeup and various SIZZZZZLE STEAKS! and ASK ME ABOUT SUPERCHOCOLATESUNDAES! buttons. I'd throw down my backpack and take my place on the couch, where we'd share a bowl, smoke some cigarettes (I was buying my own packs now), and watch *General Hospital,* some sleazy talk show, or another infomercial. This, of course, usually made me lose any motivation I had for cheerleading. If I even made it to practice afterward—and increasingly, I didn't—I was usually so tired and lazy it was all I could do to go through the motions.

The only thing worthwhile about practice was that I got to see Rina, who was currently embroiled in one of her trademark mucky love triangles. This one involved her quarterback, Bill Skerrit, a nice aw-shucks kind of guy who honestly believed he and Rina were going to get married, and the college-boy shoe salesman, Jeff, who Rina had met a month earlier when she'd gone to return a pair of platform sandals. Bill Skerrit had already bought Rina a friendship ring, which she wasn't wearing, and Jeff was a dog and never called her when he said he would. Of course, she was mad for him.

"Oh, God," she'd say to me as we sat outside the gym after practice. "I don't want to *be* like this, you know?"

"Like what?" I'd say.

"Like such a total *bitch*. I mean, poor Bill, you know?"

Bill, who assumed he *and* Rina were both saving themselves for marriage, had not the slightest inkling that she was, ahem, *involved* with Jeff. I'd only met him once, at the mall. He was tall, with a big floppy shock of blond hair he was always getting out of his face by jerking his head suddenly to the side, whiplash-style. Rina found this incredibly sexy. It made me nervous.

During all of this I was also spending as much time as I could with Rogerson, who still complained that I wasn't around enough. My grades kept slipping as he talked me into going out with him every night, always sweet-talking me into it the same way he coaxed me out of the house. And the nights when he just showed up, not talking, just wanting me to sit with him while he recovered from something he wouldn't even discuss, became more and more frequent. I noticed bruises on his face, red marks and puffiness around his eyes, but he shrugged off my concern, dodging it gracefully, again. I felt desperately helpless, unable to protect him from some awful force I couldn't even name. It kept me up nights, long after I'd watched him drive away.

I was running from one problem or place to another, with no time left to study, or sleep, or just *breathe*. I felt pulled in all directions, fighting to keep all these obligations circling in the air above me. It was only a matter of time before something fell.

It was the Friday of the Winter Athletic Ceremony that it happened. After last period I was supposed to go to a cheerleading meeting, then home to meet Rogerson, who wanted me to go to the mall to help him buy a birthday gift for his mother. After that, I would return home to shower, change, and ride back to school with my parents and Boo and Stewart for the ceremony, where I'd get a corsage from some football player. This would be followed by us all sitting through an endlessly boring speech by Principal Hawthorne detailing the "virtue of competition" and the "lessons we learn from teamwork" that we'd all heard the year before, and the year before that, while we waited for Cass to get *her* trophies. Finally I would be given a cheap plaque, my mother would take about a dozen pictures (in all of which I would have a partial—or no—head) and somehow, eventually, it would be over.

By 3:15, it was clear I needed something to help me get through this. I drove to Corinna's with one eye on the clock, just wanting a few minutes of peace.

When I got there she was in her uniform—today, her button said SUPER STEAKS! THE NEW SENSATION!—and rolling change on the coffee table while watching reruns of the *Newlywed Game*.

"I have to make at least a hundred bucks tonight after tipping out," she explained as I sat down, taking the bowl as she passed it to me, the lighter balanced on top of it. Now she didn't even bother to ask me before she packed it—we had a routine, a system. Rogerson had even begun to give me my own small supply of pot, as well as a bowl, tiny and white ceramic with a wizard painted on its tip. With it, my bag, cigarettes, and a lighter, I was like Barbie all over again, just with different accessories.

Now Corinna exhaled, blowing out smoke as she stacked pennies, tucking her hair behind her ear. "Dave's out of work at least till next week and the power bill's due Monday. Plus I wrote a check for groceries that's gonna bounce if I don't deposit something tonight."

I took the bowl and lit it, watching as one of the couples on the TV won a new bedroom suite. The woman had seventies hair, all hairspray and feathered bangs, and was jumping up and down, kissing the host. "I'm sorry," I said. "That sucks."

"Yeah, well," she said, piling pennies into a roll and twisting the ends shut. "We'll make it somehow. We always do."

Corinna always seemed to be working, but I never could quite figure out what Dave *did,* exactly. He seemed to do some carpentry work, sometimes, and for a week or two he worked at the Quik Zip, selling gas and cigarettes on the night shift. More often, however, he was in the next room sleeping, where I could hear him snoring sometimes as Corinna and I spoke in whispers so as not to wake him. I was learning that with Dave, as with Rogerson, it was best just not to ask questions.

After we'd finished smoking I glanced at the clock: four sharp. The meeting was beginning, and I could just see Chelsea Robbins taking her spot in front of the assembled squad, decreeing who would be escorted by which football player at the banquet. It seemed like a long way back to school, suddenly, and I wondered if anyone had noticed yet that I wasn't there.

Corinna looked up from stacking dimes. "Aren't you late for practice?"

I thought of Mike Evans pinning a corsage on my chest and leading me to the stage while my mother snapped pictures that would never come out. "Nope," I said, settling back into the couch. "Don't have it today."

She picked up the remote and flipped a few stations until the phone rang, leaving it on a commercial for car wax as she got up to snatch the cordless off the top of the TV. She walked into the kitchen, lowering her voice, as I heard Dave mumble something, asleep, from behind the half-open door to my right that led to the bedroom.

Then I heard music I recognized. It was yet another *Lamont Whipper* rerun coming on. It was so popular that now they'd added yet another showing, making my mother that much happier. I watched as the camera zoomed in on Lamont himself, holding his microphone. He announced the day's topic—"Better Run While You Can, 'Cause You've Been Messing with My Man!" Cass was standing behind him.

She was wearing a brown sweater and jeans, her hair up and twisted into a hasty bun behind her head, held in place with a pencil, the old Boo trick. She was holding a clipboard, her eyes glancing quickly around the studio, checking something I couldn't see. As her gaze moved across the audience, she stared right into the camera for one instant, and it was suddenly like she was looking right at me. And as she did, she lifted a finger and smoothed it across her eyebrow, turning her head slightly.

I felt a slow, creeping chill crawl up the back of my neck just as Corinna came back through the door, turning the phone off with an angry jab of her finger. "Oh, so listen to *this* crap. The five-thirty wait called in sick with a freakin' hangover, so I'm on my own till six. On a Friday, no less." She sighed, sitting back down and shaking a cigarette out of the open pack next to her stacks of coins. "Can you believe that?"

"No," I said softly, as the camera switched angles to focus on the first guest, a huge black woman in a brightly printed pantsuit. I lit a cigarette and drew in hard, my vision spinning for a second.

"Whatever. I have got to get out of this crappy job. It's about to kill me." Corinna glanced at the TV. "What's this?"

"*Lamont Whipper*," I said.

"Oh, I hate that show," she moaned, picking up the remote. "It's like white trash on parade. Do you mind if I change—"

"Wait," I said quickly, as the camera shot back to Lamont, who was now asking a thin blond woman in a Harley-Davidson T-shirt her opinion. "Just one second."

And there was Cass again, this time scribbling something on her clipboard while a guy in headphones leaned down to whisper something in her ear. Then she smiled, shaking her head, and I thought of my mother sitting at home, her chair pulled up to the screen, smiling back.

"Caitlin," Corinna said. She was watching my face. "What is it?"

Now, on-screen, Cass glanced back up, brushing her bangs out of her face with the back of her hand. "That's my sister," I said quietly.

"Where?"

"Right there. Against the wall, in the brown," I said as Cass hugged the clipboard against her chest.

"Oh, man, really?" Corinna said, leaning in closer to study the screen. "Look at that. Wow. You never even said you had a sister."

That was strange. Cass had always been such a big part of what I was, but I hadn't mentioned her—not even once. I wondered what she would think if she really *could* look through the TV and see me sitting there stoned, not recognizing the girl beside me or the place I was or even, maybe, me. I thought of the other Cassandra, the one she'd been named for, the girl who could see her own future. And I wondered if this future—Lamont Whipper and Adam and New York and leaving us behind—was the one she'd seen for herself. Or for me.

"It's so weird," Corinna was saying, still watching the screen. "She looks just like you. She could *be* you, you know?"

The camera cut away quickly, as the woman in the bright pantsuit responded to some comment from the audience. When they went back to Lamont, Cass was gone.

"I know," I told Corinna, and for once I was the only one who knew how untrue it really was. "I know."

I knew how much Rogerson hated to wait. The only time I'd ever seen him lose his temper was when Dave was set to meet us at his house and showed up thirty minutes late. Rogerson was punctual to the second.

So I left Corinna's at four-thirty-five, which gave me ten minutes to get across town to my house to meet him. I was sitting at the light by the high school, nervously watching the clock, when I saw Rina a few cars ahead of me. She'd cut the one class we had together, in fifth period, but it was just like her to skip school but show up for cheerleading practice. Rina, for all her bad judgment, was surprisingly dependable.

Watching her, even from three cars back, I could tell something was wrong. She was smoking and kept fiddling with her radio, reaching up every few seconds to wipe her eyes with her shirtsleeve or run her fingers through her hair. Every once in a while she'd start singing along with the radio, slamming her hand on the steering wheel to emphasize one chorus or line, and then her shoulders would start shaking.

It was clear. Rina was driving and crying.

After every crisis, breakup or blowout, the first thing Rina did was bolt to her car. She'd crank up the stereo and start on her standard loop—out past the high school into the country, across the highway to Topper Lake, where she'd park at one of the overlooks and feel tortured for a while. Then she'd circle through a few of her old neighborhoods, drive by her second stepdad's house to curse his front yard, and go home. It wasn't really about *where* she went, in my opinion: It was the motion she liked, which prevented just about everyone from seeing her being weak. I, however, had spend endless nights riding shotgun, listening to one of her many mix tapes of lost love/done me wrong/screw you songs and watching scenery rush by, her hiccuping sobs just barely audible under the music and the sound of the wind coming through my window.

Now, I knew I was barely going to make it to meet Rogerson on time as it was. Rina hadn't seen me, and from the looks of things she'd already done the country and was headed out to the lake. But as I watched her punch in the car cigarette lighter with a jab of her hand, then wipe her eyes, I just couldn't go home.

When the light finally changed I managed to pull up beside her after dodging around an elderly woman in a Cutlass with a handicapped sticker, who promptly flipped me off.

"Rina!" I shouted, but the radio was up loud—something sad and gooey—and she didn't hear me. I hit the horn, twice, startling the minivan with a Pro-Choice sticker in front of me, which quickly changed lanes. We kept cruising neck and neck, with Rina full-out bawling now, singing along with the radio, tears running down her face, completely oblivious to both me and the speed limit. I reached under my seat and searched around until I came up with an empty plastic Coke bottle, which I then hurled at her windshield. She jerked back from the wheel as it bounced off, then whipped her head around, eyes wide, and finally saw me.

"Shit!" she screamed, hitting the automatic window control to open the one nearest me. "What the hell you are *doing?*"

"Pull over," I yelled back. There was a Quik Zip coming up on the left. She shot me an evil look, hit her turn signal, and took a wide arc into the parking lot, coming to an abrupt stop in front of a pay phone. I pulled up behind her.

"You could have killed me," she snapped, slamming her door as she got out. She was wearing a fuzzy sweater, black skirt, and tights, her hair tumbling over her shoulders. A group of public works guys, all in bright orange vests, hollered at her as they drove past, circling the gas pumps.

"I was worried about you," I said. "What happened?"

She sighed, crossing her arms over her chest and leaning back against her car. "It's all," she began, dramatically, "over."

It was four-fifty; I was officially late. And Rina always took her time explaining herself. "Is this about Bill?" I asked.

She nodded, drawing out a piece of hair and twisting it around her finger. "Last night," she began, "I went to meet Jeff at the Yogurt Paradise at the mall during his break to discuss our relationship."

"Right," I said, trying to move her along. I could just see Rogerson sitting in front of my house.

"And we did just talk—for the most part. But then at the end, you know, things got a little physical—"

"At the Yogurt Paradise?" I said.

"We were just kissing," she snapped. "God. But, as luck would *of course* have it, Bill just happened to be walking by on his way to the cafeteria and saw us."

"Yikes."

"Oh, it gets better. He was with his *entire* family, Caitlin," she said in a low voice, as tears filled her eyes again. She looked down at her hands, picking at a pinky nail. "It was his Granny Nunell's birthday. She's, like, ninety. I met her a few weeks ago and she loved me. But you should have seen the look she shot me last night. The woman has a walker, but she meant me harm. No doubt about it."

"Ouch," I said, trying to be subtle in taking a glance at my watch: five minutes had passed.

"So I'm just *busted,*" she said, wiping her eyes. "I mean, there's his aunt Camille, and his mom and dad, his Gran-Gran—"

"Gran-Gran?"

"—and Bill, who is just staring at me, and I'm sitting there with Jeff's hand on my leg. He didn't even say anything. He just walked away. It was awful. Terrible." She crossed her arms again, tossing her hair out of her face, Jeff-style. "So of course I can't face him at school today. But I figure I can't miss the squad meeting, so I sneak in the back door."

"I missed it," I told her.

"No kidding. And as your friend," she added, changing tacks to become all business, "I should tell you that you need to be watching your back. There was a vote today, and everyone but me was in favor of a confrontation about your level of serious commitment to the school and the squad."

"Oh, God," I said. A cheerleading intervention. Just what I needed. And now, it was five after five. But Rogerson would understand. He knew about the ceremony. We could buy the present tomorrow.

"So anyway," Rina said, flicking her wrist as she switched gears again, "Bill was waiting for me after the meeting."

"What did he say?"

"What *could* he say?" she wailed. "He asked for his ring back." She put her hand on her throat, where the silver chain now hung empty, kinked a little bit from where the ring had been. "He gave me back my pictures and that shirt I gave him for his birthday. And then . . ." And she stopped, waving her hand in front of her face, unable to continue.

I waited. By now, I knew Rogerson was leaving my house, gunning up the street, wondering where I was. I could feel a slow burn starting in my stomach.

". . . then," she began again, catching her breath, "he told me he was *disappointed* in me. Which was, like, the worst. I mean, call me a bitch, or even a slut, that I can handle, you know? But to say that . . . that was just *mean.*" She crossed her arms over her chest, looking down at her feet, eyes closed. It was starting to get dark, the lights of the Quik Zip bright and warm behind her.

I walked over and put my arm around her shoulder, leaning my head against hers. "He wasn't right for you anyway," I told her, like I had so many times before. "He was too—"

"—good," she finished for me, and laughed, still crying a little bit. "Good men just don't suit me."

"That's right," I said, brushing her hair out of her face. "That's exactly right."

I stayed there with her for a while longer, letting her cry and saying all those best friend things—*You'll be okay, Don't worry, I'm here, Let it out, Screw him*—while the Quik Zip bustled with people pumping gas and rushing home, the smell of hot dogs wafting out each time the door was pushed open, mixing with the strangely warm December breeze. But all the while, my mind was on Rogerson, seeing him in my mind driving across town, angry and wondering why I, too, had somehow let him down.

When I got home it was six o'clock, Rogerson was nowhere in sight, and my parents were finishing dinner with Boo and Stewart. The whole house smelled like steak and the *Lamont Whipper Show* was on, muted, in the living room.

"Honey, where have you been?" my mother asked, turning around in her chair as I came up the stairs. "I was getting worried. The ceremony starts in less than an hour and if we want to get a good parking place . . ."

"Are you hungry?" Boo said, reaching over to poke at something in a casserole dish with a big wooden spoon. "There's plenty of tempeh goat cheese salad left here."

"I laid out that blue dress for you to wear and bought you some new panty hose," my mother added. "You should hurry and take a shower, though, because you really cut it close by—"

"I know," I said, already kicking off my shoes as I headed into my room. I was just about to shut the door behind me when my mother yelled one last thing.

"Rogerson came by looking for you," she called out over my father and Stewart talking. "He seemed to think you two had plans for this afternoon."

I eased my door open, sticking my head back out. "What else did he say?"

She shrugged, dabbing at her mouth with her napkin. "I told him you'd be back soon because of the ceremony. And he said that he'd call you later."

"Oh," I said. "Okay. Thanks." I shut my door slowly, telling myself that all this time I'd been worried for nothing. We were just going shopping, anyway. He understood. It was no big deal.

The ceremony was just as I expected: endless trophies, a flimsy certificate, and a corsage for me. Rina had recovered, at least temporarily, and was completely composed as she was escorted to the stage and our seats there, in a quick rearrangement, by a defensive back. Bill escorted Eliza Drake, while I—for punishment, clearly—was paired with the field-goal kicker, a short guy named Thad Wicker who resembled a short, stubby, chewed-on pencil with bad breath and a sinus condition.

Rogerson showed up just as Principal Hawthorne was making his final speech. I saw the door open, just a crack, and he slipped in and leaned against the wall. I was so surprised to see him, happy he was even interested enough to come. His hair was wet—the warm weather had turned to rain, suddenly, as we drove to the ceremony—and he was glancing around the room and the crowd, looking for me. When he saw me he lifted his chin, then glanced around the room and stuck his hands in his pockets.

"A lot of people," Principal Hawthorne was saying, "sometimes question the value of sports in an education. For me, the facts are clear. . . ."

I'd only known Rogerson for three months, but I could recognize instantly the subtle signs of him growing irritated: I'd been to enough parties where I'd felt him watching me, impatient, even as I tried to pull myself away from Rina so we could leave. And I knew he only looked at his watch when he thought his time was being wasted. I started to get a strange sense that maybe the afternoon had been a big deal, after all.

Principal Hawthorne kept talking and all I could do was just sit there, watching Rogerson as he fidgeted, glancing around, bored. He checked his watch again. Shifted his feet. Brushed his hand across his head. Checked his watch.

"And so, on behalf of Jackson High School I would like to thank all of these fine athletes and their families for a great season. . . ."

I looked at Principal Hawthorne, willing him to finish, even as he gripped the lectern harder, his voice rising across the faces in the audience. Beside me Rina pinched my leg, then smiled at me when I glanced at her. I smiled back, still listening, and knotted the hem of my dress up tight in my fist, squeezing it hard.

Hawthorne would not shut up. "I thank you for your hard work, your school spirit, and your good sportsmanship. We are very, very proud."

Rina was still smiling. She nodded at Rogerson, and when I looked back to where he'd been standing, just seconds before, the door was swinging shut and he was gone.

"Thank you and have a good evening!" And everyone started clapping, the auditorium seeming hotter than ever as I got up out of my chair and pushed off the stage, down the steps past the swarms and clogs of people.

"Caitlin, honey," my mother called out, and then she was right in front of me, with Boo beside her. "Let's get a picture of you in that beautiful corsage."

I stood there, forcing myself to smile.

"Oh, dear," she said, pulling down the camera to examine it. "This isn't working, for some reason. Why isn't this working?" Boo leaned over to help, both of them bending over it.

"Lens cap," I said. There were all these bodies brushing past me, and the auditorium was so hot: I could smell someone sweating.

"What?" my mother said.

"The lens cap," I said, reaching over and pulling it off. "There."

"Well, Margaret, I'm glad to see you've learned so much in photography class," Boo said, smiling at me.

"Oh, goodness!" my mother said, laughing as she stepped back to set up her shot. "I always do that, don't I?"

I nodded, feeling a hot flush crawl up my neck.

"Now, that's better . . . okay! Smile, Caitlin. Smile!"

I was smiling. And sweating. I had to go. The flash popped in front of my eyes and I saw stars.

"It was a nice ceremony," Stewart said as he came up beside me, as if I'd planned it myself. "Very uplifting."

"Show us your certificate," my mother said, prodding me in the elbow. I handed it to her; I'd forgotten I was even holding it. "Isn't that nice? Jack, isn't this nice?"

My father, who was standing a few seats down looking hot and uncomfortable in a tie I'd given him just a few years ago, green with dark black stripes, glanced at it and said, "Nice."

"I have to go," I said quickly. "Rogerson's here, so I'll just get a ride home with him, okay?"

"Well, I don't know," my mother said in a worried voice, looking at my father. "I thought we'd have coffee and dessert back at the house."

"Let her go," my father said, ready to leave himself. "The traffic's gonna be terrible. We should get going."

"Well, all right . . ." my mother said in a light voice, trailing off again. She glanced again at my father, as if wanting him to intervene, but he already had his coat and was heading to the aisle. "But, Caitlin, do try to come back to the house, so we can all celebrate together. Okay?"

"Okay." I was starting to feel dizzy.

"Let's go," my father, who had a low tolerance for crowds, repeated. He loosened his tie as he brushed past me, the crease in his forehead already folding in on itself. The room was hot and smelled like perfume mixed with sweat and people and dusty school heat.

"Very nice," Stewart said to me again as we walked up the aisle, with Boo and my mother behind us. I was hardly listening, my eyes on the crowd outside the door. "We're very proud of you, Caitlin. Really."

"Thanks," I said, stepping to the side to let a big fat lady in a pink suit between us. Once she passed I'd lost sight of Stewart and everyone else, so I slipped out the door and into the warm, moist air.

I found Rogerson parked down by the soccer fields. I knocked on the passenger side window and he looked at me, then waited a second before leaning over and unlocking the door.

I got in, shut the door, then leaned over to kiss him on the cheek, but he pulled back, turning his head away from me. The radio was playing—his music—but this time I didn't change the station.

"What's wrong?" I said.

"Nothing."

Outside, it was raining again, big drops splattering across the windshield. "I'm sorry the banquet ran long," I said. "I really couldn't do anything about it."

"Whatever," he said, running the tips of his fingers over the steering wheel. He still hadn't looked at me. "Where were you this afternoon?"

"Oh, God," I said. "I ran into Rina and she was, like, having this enormous crisis. She blew it with Bill, finally. Got totally busted." And I laughed, but the laugh sounded weird, like it was too heavy and just fell.

"Oh," he said, shifting in his seat. "I waited for you for a long time." He was looking straight ahead, to the soccer fields. I could see the rain falling sideways in the bright lights there.

"I'm sorry," I said. "She was all upset, and the time just got away from me. Okay?"

"Whatever." And he kind of smiled at me, like he was ready to let it go. Like it was all right, we were okay now.

We just sat there for a minute, both of us looking at the rain as it fell harder on the windshield.

"It's just that I wondered where you were," he said, then ducked his head, picking at a seam on the steering wheel. "Since you said you'd be there and all."

The thing is that I thought we were okay. He had smiled at me, and I'd let out a big breath, assuming it was over. Now, as he brought it up again, I stopped thinking and got careless.

"Oh, come on," I said, reaching over playfully to knock him on the knee. "Don't be such a big baby."

When he hit me, I didn't see it coming. It was just a quick blur, a flash out of the corner of my eye, and then the side of my face just exploded, burning, as his hand slammed against me.

The noise it made was a *crack,* like a gunshot. And it wasn't like in the movies, where the person just stands there and takes it. I reeled back, hitting my head against my seat. My ears were ringing, my face flushed, and already, instantly, I had tears in my eyes.

I said, out loud, "Oh, my God."

"Don't ever fucking talk to me that way," he said in a very low, quiet voice. Then he started the engine, slammed it into reverse, and fishtailed down the dirt parking lot before hitting traffic. We crawled down the slope of the main lot to the road, a line of brake lights lit up in front of us.

I had my hand on my cheek, holding it there. My face felt strange and tight and I was gripping the door handle with my other hand, as if that was all that was keeping me from flying loose from my seat and up into the air. I concentrated hard on the car in front of us, a blue Honda Accord with a bumper sticker that said *I Love My Scottish Terrier!* I read it again and again, saying the words in my head.

Someone started beeping. Traffic was bad, all backed up. Rogerson turned on the wipers as it started raining harder, the drops big and round, splashing as they hit the windshield.

"What the fuck is taking so long?" he said under his breath, looking over the car in front of us. "Jesus."

I still had my hand on my face. I was trying not to cry but the tears came anyway, bumping over my fingers and down the back of my hand, and I tried to think of something safe. But all I could come up with was trivia.

What are sometimes called Minor Planets? Asteroids. What is seaborgium? A new transuranium element. What does a sphygmomanometer measure? Blood pressure.

All the cars were going off to the median, heading around something. One by one they pulled aside, bumping across the grass and gravel. As we got closer I could see it was my parents' car in the middle of the road. My father was behind the wheel, one hand rubbing his forehead, while my mother sat beside him. Stewart was in the backseat, the door opposite him open. And then, as we crawled around them, I saw Boo.

She was crouching in the road, her braid hanging over her shoulder. Then she stood up, hands cupped and extended in front of her. She was holding something.

The rain was coming down very hard now, in sheets, but Boo moved slowly, carrying whatever it was very gently. As we wound past her, I looked back and saw her bend down by the side of the road. She put her hands into the grass, releasing what she'd been carrying, what she had saved. It was a turtle, brought out by the unseasonable rain and into peril by blind instinct. Boo stood up, hands on her hips, watching as it made its way over the grass, to its intended destination, as the cars honked and the people cursed and Rogerson, disgusted, gunned the engine across the grass median and back onto the road, while my face still burned under my hand.

"Crazy bitch," he said.

But as we turned right, onto the main road home, all I could think of as we sped away was how it must feel to be surrounded by those whizzing cars and find yourself suddenly lifted and carried, safe, to the comfort of that tall, cool grass.

We didn't talk about what happened. Instead, we went to McDonald's, just like it was any other night, where Rogerson had a Big Mac and bought me a milkshake without me even asking him to. Then he drove me home, his hand on my leg, playing my radio station like nothing had happened, nothing at all. It seemed so crazy to me, like maybe I had dreamed it, somehow, but each time I touched my fingers to my face the swelling and tenderness there reminded me it was real.

Rogerson parked in front of my house, then surprised me by reaching over and kissing me very tenderly, cupping my chin in his hand. And as much as I hated to admit it—it seemed impossible, just so wrong—I felt that rush that always came when he touched me or kissed me, the one that made me feel unsteady and wonderful all at once.

"I love you," he said, pulling back and looking very directly into my eyes. His were so green, like the ocean underwater: When he'd been angry, earlier, they seemed almost black. "Okay?"

It was the first time he'd said it, and under other circumstances it would have been important. But now, all I could think about was the pain in my face. My temple was still throbbing, my eye swollen just enough that when I blinked it stung. And I missed Cass so much, suddenly, wanted to walk up the steps to my house and find her there, ready to smooth one finger over my eyebrow, her face close to mine. Close enough to see what had happened, without me even having to say it out loud.

Rogerson was focused on me. It was as if he was asking me to make a pact with him, to get our stories straight. He brushed his finger across the back of my hand, gently. All the way home he'd kept touching me, so carefully, as if he had to keep me somehow connected to him or I'd just drift away.

I could have just gotten out of the car and walked up to my house, leaving him behind forever. Things would have been very different if I had done that. But the fact was that I loved Rogerson. It wasn't just that I loved him, even: it was that I loved what *I* was when I was with him. Not a little sister, the pretty girl's sidekick, the second runner-up. All I'd ever wanted was to make my own path, far from Cass's. And even after what had happened, I wasn't ready to give that up just yet.

"Okay," I said to him, and when he kissed me again I closed my eyes, feeling the slight sting there, like a pinprick, nothing more.

He stayed in front of my house, engine running, as I walked up the steps. I could feel him watching me and wondered if he was worried whether I'd keep up my end of our bargain. Still, I couldn't shake the image of his face, so dark and angry, his hand coming at me, with no time to stop it or get out of the way. It was like he'd become a different person, a monster from a nightmare.

He didn't drive away until I'd closed the front door behind me. I took a deep breath and started up the stairs, not even sure yet what story I would tell when my mother saw my face and flew into a panic.

When I got to the top of the stairs, I could see her standing in the kitchen, clutching the phone to her ear, the cord wrapped around her wrist. My father was standing in front of the refrigerator, arms crossed against his chest, his eyes on my mother as she spoke, haltingly, her voice seeming to echo lightly off the cabinets and bright, shiny floor. Neither of them saw me.

"Oh, baby," my mother was saying, one hand rising, shaking, to touch her own cheek. "I'm so glad you called."

My father shifted his weight, the worried crease easing into and out of his forehead, but he never took his eyes off my mother's face. Behind him, on the counter, were four coffee cups, abandoned, as well as a plate of untouched brownies.

"Oh, honey, no. No. We're not mad," my mother said softly, wiping her eyes and looking back at my father, a mild smile on her face. "We were just *worried* about you, that's all. We just wanted to be sure . . . that you were okay." Her voice cracked, slightly. "I know, sweetie. I know."

I walked into the living room and sat down in my father's chair, looking at the row of dolls lined up around the TV. They stared back at me, open-mouthed, their gazes dull and gray, as I reached up and touched my eye, feeling the slight puffiness there.

"We love you too, Cass," my mother said, her voice choked. "We just didn't want to lose you, honey. I couldn't stand to lose you."

I heard the patio door slide open, then footsteps as my father walked out onto the deck. A breeze blew in—hot and sticky-wet—before the door slid shut again. When I looked outside, through the glass, he was standing with his back to me, looking up at the few stars visible through the fast-moving clouds.

My mother sniffled, listening as Cass spoke. Then she laughed, once, and said, "We've got time, honey. Plenty of time to tell us everything, when you're ready."

I closed my eyes, seeing Rogerson again in my mind, his eyes black as his hand lashed out, the pain spreading so suddenly from my cheek to my temple. I hadn't even seen it coming, hadn't even had a chance to move aside.

My mother was talking, laughing, as I crept back down the stairs and slipped out the front door, easing it shut behind me. I didn't even know where I was going—Rina's route, maybe—as I started my car and pulled out onto the street, my headlights cutting a swath across the house. I just drove, one hand cradling my face, until I finally turned into the parking lot at Applebee's.

I could see Corinna inside, sitting at the bar, legs crossed, smoking a cigarette and counting a stack of money, her hair twisted up in a bun. The bartender slid a drink over to her, and she looked up at him, smiling, then tucked a loose strand of hair behind her ear, her bracelets sliding down her arm.

When I walked inside I had no idea of what my face looked like: I still hadn't seen a mirror. But when the bartender nodded at me and Corinna turned around, her mouth dropped open, her eyes widening.

"Oh, my God," she said, standing up and coming over to me. She reached out and touched my eye and I flinched, my own hand rising to push her away. "What happened to you, Caitlin?"

But I couldn't tell her. Instead, I just let her walk me to the bar and sit me down before she wrapped her arms around me, drawing my face to her shoulder. She smelled like fried food and grilled peppers as she drew her fingers through my hair, telling me it was all right, all right now.

Chapter Nine

Dec. 13

What's been happening is so strange, like it isn't even

Dec. 14

Last night something happened with Rogerson. He got so angry at me, and he

Dec. 14

I don't even know where to start but

This wasn't working.

I closed my dream journal, sitting back across my pillows in the slant of streetlight coming through the window. Since the night of the winter banquet I'd tried again and again to put down in words or even say aloud just to myself what had happened with Rogerson. The excuses had come easily: to my parents, Corinna, and Rina, I'd gotten bumped by a stray elbow as I made my way through the banquet crowd. The truth was harder.

I was afraid of forgetting. It seemed too easy. Already life was back to normal—I was lost in midterms and cheering practice and long, gray winter afternoons at Corinna's. But when Rogerson and I were at the pool house, inching ever closer to the inevitable, I'd feel his fingers slide up my arm, or curve around my neck and be lost in it, only to feel a sudden jolt as I remembered. His face, so angry, glaring at me. That split second as his hand moved toward me, too quickly for me to even comprehend what was about to happen.

But then he'd kiss me harder, and I'd go under again.

My mother, meanwhile, was almost giddy after her one conversation with Cass, who had still made it clear that she wanted to take things *slowly:* In two weeks she hadn't yet called back.

My mother was hoping she would for Christmas Eve. This, alone, just the possibility, was making the holidays more bearable for all of us. Before Cass broke down under endless pleading letters and phone messages, my mother hadn't even begun to prepare for her favorite of holidays: no eggnog, no tinsel, not even a tree. The day after Cass called, I came home to find her baking snowman cookies and wrapping gifts, with Barbra Streisand singing "Silent Night" in the background.

From what I could make of it, Cass hadn't explained much when she called. She said she missed us, and that she was happy. That she liked her job. That she hoped we could understand that this was what she wanted. Yale was not mentioned, and she didn't give my mother her phone number.

"She needs time," my father kept saying, each time the phone rang and my mother ran to it, her face falling the instant she didn't hear Cass's voice on the other end of the line. "She'll come around."

"I just don't understand why she doesn't want to be in contact with us," my mother kept saying. "She didn't even *talk* to Caitlin."

But the truth was, I wasn't ready to talk to Cass yet. I had a secret now, one I could keep from everyone else. But I worried that Cass, even over the phone, would recognize something different in my voice. She knew me too well.

Life was going on. I didn't even have a scar, this time, to remind me of what happened. But sometimes, when I glanced sideways at

Rogerson in the car, or right before I fell asleep at night, I would have a sudden flash of his face again, how it had literally *changed* right before my eyes. And even as life settled back to normal, and we never discussed it, there was a part of me waiting, always braced and ready for him to do it again.

My mother, Boo, and I had our final photography class before the holidays the last Saturday before Christmas. We'd just finished developing what our instructor, Matthew, called our "people series," in which we were supposed to use a portrait to convey our relationship to someone else. My mother had posed my father in front of the window in his study, with all his diplomas and various certificates behind him. He looked uncomfortable, his smiled forced, hands uneasily stuffed in his pockets, like an executive posing for the company newsletter. My mother, however, was just proud to have gotten his whole head in.

Boo's picture was of her and Stewart. They'd put the camera on a table, set the timer, and then bent over, heads down, for a full minute, yanking themselves up just before the shutter clicked. The result was striking: the two of them, hair wildly sticking up, eyes sparkling and smiling hugely while the blood rushed out of their faces. It captured the closeness and eccentricity about them that I loved—two people, so alike, caught in a crazy moment of their own making.

My picture was of Rogerson. He hadn't wanted me to shoot him, but since the winter banquet he'd been sweet and gentle with me, on his best behavior. I'd carried my camera around with me for over a week, trying to catch him at the perfect time, and taken a few shots here and there, none of them outstanding. Then, one day, we were walking down the steps of Corinna's when I called out his name and he turned around.

In the picture, Rogerson is not smiling. He is looking steadily at the camera, a trace of irritation on his face, his car keys dangling from one hand under his jacket sleeve. Behind him you can see all the bare winter trees against the light gray sky. The sun is barely bright, and farther down the driveway, at the very end, you can see Dave's yellow Lab, Mingus, sitting by the mailbox, looking out at the road. Rogerson takes up most of the picture, the landscape behind him stark and cold as if there is some part of him that belongs there.

Matthew, wearing a red wool sweater and now sporting sideburns, called my mother's picture "promising" (knowing to appreciate a subject with a full head) and Boo's "startling and emotional." When he got to mine, he just stood there, looking down at it for a long time. Then he said, "It's clear you know this subject very well."

"Oh, yeah," I said. For some reason, I always blushed like crazy when Matthew talked to me. He wasn't that much older than me—maybe four years—and had such a sweet, gentle disposition, always placing a hand on your shoulder or back to make a point. Boo said he was full of positive aura. "Well, he's my boyfriend."

Matthew nodded, his eyes still on the photograph. "It looks," he said in a lower voice, just to me, "like you know him a little better than he'd like you to."

I looked back down at the picture, at Rogerson's eyes, remembering again how dark, almost black, they'd seemed the night he hit me.

"Yeah," I said, keeping my eye on the picture. "I guess I do."

When class was over, I walked outside with my mother and Boo, who were headed off to do some final Christmas shopping. Rogerson was picking me up, but it was so cold in the parking lot, and sleeting, that I went back into the lobby of the Arts Center to wait. There was an Irish dancing class going on down the hallway, with music all jaunty and fast, and I stood listening and watching the Christmas lights strung over the front windows as they blinked on and off. Outside, the traffic was thick with last-minute shoppers, angrily beeping at each other at the stoplight. I wondered what Cass was doing for Christmas: if she had put up lights, bought a tree, hung stockings over a mantel.

"Caitlin?"

I turned around to see Matthew, standing there in a lime-green windbreaker, a backpack slung over his shoulder. "Hi," I said.

"You miss your ride or something?" he asked, glancing around the small lobby. Down the hall the Irish music stopped, suddenly, and there was a smattering of applause and laughter.

"Nah," I said. "He's just late."

He nodded, pulling up his windbreaker hood. "I can wait with you, if you want."

"Oh, no," I said quickly, as the Irish music began again, followed by the sound of feet clomping across a hard floor. "I'm fine."

"Okay," he said, putting one hand on the door and beginning to push it open. Then he stopped and said, "You have a real talent for faces, Caitlin. I've been very impressed with your work."

"Oh, thanks," I said, embarrassed. "I just mess around, mostly."

"You're very good. That one we looked at today, of your boyfriend . . . it's very moving. There's something striking there, and you caught it. Very well done."

He stood there, as if he knew something and was just waiting for me to confirm it. Instead, I realized I was blushing, clutching my folder with the picture in it so tightly I was bending the edges. "Thanks," I said again. "Really."

He nodded, smiling, and reached into his windbreaker pocket to pull out a pair of red knit mittens. "Have a good holiday."

"You, too," I said, as Rogerson pulled in to the far side of the parking lot. "Merry Christmas, Matthew."

He smiled, then reached forward and took my hand, squeezing it tightly between the warm wool of his mittens. They felt scratchy yet comfortable, like the kind Cass and I both had as kids, clipped to our jackets so we wouldn't lose them. "Merry Christmas," he said.

There was something so nice about standing there with him, under all those blinking lights, his mittens closed tightly over my fingers. I felt safe with him, strangely, with this person I hardly knew—safer than I'd felt in a long time, as if some part of me that had been churned up and crazy had finally come to a stop.

We couldn't have stood there like that for more than five seconds before Rogerson pulled up in front of the window and beeped the horn.

"Well," I said, and he dropped my hand. "There's my ride."

"Right," Matthew said. "See you later."

We walked out the door together, and Rogerson leaned over to unlock my door, keeping his eyes on Matthew as I climbed inside.

"Who's that?" he asked as I put my seat belt on.

"He teaches my class," I said. "Where've you been?"

He just shook his head as he put the car in gear, gunning across the parking lot. "Dave said he could get us a good deal on this ounce, but the guy never showed. Waited for an hour."

"Oh, man," I said. "You must have been really mad."

He didn't say anything, instead looking past me out my window to the sidewalk beside us. When I turned my head, I saw Matthew walking, his backpack over both shoulders and hands in his pockets, head ducked against the falling sleet.

I was about to change the subject, but something felt strange to me, an unsteady feeling like before lightning strikes. Rogerson still had his eyes on Matthew, even as he disappeared around a corner, and

I thought again of the picture I held in my lap, the irritation in his eyes, the stark trees, with barely a sun at all in the sky behind him.

He didn't say a word the whole way home. But when we pulled up in front of my mailbox, he cut the engine and just sat there, looking straight ahead. I slid my fingers down to my door handle, telling myself he was just in a bad mood, not my fault. Dave had made him wait, and then he'd seen—or had he?—Matthew holding my hand. I could slip out, he'd go burn off steam, and then later everything would be okay. It would. If I could just—

"So," he said suddenly, and I felt that crackling electricity again, a whooshing in my ears, "what's going on with you and that guy, Caitlin?"

"Nothing," I said, and my own voice sounded strange to me, like it was weightless, drifting up, up, and away.

"I saw you." The words were clipped and low. "Don't lie to me."

"I'm not lying," I said quickly, and I hated the way I sounded, so weak and pleading. "I just wished him a Merry Christmas and he shook my hand . . ."

"Don't lie to me!" he yelled, and in the small space of the car it was so loud, hurting my ears.

"I'm not," I whispered. "Rogerson, please. It's nothing." And then I reached out and touched his arm.

He was coiled and taut, a mousetrap set to spring at the slightest touch. As soon as my fingers brushed his sleeve, his fist was in motion, springing out at me and catching my jaw, knocking me backward so hard the door handle dug into my right side, twisting the skin.

I felt like I couldn't shut my mouth, but even so I was still trying to explain. "Rogerson," I said. "I—"

"Shut up, Caitlin," he said.

"But—"

He slapped me hard, across the other cheek, and it felt like part of my face was shattering into tiny pieces. I covered my face with my hands, stretching my fingers to cover the span from my forehead to my chin, as if without them I would fall apart altogether.

"This isn't my fault," he said in a low voice, as I tasted blood in my mouth. "It isn't, Caitlin. You know what you did."

I didn't say anything. I didn't think I could take another blow. Instead, I closed my eyes and thought of trivia, again: questions and answers, the solidness and safety of facts. When the biggest secret about Rogerson was the limitless stretch of what he knew.

What instrument do sailors use to measure time?

I told myself to breathe. *A chronometer.*

Where in Italy did pizza originate?

My cheek was still burning, all the way up to my temple. *Naples.*

I turned my head, resting my sore cheek against the cold glass of the window, and looked at my house. We had a fat plastic Santa standing by the front steps, white lights strung in the tree by the walk, and a row of tiny reindeer mounted on the roof of the garage. Upstairs, I could see my father sitting in his chair in the square of one window, reading the paper, just like he had in a million nights of my childhood.

I closed my eyes, willing him somehow to look through the dark car windows and rush out and save me from Rogerson, and from myself. But he didn't. Instead, my father did what he always did: He folded the paper, picked up the remote, moving across channel after channel, waiting for me—and Cass—to come home.

When I came inside twenty minutes later my mother was taking a casserole out of the oven.

"Oh, my goodness!" she said, her eyes widening. She plunked it down on the counter and started across the kitchen, wiping her hands on a towel decorated with tiny Christmas trees. "What *happened* to you, Caitlin?"

"I fell," I said quickly, even as she leaned in close, brushing my hair off my forehead. In Rogerson's rearview mirror, after we'd smoked a bowl, it hadn't looked that bad: just a bit red, puffy in places.

"Fell?" she said. "Jack, come in here!"

"Mom, I'm fine." My father appeared in the kitchen doorway, the line in his forehead already creased and deep. "There was just some ice by the mailbox and I slipped."

"Oh, I just knew it!" she said, pushing me down into a chair: The sore spot on my side hit against the armrest and I cringed, sucking in a breath. She didn't notice. "Jack, didn't I tell you walking back from Boo's I slipped there? Didn't I? Caitlin, was Rogerson with you?"

"No," I said, shaking my head. "He dropped me off and then when I started up the walk my feet just flew out from under me."

"Well," my father said, his gaze steady on my face, "it looks like you hit right there on your jaw. Get that ice pack out of the freezer, Margaret, before the swelling gets any worse."

"I'm fine," I said again. "It doesn't even hurt anymore."

It was strange that I didn't even consider telling the truth. I was just stoned and bleary, so cried out that all I could think of was curling up on my bed and going to sleep. Rogerson had lit the bowl without even a word, even as I sat there beside him, my ears ringing, and after a few hits everything just seemed to fade out. Increasingly, that was the way the pot worked with me lately. After a couple of hits, whatever had been bothering me drifted to arm's length, like the end of a song on the radio you can just barely hear, just fading away.

And then he pulled me close to him, told me he loved me and

kissed me hard and urgently, his hand curling around the back of my neck, the way he knew I liked it. As if somehow, that way, he could give back what he'd taken from me. And I let him.

Now, I closed my eyes as my father pressed the ice pack against my face, making it sting as the coolness seeped in slowly. I told myself I had too many secrets already: the drugs, cigarettes, my downward cheerleading spiral. If I let one out, the rest would tumble behind it, out of my control, like wild horses let loose to stampede.

It was funny. What I'd loved most about Rogerson was that he took me to a place so far from anywhere Cass had been. And now, him hitting me was the same thing. Cass wouldn't have taken up with Rogerson, just like she never would have stayed with anyone who hurt her. But I wasn't Cass, not even close. I was weaker. And I'd keep this secret before I'd prove that again.

"You need to keep this there until the swelling goes down," my father said now, taking my hand and pressing it against the ice pack. "Okay?"

"It's just so red," my mother said in a worried voice. "You must have hit so *hard*."

"Yeah," I told her, averting my eyes. "I did."

My father was putting on his jacket. "I'm going to go put some salt on the walk," he said to my mother. "I think we've got some left over from last year out in the shed."

"Yes, yes, it's behind the potting soil," she said, following him down the stairs. "And Jack, make sure you check the whole spot, won't you? I'd hate to see anyone else get hurt."

I moved the ice pack to my cheek. I could still taste blood in my mouth.

"Now, Caitlin," my mother said as she came back up the stairs, the door clicking shut behind my father. "I'm going to run a hot bath for you. Won't that be nice? And when you're done, I'll bring dinner to your room so you can eat in bed, and rest. Okay?"

"Mom, you don't have to—"

"Hush. Go get undressed and I'll let you know when it's ready." She started out of the kitchen, then stopped and put her hand on my shoulder, bending down to kiss me gently on the forehead. She smelled like vanilla and Joy perfume, and suddenly I felt like I might start crying again. "You really scared me, Caitlin," she said, smiling as she brushed her fingers through my hair. "I don't know what I would do if something happened to you."

I could tell her, I told myself. *I could tell her right now and fix this. I could say that he hits me and I hate cheerleading and I miss Cass but I know why she left and I wish I could make everything better but I can't, I can't, I can't even tell you where it hurts, not now.*

"Don't worry," I said instead, as she ruffled my hair and walked away, my mother, to do what she did best, to take care of me. "I'm fine."

When I went to my room to change into my bathrobe, my father was still outside, scattering salt by hand down the length of our walk. When he reached the front steps he went back, across the grass, to the spot by the mailbox where I'd told him I'd fallen, and scattered another handful there. Then, as I watched, he spent a good five minutes scraping his foot back and forth across the pavement, searching for slick spots, as if that was all it would take to keep us safe.

When my mother tucked me in that night, I was half asleep, my face sore, my belly full of chicken-broccoli casserole. She kissed my cheek carefully, not wanting to hurt me, then walked to my doorway and stood there in silhouette, her hand curled over the doorknob.

"Good night, honey," she said. "I'll see you in dreamland."

I was too tired to answer her.

That night, I didn't find my mother in my dreams. But for the first time since she'd left, I saw Cass.

The dream itself was long and complicated. Eliza Drake was there, and Corinna, and Mrs. Garver, my fourth grade teacher. We were in the Lakeview Mall, searching for something having to do with aluminum, running to the far end, near the Sears store. I was passing an empty storefront, just glass and empty inside, when I saw Cass. She was standing a few feet away, on the other side, but when I stopped she came closer.

"Cass?" I said, and Mrs. Garver was yelling at me to come on, hurry up, now, now.

She smiled at me, cocking her head to the side. She was wearing this bright red sweater and I remember wondering if she was stuck in there, trapped somehow. "Good luck," she said to me, raising one hand and pressing her palm against the glass separating us. As if she could see the future, hers and mine, everything.

"Wait," I said, "Cass—"

"Go," she said, as Mrs. Garver grabbed my arm, yanking me away. "Go ahead, Caitlin. Go."

"Cass—" I said again, but I was already running, looking back to find her, but now all the storefronts were empty glass, and I knew I could never find her, even if I tried.

When I woke up I was sweating and my jaw ached, a throbbing pain that seemed to match my heartbeat. I sat up in bed and turned on the light: It was only 10:30. I could hear the TV on in the living room as my father watched the early news, and next door Boo's kitchen light was on and she was sitting at the table, reading a book.

I lay back against my pillows, still seeing Cass in that red sweater, her hand pressed against the glass. *It was just a dream,* I told myself. *That's all.*

When I pulled my dream journal from under the bed and flipped to a blank page, I didn't know yet what I would write. I put a hand on my aching cheek and just began:

Dec. 20

Dear Cass,

I don't know if you'll ever read this. Maybe I won't want you to. But something's happening to me and you're the only one I can tell. I had this dream about you tonight and it scared me into doing this: In the dream, I lost you for good. Lately I've been feeling like I'm losing myself, too. This is why.

My boyfriend, Rogerson, hit me tonight. It wasn't the first time. I know you can't believe I'd let this happen: I can't either. But it's more confusing than you'd think. I love him. That sounds so weak and pitiful, but lately, it's been enough for me to forgive anything. But after tonight, I'm not so sure. He really hurt me, Cass. It still hurts now. . . .

Chapter Ten

"Caitlin?"

I blinked, opening my eyes. My English lit teacher, Mr. Lensing, was standing over me, a well-worn copy of T. S. Eliot's collected poems in his hand. All around us the room was quiet and I could feel everyone watching me.

"Yes?"

"Did you hear the question?" He shifted the book to his other hand, then lifted his glasses off his head and put them on while flipping a few pages with his fingers. "I asked you about the symbolism of the mermaids in Eliot's 'The Love Song of J. Alfred Prufrock.'"

"Oh," I said, looking down at my own book, which was closed, and frantically flipping through the pages, the words blurring. "I, um, think—"

"Page one-eighty-four," Richard Spellman, class president, whispered from behind me. "Bottom of the page."

"Right," I said, *One-fifty, one-sixty-two, one-seventy-four.* Where the hell was it? "Um, the mermaids. Well—"

A few rows back, someone snickered. Then coughed. Mr. Lensing took his glasses off again. "Can anyone help us out here?" he asked, a tired look on his face. "Yes. Richard."

"The mermaids represent what is ultimately unattainable by the speaker," Richard said, and the same person in back snickered again, at him. "When he says they won't sing to him, he's talking about his separateness from the rest of the world, the kind of dream-state he is in, all by himself. He says he's underwater, with these mermaids who both accept and reject him. But it is the human element—the real world—that ultimately does him in, as is seen in the last line."

I had finally located the right page, my eyes quickly scanning the very end of the poem: *Till human voices wake us, and we drown.*

"Very good," Mr. Lensing said, clapping his book shut just as the bell rang. "Read—and be ready to discuss—*The Waste Land* tomorrow, people. And don't forget, papers are due in one week!"

Everyone was talking now, books closing, backpacks zipping up, the sound of voices and shuffling in the hallway coming in through the open door. I shut my notebook and stood up, looking out the window at the parking lot and the gray, February sky above it.

"Caitlin."

I looked up. Mr. Lensing, now behind his desk, was watching me. "Yes?"

"Wake up," he said. "Okay?"

I nodded. "Yeah, sure. Okay."

I walked out into the hallway, past the lockers and into the girls' bathroom, which was thick with the smell of cigarettes and hairspray. A group of girls were crowded by the mirrors, checking lipstick and gossiping, but I pushed past them and went into a stall, locking it behind me.

"My point is," one of the girls by the sinks was saying, "I just can't even *think* about the prom yet."

There was a hiss of hairspray, and then someone else said, "I heard Becca Plaser already bought her dress, in New York. It cost, like, five hundred dollars or something."

"Oh, please," the first girl said. "It doesn't matter if you spend a million on your dress if you can't get a *date*."

I sat down on the toilet, then reached over with my right hand to carefully roll up my left sleeve. And midway up my forearm, I could see the bluish-black edge of the bruise coming into view.

"Well," another girl said, "all that matters is that we will be beach-bound the night of the prom. It's gonna be so cool!"

"So your parents said yes?"

"Yep. I mean, I was subjected to the whole Trust Talk and all that. But we are *in,* for sure. No worries."

I kept rolling up my sleeve until I could see the whole bruise. It was turning yellow in the center, less black than the day before.

"Yes!" I heard a slapping of palms, then someone laughing. The bell announcing the next period rang, ear-splittingly loud in the small space. I touched the center of the bruise with my finger, smoothing my fingers over its width. It still hurt, but the swelling was down.

I sat there, listening as the girls left, then ducked my head to check for feet under the other stalls. Nobody. I was alone.

I rolled down my sleeve, pulling it tight to the edge of my wrist. As if by silent agreement, since the night I'd told my parents how I had "slipped on the ice," Rogerson had taken to only hitting me where I could cover it: arms, legs, shoulders. I wore only long-sleeved shirts, big sweaters, and turtlenecks, but at least now my face was off-limits.

After that night it was okay for a little while. He seemed sorry—although he never said so out loud—but I could tell. It was in the way he kept his hand on my knee, or placed his fingers in the small of my back, always keeping me close. In the Cokes and candy bars he bought me without being asked, CDs or magazines I liked dropped like offerings in my lap, surprising me. And most of all it was in the way he kissed me, his lips on my neck, or trailing down across my collarbone, as if I was beautiful or even sacred.

On Christmas Eve, I went to the pool house, where Rogerson

cooked me dinner. Afterward, he slid a box across the table to me: it was white, and long, tied with a red bow. Inside was a silver necklace made up of tiny, interlocking squares, so shiny it glittered as he lifted up my hair to do the clasp. I thought then, as I had so many times before, how impossible it seemed that he could ever have hurt me.

That night, I slept with him for the first time. And it hurt, too, but in a different way, one I'd been expecting. And the pain didn't linger, easily overshadowed by how good it felt to lie in his arms afterward, my head on his chest. I could see my necklace shining in the moonlight that was slanting through the window, and made a wish on it that things would be better now.

Each time we had sex from then on, I told myself that this was the closest you could get to another person. So close their breaths become your own. So I gave him all of me, believing I could trust him.

Then, on New Year's Eve, I talked too much to a guy at a party while Rogerson did business in another room. Outside he yanked me by my hair and pushed me against a wall, where I'd clocked the back of my head against a planter, making it bleed. I saw in the New Year at Corinna's, stoned, with a warm washcloth pressed against my head—Rogerson explained how I'd been tipsy, too much beer—while everyone counted down and clinked champagne glasses. Corinna gave Dave a long, sloppy kiss and said, "This is our year, baby."

"You say that every year," he said, laughing.

"No. This year, it's true. I can feel it," she replied. "California, here we come!"

"Happy New Year," Rogerson said, and then he kissed me. But for the first time since all of this had started—the hittings, and the sex—it was different. I still felt something, but not like I had before. I was wary now.

"Happy New Year," I'd responded, like the robot I felt I was becoming. I looked down at my necklace, running my fingers over the patterned squares. Even though it had just been days earlier, Christmas Eve—and those gentle hands on my neck—already seemed like another world.

The next day he bought me a CD and took me to the movies, where he held my hand, his fingers locked around mine. I couldn't focus on the film, something about the apocalypse and only one man who could save all humanity. Instead I kept looking at Rogerson, the light flickering across his face, and wondering what lay ahead for us, and me.

There was no pattern, no way of knowing when to expect it. After New Year's a week passed until the next time, then just a couple of days, then two weeks. Whenever he did hit me, I could count on him being sorry for at least twenty-four hours: a safe period on which I had come to rely, like home base. Those were the good days. But once they were over, all bets were off.

But no matter what we were doing, the fact that he hit me was always on my mind. When we had sex, especially, I couldn't push it out of my mind, however badly I wanted to. The Rogerson kissing me or stroking my stomach couldn't be the same one who lashed out so easily, who pushed me up against walls or smacked me. It seemed incongruous, against all logic, like a theorem you could never prove in geometry. And in the moments afterward, as we lay there together, I'd hold him so close, as if just by tangling myself with him I could keep that Rogerson with me, banishing the other forever. But no matter how hard I tried, he always managed to slip away.

It got to be that sex was the only time I could count on being safe. And it never lasted long enough.

Then we'd be driving, stoned, on our way somewhere, and then somewhere else after that. Before it had been exciting, new, to always be in transit. But now I felt like I was drifting, sucked down by an undertow, and too far out to swim back to the shore. I never even tried to change the station anymore, instead letting his music fill my ears and all the spaces between us, heavy and thick, like a haze.

Wake up, Caitlin. Mr. Lensing wasn't the only one who'd noticed.

"Caitlin?" my mother would say to me at the dinner table, as I pushed around my food, my sleeves pulled tight to my wrists even though she kept the heat cranked and there was a fire crackling and snapping right behind me. My mother was cold-blooded. "Honey, are you okay? Aren't you hungry?"

"Caitlin!" the dance coach would bark as I flubbed another cartwheel or missed a step, finishing out the clumsy death throes of my cheerleading career. "Get with it, O'Koren! What's the matter with you?"

"Caitlin," Boo would say, trying to hide the hurt in her face as I shrank back from her in photography class—the only time I ever saw her anymore—when she tried to squeeze my arm or shoulder, saying hello in her touchy way. "I *miss* you."

"Caitlin?" Rina would ask in our one shared class, history, fanning her hand over my eyes as I zoned out, half-listening to her detail another dramatic blow-up with Jeff. "Hello?"

"Caitlin," Corinna would say. "Hand me that lighter."

"Caitlin," Stewart had said more than once, "you look like you really, desperately, are in need of some wheat germ. Seriously."

And finally, the one voice to which I snapped to attention, every time.

"Caitlin," Rogerson would say, and I'd listen so hard, trying to tell just by the cadence what might happen when we were alone. "Come on."

Wake up, Caitlin, Mr. Lensing had said. But what he didn't understand was that this dreamland was preferable, walking through this life half-sleeping, everything at arm's length or farther away.

I understood those mermaids. I didn't care if they sang to me. All I wanted was to block out all the human voices as they called my name again and again, pulling me upward into light, to drown.

I had known since December that punctuality could mean the best or worst of things for me with Rogerson. But now things were getting harder.

Rogerson picked me up for lunch every day right at noon. This gave me exactly five minutes to get from my trigonometry class, which was on one side of campus, through the packed hallways and crowded courtyard to the small turnaround near the auto mechanics classroom where he always waited for me.

But no matter how quickly I left class—even after changing my seat, so I was right by the door and could leap up the second the bell rang—he always managed to get there first. I'd round the corner, out of breath, to see the car parked there, engine idling. I'd know Rogerson was behind those tinted windows, waiting and watching.

Sometimes, it was just a little rough: a blocking bruise. Other times, a hard foul. And if things were really bad—full contact.

It was always easier for me to think about it this way. Sports was my father cheering Saturday morning football, Cass lifting the all-state trophy over her head, our entire family at university basketball games, roaring with the crowd. Sports were safe, even when Rogerson wasn't.

Even the days that I skipped fourth period so I was there first, sitting under the little scrubby tree by the curb when he pulled in, it didn't seem to make him any happier. It was like he wanted to be mad, so he'd have an excuse to do what he did to me. And he was doing it more and more often, as winter headed into spring. The bruise on my arm I'd gotten courtesy of Mrs. Dennis, my trig teacher, who insisted on keeping me after class a few days earlier to discuss my lack of class participation and a failing quiz grade.

I started skipping her class, because it was easier. I'd sit under that tree, my knees pulled tight against my chest and smoke cigarettes, my eyes fixed on the entrance to the turnaround. There were rules of play here, technical fouls, illegal movements. I had to be careful.

I couldn't talk to anyone because if Rogerson saw me he'd assume I was (A) flirting or (B) discussing him. One day Richard Spellman, class president, tried to sit down and talk to me about some stupid group project we were doing for English. I just shook him off, edging farther and farther away: I knew I could guarantee myself full contact plus a few hard fouls if Rogerson saw us there together. But Richard just kept talking, oblivious, while I picked at grass blades, my stomach churning, and hid behind my sunglasses, pretending I was invisible. I was getting good at that. When he finally left it was only a matter of seconds before Rogerson pulled in. So close. So, so close.

The only person I ever really spoke to at school anymore was Rina, and not much at that.

"Let's go out tonight, just us girls," she said to me one day, as we sat together under my tree. The bell had just rung and she'd plopped down next to me, stretching her long legs out in front of her.

"I can't," I said.

"Why not?" She fumbled in her purse for her sunglasses—black with cat's-eye-shaped frames and tiny rhinestones in the corners—and put them on, leaning her head back to look up into the mild winter sun.

"I've got plans with Rogerson," I said.

"You *always* have plans with Rogerson," she said. "We haven't done a girls' night in forever, Caitlin. I'm in withdrawal here."

"I'm sorry," I said, watching as a black car—not him—sped past on the road in front of us. "But I made plans already."

"Oh, come on," she said, popping her sunglasses up on her forehead and looking at me. "What could be so important to blow off your best friend? *Again.*"

I sighed. Rina always made this hard for me. "I'm not trying to blow you off," I said. "I just already told him we'd do this thing together."

"Okay, fine," she said, flipping her hand. "How about this . . . we'll go out early, get a burger or something, and then you can meet him later somewhere."

"I can't," I said again.

"God, Caitlin!" she said, exasperated. She pulled her purse onto her lap and started digging for a cigarette, grabbing my lighter with her other hand. "Look, just let me talk to him, okay? I'll tell him you really need some girl time and I'll promise to have you back home at a decent hour. Let me handle it. I'll tell him—"

"Rina."

"I'm serious," she said. "I know how to handle this. He'll understand. He's coming to pick you up right now, right? So I'll just talk to him now."

She just *didn't* understand. "It's not a good idea," I said.

"Sure it is," she said easily, tossing back my lighter. "I can deal with Rogerson. No problem. By the time I'm done with him he'll be putty in my hands."

"Rina, I said no." She didn't know what she could do to me. What kind of full contact I could expect at the slightest intervention. My stomach already binding tight, a burning there that seemed to grow each day.

"Not another word," she said lightly, blowing me off while exhaling a long steam of smoke. "It's taken care of."

"Rina—"

"Hush. I told you. It's—"

"No," I snapped, louder than I meant to, and she jerked back, surprised, like I'd slapped her. "I told you, I can't. That's it."

She cocked her head to the side, her face hurt. "What, you're not allowed to hang out with me anymore or something? He's telling you what to do now?"

"No," I said, as another black car passed by, the light glinting off it. "He's not."

"That's sure what it sounds like," she said, an uppity tone in her voice.

"Well, it isn't," I said.

We sat there for a few minutes, not talking. All around us people were passing by, on their way to the parking lot or their next class, voices high and laughing. I was thinking back to all those nights of driving and crying, when I listened to Rina wail as the scenery sped past. She could tell me anything, as long as we were in motion.

"What's going on, Caitlin?" she said suddenly, moving a little closer and lowering her voice. "Tell me."

I look at her—my best friend—with her strawberry-blond hair and pink Coral Ice lipstick, and for a split second I wanted to let it all spill out. About the importance of time, and the helpless feeling I got every time I saw that black BMW, not knowing what waited on the other side of the tinted windows. About hard fouls, and full contact, and those mermaids, pulling me up to drown.

But I couldn't tell her. I couldn't tell anyone. As long as I didn't say it aloud, it wasn't real.

So I smiled my best cheerleader smile, shook my head, and said, "It's nothing, Rina. You worry too much." I concentrated on keeping my voice chipper, all pep: *I've got spirit, yes I do, I've got spirit, how 'bout you?*

Rina cocked her head to the side, studying me. She wasn't a dumb girl; she knew something was up. But she still had faith in our friendship, forged in the war zone of junior high. She thought I'd never lie to her.

"Okay," she said finally, as if we'd bartered out some kind of agreement. "But if you need me—"

"I know," I said, cutting her off. It was right at noon: My safe time was up. The muscles in my stomach and shoulders were clenching harder as I picked up my backpack and began to move closer to the turnaround. I looked at her, sitting cross-legged there in her sunglasses, popping her gum, with no greater concern in her life right then than me. And I envied her, quickly and quietly, in a different way than I had all those years we'd spent together.

"I gotta go," I said, and she nodded as I backed away, turning my head to look over at the parking lot entrance where Rogerson was pulling in. I was on time, but just a few feet too far out of sight. I knew she was watching me as I walked toward the car, the engine purring, low and growly, like a dog just warning you to stay back.

I didn't know what to expect this time. Trash talk, a hard foul. Full contact. I took a deep breath, walked up to the car, my reflection staring back at me in those black, black windows, and stepped across the sidelines, into the game.

While I was working on being invisible, Cass was slowly coming back to us. She hadn't called on Christmas Eve, which had made my mother teary the entire time we opened gifts and had our annual pancake breakfast with Boo and Stewart the next morning. Cass did send a card, with a picture of her and Adam inside. They were standing in front of their own tree, a small scrubby pine with a few lights, one of those homemade paper chains, and a tinfoil angel on top. He had his arm around her and they were both smiling; Cass looked as happy as I'd ever seen her. My mother put the picture in a frame, immediately, and parked it on the coffee table, displacing a series of glass teddy bears and a small basket of potpourri.

"I'm trying to understand what she meant about keeping her life her own, about boundaries," I heard her say to Boo Christmas day as they cleaned up the kitchen. My father was parked in his chair, watching a game, with Stewart dozing on the couch, one hand on his stomach. "But this is *Christmas,* for goodness sake."

"She's coming around," Boo said reassuringly.

"She seems to think that we controlled her somehow, that we were too involved in her life." I could hear my mother washing dishes, the water splashing. "And now, I guess, we're not. Or something." And she sighed, again, that low, sad Cass-sigh I'd heard daily since the summer.

Cass's gifts sat under the tree until we dismantled it. My mother, always fair, had even bought one—small, but still there—for Adam. Then they were moved to the hall closet, still in their brightly colored paper and ribbons, and stacked behind the vacuum cleaner.

When she had finally called, about a week into the New Year, I was lying in my bed, sleeping after another late night, as well as a fresh wrist-wrenching bruise, courtesy of Rogerson. I knew it was Cass just by the way my mother's voice jumped from its normal, polite hello to a gasp of excitement I could hear clearly through my door and down the hallway.

"Happy New Year to you, too!" she cried out, and I could hear her moving around, looking for my father so she could get him on the extension. This was harder for him. He'd get on the line and listen, talking to Cass only when prompted, and then in short, formal sentences, his voice low, as if she was someone he knew only formally. "How are you, honey? How was your Christmas?"

I could hear her going through the kitchen to my father's study, her heels clacking across the floor. I rolled over and closed my eyes.

"Oh, yes, we had a wonderful time. You missed the blueberry pancakes. But you were on our minds. It just wasn't the same without you." A pause, and then she whispered, "Jack, it's Cassandra. Pick up that extension."

My mother made affirmative noises as Cass described her Christmas, and then I heard my father say, "Hello, Cassandra."

"Oh, it's so wonderful you called!" my mother chirped, her voice so full and happy. I pulled my pillow over my head trying to block out the sound.

"How's the weather up there?" my father asked, and it was quiet as Cass responded. "Well, that's New York in January for you."

"It's been lovely here," my mother added. "What? Oh, she's fine, so busy. Her cheerleading is just going wonderfully, and she's so caught up with school and this new boyfriend of hers, Rogerson, she's busy every night. She's just *wonderful.*"

I reached up and examined my wrist, feeling the tenderness right by my watchband. *Wonderful,* I thought.

"I'm sure she'd want to talk to you," my mother went on, and I could hear her starting down the hallway toward my room, the cordless in her hand. "I think she's still sleeping, but I can—"

I pulled the pillow tighter, letting my body fall slack just as she opened the door a crack, peeking in.

"Caitlin?" she whispered. "Honey?"

I stayed perfectly still, concentrating on breathing evenly: in, out. In, out.

"Oh, my," my mother said softly, "she's still asleep. She'll be so sorry she missed you."

I waited until I heard the soft click of the door shutting again before I opened my eyes. Her voice faded as she walked back to the kitchen, still cooing as she took in Cass's every word.

The truth was, I didn't want to talk to Cass. So far everyone who had noticed *something* was different in me had been distracted enough by their own problems—Rina with Jeff, my mother with Cass, even Corinna with Dave and her work—that they accepted my easy explanations about falling or clumsiness and didn't look too closely. The only one who acted as if she might have sensed something was Boo, but she'd never try to pry it out of me. It wasn't her style. So it was easy, in photography class or over dinner, to ignore her thoughtful glances, to sidestep her questions with the standard dinner table answers: *Fine. Busy. Nothing special. I'm just tired.*

But my sister was different. We were too alike, and I was scared that she'd be able to tell something was wrong with one word, one sentence, instantly guessing everything. And I couldn't be found out, not by Cass. She was the strong one, the smart one. She would never have let this happen to her.

I reached under my mattress and pulled out my dream journal, flipping through a few full pages to find the first blank spot. And as my mother laughed and trilled from the kitchen, soaking up every bit of Cass she could, I talked to my sister the only way I had left.

Jan 7

Dear Cass,

Remember when we were kids and Mom always made us come up with one resolution for New Year's we had to keep, no matter what? Like flossing your teeth every day, or not fighting so much, or reading one book every month. It seemed like anything was possible when you had a clean slate to start with.

Well, it's New Year's now but I don't feel that way anymore. I wonder if you do either. Something's happening to me. It's like I'm shrinking smaller and smaller and I can't stop it. There's just so much wrong that I can't imagine the shame in admitting even the tiniest part of it. When you left it was like there was this huge gap to fill, but instead of spreading wide enough to do it I just fell right in, and I'm still falling. Like I'm half-asleep, and I can't wake up, can't wake up. . . .

I went to Corinna's one afternoon in late February to smoke a quick bowl before practice and found the entire house dark, a bunch of candles lined up and lit on the coffee table. She was on the phone, pleading with the power company and chain-smoking.

"I understand that," she said, handing my bowl back to me. Without the TV on, it was strangely quiet: I could hear their cat purring from across the room. She was sitting on the couch with her checkbook and a calculator, crying and trying to figure out what happened to the money that was supposed to cover the bills. "But I've always paid them before. I mean, I specifically remember giving the money to my boyfriend to deposit, so I don't see how—"

I lit the bowl and breathed in deep. Corinna was listening, shaking her head. She grabbed another Kleenex out of the box on the table and wiped at her eyes impatiently.

"Yes, okay. Fine. Thank you." She dropped the phone on the coffee table and raised her hands to her face, covering her eyes. Her bracelets slid down her arm, clanking against the ASK ME ABOUT SIMPLY SOUP-PERB COMBOS! button on the front of her uniform.

"I hate this," she said, her voice muffled.

"I'm so sorry," I said.

She looked up at me, half-smiled, and reached out to pick up her cigarettes. "Did you know that today in L.A. it was seventy-two degrees? In the middle of winter?" She sighed. "It's like a paradise out there."

"Sounds nice," I said. "But I'll miss you when you go."

She put the cigarette in her mouth. "You'll come visit. We'll go to the beach, and find movie stars, and get a tan in the middle of February."

"All right," I told her. "I'm there."

"I wish I was, right now," she said. "It's like all I think about anymore. All I want, you know? Just to be there."

I nodded, but to me California was so far away as to not be real, just like so much else these days.

I was late for practice as usual, and when I walked in everyone was waiting for me.

"Caitlin," Chelsea Robbins said. "Glad you could join us. Have a seat; we need to talk to you."

I blinked, hard, and started to walk over to the bleachers. Everyone except Rina—who was pretending to be preoccupied with tying her shoe—was watching me. They were all in their practice clothes, shorts and T-shirts, bright white Nikes with white socks. I was in sweats. Even when I was in uniform, I always wore tights and a sweater—I couldn't remember the last time I'd let anyone see my arms or legs bare.

This would have been bad even if I *hadn't* been stoned. With that added element, however, it was all I could do to sit down and remain calm as all eyes stayed on me.

The cheerleading intervention, I thought, looking around me at all those perky faces, staring at me flatly as if I was a specimen about to be slapped on a slide. *Here we go.*

"Caitlin," Chelsea began as she sat down, folding her hands in her lap, "we thought it was time we discussed what you see as your role in the future of this squad."

All those eyes, on me. I swallowed, and it sounded louder than God.

"My future," I said.

"Yes." Chelsea's lips were pink and glossy, and she pursed them a lot when she talked. I had not noticed this before. "It's no secret that your participation and commitment of late has been, well, lacking. Am I right?"

There was a low murmur from the pack as everyone agreed.

"You show up late, you have no energy, you barely make it to games," Chelsea continued, ticking each reason off on a slender finger. "You don't attend squad functions. And there's been some speculation that you may . . . have some kind of problem."

More murmuring. Eliza Drake nodded her head, her ponytail bouncing. The lights in the gym were so bright and I could hear them buzzing, like a swarm of angry bees about to sting. I looked up at them, wincing in the glare.

Problem, I thought. *You don't know the half of it.*

"Caitlin." Chelsea was losing patience. Beside her, Lindsay White, whose teen modeling career had been lost when I fell on her, rolled her eyes. Bitter. "We wanted to give you a chance to respond. To make your case."

I looked around at them, all so pretty and healthy, the best and the brightest. I saw Rina, looking sadly at me, and Eliza Drake, who had lost those nagging fifteen pounds and was ready to make top of the pyramid again. And then I thought of Corinna, crying in the dark at her house as the sun went down and it grew colder and colder.

"Caitlin," Chelsea said as she shook her head, her ponytail bobbing from side to side, "don't you even *care* anymore?"

I didn't belong with these people. I never had. Next to my life with Rogerson and the ongoing struggle to avoid full contact, cheerleading seemed even sillier and more unimportant than ever. It was like another world, another language that I'd hardly learned and already forgotten.

Don't you care anymore? Don't you?

This question seemed ludicrous to me. Of course I didn't care. If I did, I wouldn't be hiding a bruise on my arm and one on my back. I wouldn't be shrouding myself in long sleeves and chain-smoking, watching myself shrink down to nothing as I tried to be invisible.

Don't you care, Caitlin?

They were all still watching me.

"No," I said bluntly to Chelsea Robbins and her pink, pink lips, then lifted my eyes to look across all their faces. "I don't."

I could feel them all reacting to this as I walked down the bleachers and started across that shiny gym floor, where I'd done a hundred cartwheels and climbed atop so many pyramids what seemed a million years ago.

"Caitlin," Rina called after me. "Wait."

But I was already gone, pulling my arms tight against my chest as the door slammed shut behind me.

I walked out to my car, got in, and locked the door. Then I sat there, in the empty parking lot, and cried. It was the worst kind of sobbing, the kind that hurts your chest and steals your breath. No one could hear me.

I couldn't believe I was upset about being kicked off the cheerleading squad, since I'd hated it right from the start. But it wasn't just that. It was that at least while I was on the squad I had some semblance of a normal life: my old life. But now, I was just a girl with a boyfriend who beat her, who smoked too much. I was drowning in broad daylight and no one could tell.

I was due to meet Rogerson at my house right after practice, at six sharp, so I had time to take the long way home, following Rina's driving and crying path. When I passed Corinna's, all the windows were dark and her car was gone. I thought of her coming home that night to a pitch-black house, holding her hand out in front of her face as she found her way to a candle and a match. The dark might not be so bad when it was everywhere, even outside.

I drove out to the lake, then back into town through Rina's old neighborhood, pausing for a minute in front of her second stepfather's house to curse him, just like she did. Then I headed home, taking my time, and passed my house, driving up the street to hang a right and pull into Commons Park.

I hadn't been there in years. The slide and the swing set were new, but the sandbox—where Cass had reached out with a shovel and changed my face forever—was the same. I went and sat on its edge, reaching down to scoop up a handful of the grainy, wet sand, imagining the layers beneath it, full of lost buttons and action figures and

Barbie shoes, all buried and fossilized like dinosaur bones. There was something of mine here, too.

I reached up with my finger and traced the scar over my eyebrow, remembering when that was the greatest hurt I'd ever known. When I closed my eyes, I pictured my mother carrying me all the way home, and my father holding my hand while the needle dipped in and out, outlining the arc of my scar. And finally, with my own memory, I saw the way Cass's expression changed whenever her eyes drifted across my face, taking it as hers as much as my own.

That had been a different time, a different hurt. I couldn't even remember that pain, now.

I sat at the park for a long time, running my fingers through the sand. I thought about everything: cheerleading, my bruises, Rogerson's face in the picture I'd taken of him, my mother's chipper voice on the phone, and Corinna at Applebee's, pushing Super Sundaes and dreaming of California. But mostly I thought of Cass, and how I wished she was here to claim this hurt, too.

I was still there when Rogerson slowed down, seeing my car, and pulled in. His headlights moved across the swing and slide and monkey bars to finally find me, staying there like a spotlight. He didn't get out of the car, but just left the engine idling as he waited.

I squinted as I stood up, pulling my jacket around me. Like always, I didn't know what to expect from him. I slid a handful of that sand into my pocket, wondering what relics it had once held. I rubbed the grains between my fingers, like charms, then took a deep breath and stepped into that bright, bright light.

Chapter Eleven

I didn't tell my mother that I'd been kicked off the squad, exactly. In fact, she was so busy winning Cass back—phone call by phone call—she didn't even question my flimsy explanation about how in the lull between winter and spring sports there were fewer practices. So I began spending more time in the darkroom at the Arts Center when she thought I was doing cheerleader stuff: sticking to my former schedule and going there after school, then showing up at the same time for dinner. On game nights, I'd just call Rina from wherever I was with Rogerson to find out who'd won before I went home.

This was surprisingly easy. My mother was distracted not only with Cass but also with her annual April Fool's party, my father with a new semester, a chancellor search and the men and women's basketball teams in the thick of March Madness. Now it almost seemed that I *was* becoming invisible, passing through the house in my long sleeves and jeans—even as the weather heated up—my eyes red regardless of Visine, hardly talking except to answer their standard queries: *How was school? Who won the game? Would you please pass the potatoes?*

And the answers came easy, automatically. *Fine. We did. Yes.*

The only time I ever felt safe anymore was when I was at the darkroom, in the half-light with the door locked, everything quiet as I worked developing my pictures, watching each of the images come into being right before my eyes. Since Christmas I'd focused mostly on portraits of people. I was fascinated with the way light and angle could completely change the way a person looked, and I'd spent the last two months taking pictures of everyone I knew, trying to capture each one of their different faces.

Behind the camera, I was invisible. When I lifted it up to my eye it was like I crawled into the lens, losing myself there, and everything else fell away.

I'd shot Corinna sitting on her front steps in the sunlight with the dog, Mingus, lying beside her. She was wearing a long, gauzy skirt and a big wool sweater fraying at the cuffs. She'd cocked her head to the side and propped one hand under her chin, her bracelets glinting in the sunshine, the TV in the distance behind her showing static. Her hair was blowing around her face and she was smiling, with Mingus looking up at her adoringly. I'd had the picture framed and gave it to her as a gift. She'd hung it on the wall in the living room, next to a huge Ansel Adams print of a canyon. She said she couldn't remember the last time she'd seen a picture of herself that she liked, and sometimes when we were sitting on the couch just hanging out I'd catch her looking at it, studying her own face as it smiled back at her.

I posed Boo sitting in the grass of her backyard, cross-legged, right beside her chipped cement Buddha, both of them smiling and content. And I found my mother, her chair pulled up close to the TV, leaning forward to scan the screen during *Lamont Whipper,* looking for Cass. She'd been so absorbed she hadn't even heard me take the picture, her face hopeful, intent, watching carefully so as not to miss a single thing. That picture I buried deep under my sweaters in a drawer: it just hurt me, somehow, to look at it.

Rogerson didn't have much patience for getting his picture taken, but occasionally I caught him: bending over the engine of the BMW with the hood up, reaching with one hand to brush back his hair.

Standing in Corinna's kitchen drinking a Yoo Hoo with that big velvet Elvis taking up the whole frame behind him. Lying on his bed right next to me, the lens just inches from his face, smiling slightly, sleepily, as I clicked the shutter.

These were pictures I rushed to develop, holding my breath as they emerged before me. I'd examined them so closely, as if they were proof, absolute documentation that he wasn't a monster, that he was still the guy I'd fallen in love with. I'd bring them home and stick them in my dream journal, as if him smiling here or looking at me nicely there would balance out the truths I'd written to Cass in those same pages.

I kept collecting faces, as if by holding all these people in my hands I could convince myself that everything was still okay. So I had Dave, rubbing his eyes with hair askew, half a frozen burrito in one hand. Rina in her cat's-eye sunglasses and cheerleading uniform, smoking a cigarette and sticking out her tongue. My father in his chair, watching a basketball game, his face so expectant as the seconds ticked down and his team took a last-chance, do-or-die shot. And Rogerson, again and again, smiling, not smiling, scowling, laughing, glaring. The only expression I didn't have of his was the one I knew by heart: the dark eyes, angry face, flushed skin—the last thing I usually saw before squeezing my eyes shut and bearing down.

My favorite picture, though, was one I hadn't even taken. Rogerson and I had been at Corinna's, sitting at their kitchen table, when she'd picked up my camera and leaned in close to us, telling us to say cheese. The day before, Rogerson had gotten upset with me for some reason—it was easier, sometimes, to just forget the specifics—and punched me in the arm, which meant in the picture I was in my safe zone, when he was trying to make up with me. In the picture I'm on his lap as he sits at the table, my head against his chest. He has one arm around my waist, and just as Corinna hit the shutter he'd tickled me, making me burst out laughing, and he had, too. It is one of those great moments, the kind you can't plan. Sometimes the light or the expression is just perfect, and you're lucky enough to catch it, usually accidentally.

I spent a lot of time looking at that picture. Wondering what I'd think of that girl, if I was someone else, seeing how easily she sits in her boyfriend's lap, laughing, with his arms around her. I would have thought her life was perfect, the way I once thought Cass's was. It was too easy, I was learning, to just assume things.

One day I took all my pictures and hung them around my room, tacking them to the walls, the mirror, even the ceiling. Then I stood and stared at each of the faces, studying them one at a time. I learned them carefully, aware of every nuance in their expressions. They stared back at me, frozen, but even though I could read their entire world in their faces, none of them were looking that closely at me.

Cass usually called after dinner, when I was already long gone out the door to another "cheerleading meeting," or on the weekends, when I was locked in the darkroom or with Rogerson. But one late Sunday afternoon I was the only one home when the phone rang.

"Caitlin?"

It was so strange to hear her voice, and I felt myself catch my breath. But I didn't say anything.

"Caitlin. It's me," she said. She sounded so far away. "It's Cass. I can't believe you're finally there when I called. How are you?"

I swallowed, hard, and looked out the window. I could see Boo in her backyard, misting a row of ferns.

"Caitlin." She sounded confused. "Hello?"

I ran a finger up and over my neck, feeling down to the spot below my collar where I'd hit the top of my seat belt the night before when

Rogerson had pushed me. I pressed down on the bruise: It didn't hurt that badly. I was learning even the smallest push could bring a swelling, blue-black spot, the body infinitely more dramatic than it needed to be.

"Hello?" she said again, and I closed my eyes. "Caitlin? Are you there?"

I could see her in my mind, that time on the *Lamont Whipper Show,* ducking her head and smiling as she wrote something on her clipboard, and the way she glanced up for that one second, like she was looking right at me. Like she could see me, sitting on Corinna's couch, stoned and lost.

"I understand if you're upset with me," she said, suddenly. "But I had to leave. My whole future had been planned but it wasn't what *I* wanted. It was like I had no choice anymore. That's a terrible feeling, Caitlin."

I could see her reaching out with a finger, smoothing over the scar, and sighing.

She looks just like you, Corinna had said. *She could be you.*

"Caitlin?" Cass said, and I turned away from the window, looking down the stairs and out the front door, trying to picture her making that walk away from this. It seemed like so far, and I was so tired. Tired of keeping time, of studying faces, of hiding bruises. Of disappearing, bit by bit, while my world kept going without me, even as I slipped farther beneath the water, drowning.

"Come on," she whispered. "Talk to me."

I wanted to. But the words just wouldn't come. And when I hung up, she didn't call back.

The next day, when I pulled up to Corinna's after school, the front door was open. As soon as I stepped into the living room, I could hear them.

"I just don't understand *why* you took the money out," Corinna was saying. "This was, like, our last chance with them."

"It'll be all right," I heard Dave say. "Calm down. We'll get the money."

"How? Tell me."

"I told you I know that guy at the auto shop. He said to come in anytime, he'd hire me. I'll go tomorrow. It's no big deal."

Corinna sighed, loudly, and I heard her bracelets jingle. I stepped back out on the porch, easing the door shut behind me. Mingus, lying next to the rocking chair, closed his eyes as I leaned over to scratch his ears.

"They needed the rent today, David," Corinna said. "The check bounced last week."

"I thought we had it covered."

"We would have if you hadn't taken the money out," she said, exasperated. "I mean, we've *talked* about this. More than once."

"I told you, Corinna," Dave said, and now he sounded irritated, "I needed it. Okay?"

"Just like you needed the power bill money. And the money I set aside for Mingus to go to the vet." Corinna strode into the living room, snatched her cigarettes off the table, and then walked back through the swinging door to the kitchen. "David, I'm working my butt off in this crappy job for that money. There's no way I can do more than I'm already doing. And we'll never get to California if we don't start—"

"Oh, man," Dave said. "Don't bring that California shit up again."

"Well, if you could just find a way to bring in some money we could save up enough—"

"I knew it," Dave said angrily, his voice rising. Mingus lifted his head. "It *always* comes back to me. I can't keep a job, I can't bring home the money you need for La-La Land. Well, Corinna, I'm sorry I'm such a *failure* to you. I guess your mom was right, huh?"

"David, no," Corinna said, and her voice sounded choked. "It's just that we'd do better if you could just—"

"You don't seem to have any trouble smoking the pot I get for you," Dave went on. I felt uncomfortable: I'd never heard him yell before. "You take that with *no* problem. But you want me to go work at the Fast Fare for six bucks an hour *before* taxes just so you can take the damn dog to the vet?"

"I don't want us to have to struggle so much," Corinna said, and now I could tell she was crying. I remembered how they'd looked that day in the kitchen, dancing around the dog bowl, how happy she'd been. So in love, like I imagined Cass was. Like I wanted to be.

"Well, I'm sorry I can't give you everything you want," Dave said, and I could tell he was coming closer even before he pushed the kitchen door open with a bang. I tried to step out of sight but he saw me, stopping suddenly in front of the TV. "Oh—hey, Caitlin."

"Hi," I said, as Mingus wagged his tail beside me, thumping against the porch. "I was just—"

Corinna stepped out of the kitchen, her arms crossed against her chest. Her face was streaked with tears and she wouldn't look at me. "Caitlin," she said, tucking her hair behind her ear, "this isn't a good time, okay?"

They were both just standing there, and I suddenly felt stupid and helpless, like I didn't belong anywhere. "Yeah," I said. "Sure. I'll just, um, see you later."

I turned around and started down the steps, and Mingus followed me across the yard. He ran behind my car all the way down the bumpy dirt road, stopping to sit by the mailbox, as if he knew he couldn't go any farther. After I turned onto the highway I looked back and could barely make him out in the settling dust, watching me as I left him behind.

There were some times—when things got bad—that I saw something flash across Rogerson's face, like he couldn't believe what he'd done. Like he'd just woken up and found himself standing over me, fist still clenched, looking down in disbelief at the place on my shoulder/arm/stomach/back/leg where he'd just hit me. I wondered if he was thinking of his father, and the marks he'd left behind. And even as I felt the spot with my own fingers, knowing already what the bruise would look like, I felt *sorry* for him, like for that one second he was just as scared as I was. It was so strange. *Sorry* for him.

By the last weekend in March, preparations for my mother and Boo's annual Fool's Party were in full swing. They'd been throwing it since before I could remember, to celebrate the day that Boo and Stewart had moved in next door way back before I was even born. What had begun as an intimate, chips-and-dip, cheese-and-crackers sort of event had swelled with each year to include all of my parents' and Boo and Stewart's friends, as well as most of the neighborhood. The mix of academic types and yoga-instructing New Agers guaranteed that the party, which always seemed to fall on the first warm weekend of spring, would be interesting.

For a full week before, my mother and Boo were in serious cooking mode. Our freezer and fridge were packed with cheese balls and baklava, shrimp waiting to be peeled, bags upon bags of sliced cucumbers and radishes shaped like rosebuds. My mother handled the meat eaters, while Boo and Stewart made marinated tofu, tempeh salad, vegetarian gumbo, and vegan cookies (which tasted thick and dry, like eating straw). The food was politely segregated, ever since the episode a few years ago when one of Stewart's friends, a Buddhist vegan, accidentally mistook a crab puff for a wheat-free biscuit. There was a huge scene and no crab had crossed our threshold since.

If my mother had been distracted before, the party took whatever was left of her attention. She was like a whirling dervish, zooming around the house with a dustrag in one hand and a bowl of seven-layer dip in the other, while my father busied himself fixing up the yard and scraping the grill to prepare to make shish kebabs. It had always been Cass's and my job to stay out of the way and *not* eat any of the things made for the party in the days before, though she was an expert at picking a shrimp or snarking some dip without my mother noticing. The night of the party we collected coats, snuck a glass or two of champagne, and camped out in Cass's room, which had the best view of the backyard. From there we'd smuggle in food and take bets on the exact time my mother and Boo would get tipsy enough to start singing show tunes, accompanied by Stewart on his ukulele. We were never off by very much.

This year, I didn't even want to go to the party. I just concentrated on staying out of the way, dodging my mother as she vacuumed beneath my feet or asked me to taste the new and improved batch of her famous spinach-artichoke dip. I just drifted through the house, my sleeves pulled tight, concentrating on becoming more and more invisible, fading to nothing. I knew that soon I could slip away and no one would notice—if they'd even known I was there to begin with.

The Thursday before the party, Rogerson and I were at McDonald's for lunch. It was beautiful out, finally warm, and I'd made it to meet him at the turnaround early. A good day.

He had the hood popped on the BMW and I was sitting on the curb, my history book open in my lap, when I caught a whiff of the first spring breeze: the smell of pollen, and grass, and sunshine. I took a sip of my milkshake and looked up at Rogerson, just as that same breeze ruffled back his hair. He glanced up, smelling it too. Then he looked at me, lifting his chin, and smiled.

"Hey, Rogerson," I said, as he ducked his head back under the hood.

"Yeah."

I glanced down at my book, then looked back at him, lifting a hand to block out the sun so I could see him clearly. "How long's an eon?"

As he took a minute to answer, I thought back to how amazed I'd been, at the beginning of all of this, by how much he knew. Back then he was just a brilliant, good-looking boy who liked me and made me feel special. We could have gone anywhere from there.

But as I looked at my reflection in the chrome of the bumper in front of me, I saw myself as I was, now: skinny, long baggy shirt pulled tight over my wrists, jeans, and sunglasses. Fingers smelly from smoking, the topography of bruises across my skin and bones like a road map of all that had happened, every mile of the journey.

"An eon," Rogerson repeated, lifting his head up and looking at me again. There were moments when my heart ached for him: I loved him so much. It was strange. "A billion years," he said. "Right?"

"Yeah," I said. "You're right."

He nodded, then let the hood fall gently shut. I closed my eyes as the breeze blew through again, smelling like summer.

"That's a long time," he said, and I opened my eyes, remembering how he'd stood in the doorway of that party, all those months ago, lifting his chin in that same way and calling to me. *Come on,* he'd said. *Come on.*

A billion years. It was long enough to learn a lot about someone.

"Yeah," I said, as the breeze blew over us both, sweet and fresh and so brand-new under a perfect blue sky. He was smiling at me, and for some reason it almost broke my heart. "It is."

On the Friday before the Fool's Party, my mother came into my room and sat on the bed with a bag in her lap from Belk's department store. Then, she took a deep breath.

I was lying on my bed, still a little stoned from the bowl Rogerson and I had smoked on the way home from school.

"Honey," she said, scooting a little closer, "I've been worried about you."

Instantly, even in my detached state, my interior alarms started to flash. Cover, cover, cover. Set the play, keep the defense going. Run and shoot.

"I'm fine," I said.

"Caitlin," she said, cocking her head to the side. "There are some things a mother can't help but notice." She crossed her legs, her panty hose rubbing against my elbow. She still dressed like the perfect housewife, in nice skirts, flats, and lipstick at all times. She was like one of her dolls: delicate, lovely, and somewhat dated.

"I'm okay," I said. "Really."

She sighed again, and I wondered if this was how it would all end. That maybe she wasn't as blind as I'd thought and had been watching me as closely as she scanned that TV screen each day for a glimpse of her other lost daughter. April Fool, on me. Surprise.

"I'm concerned," she said, and I realized I was holding my own breath, bracing myself for what was coming next. Maybe I would tell her everything, roll up my sleeves and jeans to detail each bruise and blemish. Crumple into her arms and cry as hard as I did that day she rescued me from the park, holding me tight against her as she ran block after block. Swim up through that water, higher and higher, and burst out to grab her arm before I drowned.

I looked up into her face, my own heart aching. Maybe this was it. Maybe she *could* save me.

"I'm concerned," she repeated, "that you seem to have completely abandoned primary colors."

"What?" I said.

"Primary colors," she repeated. "Caitlin, all you ever wear now is black. An occasional red or white, but that's it. You know how nice you always looked in blue."

I still do, I thought. *Look here, on the back of my wrist, those two spots the size of fingertips. Or here, at the base of my back: That's blue, too.* "Mom," I said.

"Well, I just think with a face as pretty as yours color can only make you look better. Black washes you out, honey. Color adds. Color *enhances.*"

I looked up into her face, but she didn't seem to see me, even as I pleaded that she would.

"So, with that in mind," she went on briskly, "I saw this dress today and I just *had* to buy it for you for the party tomorrow night. Look at this!" She opened the Belk's bag, pulling out a short white dress with a swooshy skirt, covered with a green ivylike print. It was the kind of dress you wore with bare legs and bare arms, white strappy sandals and your hair loose and long. "What do you think?"

I rubbed the fabric between my fingers: It was smooth and stretchy. A summer dress, like so many others in my closet I wouldn't wear this year.

"It's beautiful," I said, and looked up at my mother, with her hair in its little flip, her pearls, her pumps with the scuffs on the heel. I looked at her hard, right in her eyes, and dared her in that one second to see something else in me. Not the bruises, which I could hide well, or the shame, which I hid better. But something else at the very heart of me that she should have seen from miles and miles away.

And my mother looked right back, blinked happily, and then patted my leg, standing up. "Good, good," she said, smiling down at me. "I just wanted you to have something bright and cheerful to wear."

"I know," I said. "Thank you."

When she left I locked the door behind her and stood up, sliding off my jeans and shirt and pulling the dress over my head. It *was* beautiful: The summer before, it would have looked great on me. But now my legs and arms seemed thin and spindly, marked here and there by blue-black or black-yellow bruises in different phases of healing, scrapes and spots where the skin had been twisted and yanked that someone else wouldn't notice but I could not miss.

I stood in front of my mirror and turned slowly, watching the skirt twirl up and fall around my knees. I wanted to be a girl that could wear a dress like this. Instead, the girl in the mirror looked back at me, and I hardly recognized her. She was just some strange girl who'd tumbled off a pyramid, falling into a dream, and now waited, in a beautiful dress, like some princess in a forgotten fairy tale, for someone to come save her.

That night, my parents, Boo and Stewart and I all went outside to help put up the tent my father had rented for the party. The rental place always offered to set it up for a fee, but my father insisted we could do it ourselves. After the year before, when my mother had been reduced to tears and Stewart had been clocked in the head with a pole, rendering him temporarily unconscious, my father had broken down and recruited a few fraternity brothers who were on thin ice for hazing infractions to help us.

It was just dusk and we were all standing around with poles and bindings, waiting for my father—who was already grumbling under his breath—to get things started.

"All right, Buckley, I need you over here," he shouted, and one of the brothers nodded and crossed in front of us diagonally, dragging the tent behind him. "And Charles, get that end piece and stand right across from him."

"Jack, should I put on the back light?" my mother called out.

"No, no," he said, irritated, even though now it was almost too dark for us to see each other. We all stood there, silently, waiting for orders. "Caitlin, go stand directly across from Buckley. And Margaret, you get five feet down from her."

"Okay!" my mother called out cheerfully, looping her arm in mine as we walked across the grass together. "I'm so excited about the party," she said, squeezing my shoulder. "Aren't you?"

"Sure," I said. There was something nice, actually, about being there in the falling darkness with my family's voices all around me. It was the same time of night Cass and I had always played tag and kickball, running across yards and over fences until we were called in to dinner, smelling of sweat, our knees muddy and grass-stained.

"Stewart!" my father yelled.

"Yes," Stewart said cheerfully from right behind him.

My father jumped, startled, and then smoothed down his hair over his small bald spot, calming himself. "I need you," he said slowly, "about one foot down from where you are."

"One foot," Stewart said in his soft voice, measuring it carefully with one step. Boo, to his right, scooted down a few feet and planted herself, already onto my father's system.

"Okay," my father said, after distributing stakes and bindings to all of us. "Now what we're going to do is plant this center stake, and then connect all of the bindings to it, therefore raising the tent."

"Sounds good!" my mother, the cheerleader, said.

"Ouch! Christ!" someone said loudly.

"Buckley!" my father said.

"Something bit me," Buckley protested, and we could hear a few slapping noises. "It was big, too."

"Oh, my goodness," my mother said. "I'm sure I have some bug stuff inside. Let me just—"

"*We're raising the tent now!*" my father bellowed, and we all snapped to attention, taking a few steps back as the white material of the tent lifted up, higher and higher, stirring up a breeze underneath it.

"Shit!" someone said again.

"Buckley," my father bellowed. "One more outburst—"

"No, sorry," Boo said apologetically. "That was me. Something *is* biting over here."

"I told you," Buckley said.

"Shut up, you wimp," Charles, his frat brother, said. "Big baby."

"Pay attention to the *tent,* people," my father said sternly. "This is *not* a joking matter."

So we all concentrated, or tried to, until Stewart said thoughtfully, "This reminds me very much of a film I saw recently on Amish barn raising. Did anyone else see that program?"

"I did," Buckley called out.

"Did you?" Stewart said. "Because what I found really fascinating, other than just the craftmanship, was—"

"Uh, actually," Buckley said sheepishly, "I was, um, kidding. I didn't see it."

"The *tent!*" my father said again, as he moved around tying the bindings while we all tried to be serious.

"What I found most fascinating, anyway," Stewart continued, "was the sense of community these people found in a common task. Strangers working together. It's a rare thing these days, you know?"

"If this tent comes down on all of you tomorrow night," my father grumbled, from down low somewhere checking a binding, "you will have only yourselves to blame."

"It looks wonderful!" my mother said, stepping back and clapping her hands. "Doesn't it?"

"Wonderful," Boo agreed, wrapping her arm around Stewart's skinny waist. "See what a sense of community can do?"

We all laughed and Charles and Buckley waited to be dismissed while my father, still grumbling, checked the bindings again. It was warm and dark in the yard, and I looked up at the sky, thinking back to all the early evenings I'd spent out there, with Cass, begging and pleading for just a few more minutes of light before we had to go inside.

Then, out on the street, I heard a familiar rumbling, slowing down in front of the house, and I snapped back to my reality. I slipped around the house, and as I glanced back I couldn't make out anyone: I saw only the tent, so white and big and empty. I knew I should have said good-bye. But I couldn't. I just kept moving, watching my game, because it was fully dark now and Rogerson was waiting.

Chapter Twelve

It was three in the afternoon on the day of the Fool's Party when Rina showed up at my house. My mother, who was having a minor breakdown over the lack of citronella candles at Home Depot—she was convinced someone would get malaria—let her in. I was in my room, trying to decide which of my pictures to exhibit at the Arts Center during the wine-and-cheese reception that was our last official class. I could only pick four, so I had all the faces I'd collected spread out across my bed in a fan shape, examining each one and trying to make a decision.

"Hey, stranger."

I looked up and Rina was standing in the doorway of my room, her arms crossed over her chest. She had on a short, pink dress and strappy high-heeled sandals, and her skin—thanks to her mother's tanning bed—was already a deep brown. Her blond hair was down, curling over her shoulders, a pair of white sunglasses parked on top of her head. She looked so healthy and alive it was like she was almost sparking, right there in front of me.

"Hey," I said, as she crossed the room and plopped down on the bed, swinging one leg to cross it over the other. "What's going on?"

"I have come," she said, plucking her sunglasses off her head and expertly folding them shut, "to kidnap you."

"Kidnap?" I said.

"Yes." She leaned back on her hands, narrowing her eyes at me.

Her lips were done in a perfect pearly pink, the color of cotton candy. "Caitlin, you never do anything with me anymore."

"Rina," I said, "I've just been—"

"You don't," she said, waving me off with one hand. "You can't deny it, so don't even try. And frankly, I'm not going to stand for it anymore."

"You're not," I repeated, reaching to eliminate a shot of Dave—half a burrito hanging out of his mouth—from my collection.

"No." She glanced down at my stack of pictures, spreading them out with her hand. "Wow, Caitlin. These are awesome. This one—" and she pointed at the portrait I'd done of her, sticking out her tongue—"is especially striking."

"Thank you," I said, watching as she picked it up and smiled at her own image. "I think."

She kept going through, making approving noises, until she came to the first one I'd taken of Rogerson, standing outside Corinna's with that bleak winter sky behind him. She studied it, saying nothing, before sliding it to the bottom of my stack of discards. Then she looked at me.

"You," she said decisively, "are coming out to the lake with me for the afternoon."

I opened my mouth to say something, but she held up her hand, stopping me. "No arguments."

"But Rina," I said. "I can't. I'm supposed to meet Rogerson here later and there's the party tonight."

"Rogerson," she said, a slight hint of irritation in her voice, "can do without you for one measly afternoon, since I have done without you since God knows when. With little complaint, also, I might add. And you and I both know the party won't be in full swing till at least seven anyway."

"Rina, I can't. I'm sorry." Rogerson hadn't said specifically when he was coming over, but I knew better than to try to predict when he'd show. "I would love to do it—"

"Then do it," she said firmly, standing up like it was decided. Then, softening, she added, "Come on, Caitlin. It's a gorgeous day. We'll go out and eat some chips, soak up the sun, and complain endlessly about our lives. Just like old times."

Old times. Rina's lake house was where we'd spent most of our summer the year before, sneaking her stepfather's beers and lying out on the huge wooden deck while the sun sparkled wildly on the water before us. There was a dock, a hot tub, and every fish her stepfather had ever caught stuffed and hanging on the living room walls: They stared out at you with dead eyes, their expressions somewhat shocked as if they'd believed, to the end, that they'd be thrown back in to swim away safe.

"I don't know," I said, still hedging. I could see the lake in my mind, remembering sitting at the end of the dock in a thick sweatshirt as the sun went down, my feet dangling in the water. That summer seemed like forever ago, now. "My mom probably needs me to stick around."

Rina sighed, stood up, and walked to my door, yanking it open. "Mrs. O'Koren," she yelled down the hallway, and seconds later my mother appeared, holding her School Marm doll by the leg, a bottle of Pledge in her other hand. She'd been moving the dolls around all week, trying new arrangements: One had even popped up in the bathroom, on the floor by the heating vent, causing my father to shriek like a schoolgirl when he mistook it for the toilet brush.

"What do you think, girls?" she said, hoisting the doll up so we could see it. "Should I arrange all the townsfolk in one place, or break them up into smaller, more intimate groups? I can't *decide.*"

We just looked at her.

"I have no idea," I said finally.

"More intimate groups," Rina told her. "Less is more."

"Oh," my mother said, adjusting the School Marm's little slate, "I guess you're right."

"Now, Mrs. O'Koren," Rina went on briskly, "don't you think Caitlin should come with me out to the lake for the afternoon instead of sitting around here waiting for Rogerson to call?"

My mother looked at me. "Absolutely," she said. "It's so lovely out! And Caitlin, honey, you could use a little color. You've been so pale lately."

"Exactly," Rina said, winking at me. "See? We'll go out there, have a late lunch, and be back in plenty of time for the party. I promise."

"I really can't—"

"I told you, no arguments," Rina said right over me, walking to my closet and yanking it open. "Now I am going to the store to buy some snacks and suntan lotion, and while I am gone I want you to take a shower, find your bathing suit, and put on—" and she reached into my closet, rummaging around before finally pulling out the white, ivy-patterned dress my mother had just bought me—"this dress, right here. It's pretty and you can wear it and still get good sun. I'll be back in twenty minutes. Be ready." And then she threw the dress on the bed beside me, put on her sunglasses, and walked out of the room. A few seconds later we heard the front door slam behind her.

I looked down at the dress, feeling a bit of the swishy material between my fingers. Of course Rogerson hadn't *said* when he was coming: I always had to wait around to find out what our plans were, which usually meant putting off any invitations to do anything else until it was too late. I didn't think he'd mind if I could just tell him where I was going—no surprises. I just had to let him know.

"Oh, I can't wait to see how you look in that dress!" my mother said, tucking the Pledge under her arm. "You know, I have some tuna salad I made for the party, plus this great pimento cheese spread. With some crackers you'll have a wonderful meal and you girls won't even have to cook anything. I'll just pack it up for you right now."

"Oh, Mom, you don't have to—"

"I want to. It'll just take a jiffy." And she turned around, so happy to be involved, somehow, in getting me out of the house, back to my old life again. I could hear her fussing around, ripping plastic wrap out of the box, shaking out grocery bags, the same noises I knew from the preparation for all those bake sales and Girl Scout camping trips.

I took a quick shower, then tried to call Rogerson. I had my easy tone ready: *Just doing a girl thing, no big deal, I'll be back in an hour or two*. But the phone just rang and rang. After I dried my hair, I tried again.

Still no answer. I called Corinna's, then the main number at his parents' house. Nobody was home either place.

Relax, I told myself. *Get dressed and then try again.*

When I put the dress on, it felt good: light and airy, like wearing summer. I had a pretty big bruise on my leg, which it covered, and one fading on my arm that it didn't; there were a couple of others, one on my back, a very old one at the base of my neck, but when I put on my jacket you couldn't see any of them. Then I sat down and called Rogerson again.

Five, six, seven rings. Still no answer, and of course he was the only one in the *world* without a machine. Where was he? Halfway across town? Or—the worst case scenario—on his way, ready to pull up the minute I left with Rina? I hung up the phone, took a deep breath, and hit redial.

No answer.

I was still trying when I heard a beeping outside.

"Rina's here!" my mother called out cheerfully from the kitchen.

"Okay," I said, hanging up and dialing again. I could feel my heart beating, that same trapped feeling I had every day at lunch as I rushed through the hallways, trying to make it to the turnaround on time. I'd been so stupid to let Rina convince me to do this. *Come on, come on,* I thought. *Just be there.*

"I've packed some food for lunch," I heard my mother saying to Rina. "I just made gobs too much for tonight anyway."

"Great," Rina said. "Wow, is that pimento cheese?"

"Caitlin! Rina's here!"

"Okay," I said. "I'll be there in a second." And I listened to them talking in the hallway, my mother explaining the best way to serve the tuna salad, on lettuce, while Rina made listening noises and popped her gum. And Rogerson's phone rang, on and on. No answer.

"Hey, O'Koren, get the lead out!" Rina yelled. "Let's go!"

"Honey," my mother said, "I'm putting one of these two-liter Cokes in this bag, too, since I overbought for the party."

"Caitlin," Rina said, "don't *make* me come get you."

"I'm coming," I said, and now I was getting nervous, shaky, trying to find a way out of this. I kept dialing, again and again, while my mother and Rina talked on, cheerfully, their voices bouncing down the hallway and off my closed door.

"God, Rogerson, pick up the phone," I said under my breath, even as I heard Rina coming down the hallway, her fingers already rapping on the door as she pushed it open.

"Let's go," she said impatiently. "You can call him from the lake if you want. Okay?"

"And I will tell Rogerson where you are if he calls," my mother called out from the kitchen. "I promise."

"Okay," I said, but even as I hung up the phone my stomach was aching, twisting in on itself.

"Come on then," Rina said, and stuck out her hand just like we used to do as cheerleaders, pulling each other to our feet, one bouncy move. "Let's go."

"Oh, honey!" my mother said as I came down the hallway, clapping her hands excitedly. "That dress looks just *wonderful.* But you certainly don't need that jacket. You can hardly see the lovely neckline."

"I'm kind of cold," I said, glancing outside quickly, wishing Rogerson would just pull up, so I could explain everything while I still had the chance.

"Oh, nonsense, it's over seventy out," she said, walking over and beginning to tug at my sleeve. "Let us see the dress by itself."

"Mom, I don't want to," I said, clinging to my cuffs even as she tried to pull it off of me. Rina looked at me, raising her eyebrows.

"Oh, don't be silly," my mother said, laughing easily. "It's a sleeveless dress, Caitlin, and you have such lovely arms. You should show them off!"

"Mom—"

"Just let me see for a second." She just would *not* let up, reaching behind me to pull at the collar, her thumb brushing the tender spot I had back there, and it hurt.

"I'm cold," I said again.

"Oh, please. Do this one thing for your poor mother," she said, jabbing at the bruise now, and I winced, pulling myself—hard—out of her grasp.

"I said *no,*" I said firmly, and her face fell, shocked, as if I'd slapped her. She dropped her hands and they just hung there, limp, in front of her. "Aren't you listening to me?"

Her mouth opened, but no sound came out. Then she swallowed shakily and said, "I'm sorry, Caitlin. I . . . I just wanted to see how it looked."

She was looking at me as if I'd somehow become possessed, changing right before her eyes. As if just then, at that second, she saw who I'd become over all these months, and it scared her. I felt like some prickly animal, lashing out, scared as those ugly possums that sometimes stumbled out into daylight.

"We should go," Rina said quickly, picking up the bag my mother had packed for us. "Thanks for the food, Mrs. O'Koren. We'll be back by six-thirty at the latest."

"Fine," my mother said, one hand fluttering to her mouth as she forced a smile. "Have fun."

I was only half-listening to Rina as we drove out of the neighborhood and she kept up a constant chatter, talking about Jeff and her life, her voice floating out behind us. But all I could do was feel my dread building as I watched the road whisk by in the side mirror, miles and miles of it, each one taking me farther from home.

By the time we pulled onto the highway that passed Corinna's, there was a part of me I was afraid would explode. I kept thinking of Rogerson showing up at my house, beeping the horn. Waiting. And the penalty I'd pay, the hardest of fouls, when he found out I was gone.

"Rina," I said quickly as Corinna's came into view, "turn in here."

"What?" she said. I'd interrupted her in mid-story, something about Jeff's ex-girlfriend and a series of mysterious earrings she kept finding in his couch cushions. "Here?"

"Yes."

She hung a hard left, spinning out gravel as we started down the dirt road to their driveway. Mingus was sitting on the porch, and he started barking when he saw us. I didn't see Corinna's car.

"What is this place?" Rina said, cutting off the engine. She glanced around, taking in the trailer next door and the huge field to our left that always smelled like manure.

"Just a friend of mine's," I said, getting out of the car. "I'll be right back."

I started up to the house, praying that Corinna was home. She would understand this, could get in touch with Rogerson or explain if he showed up there before coming to look for me. I was already planning what I'd say to her, how she'd shake those bracelets and fix everything, as I started up the stairs, glanced through the screen door and saw the living room.

It was mostly empty. The couch was still there, and the TV, but all the knickknacks—the blue glass in the windowsill, the framed Ansel Adams prints, the clock where the numbers were marked by steaming coffee cups—were gone. As were the afghan from the couch, all of Corinna's buttons from the coffee table, and the picture I'd taken of her sitting on the front porch with Mingus.

It was all just gone.

I stepped inside, letting the door fall softly shut behind me. Outside I could see Rina in the car, picking at her bangs impatiently, fingers drumming on the outside door.

I pushed the kitchen door open: it, too, was stripped of just about everything, even the velvet Elvis. Mingus's bowl was still there, on the cracked tile, and the sink was full of dishes, the window over the small table open, drapes blowing in the breeze.

"She's gone," I heard Dave say behind me, and I turned around to see him standing there, in a pair of shorts, barefoot. He was holding a pack of cigarettes, his hair sticking up in all directions, a crease mark across his face from sleeping. "She left yesterday."

"What?" I said. "Where did she go?"

He looked down at the cigarettes, shaking one out of the pack and sticking it in his mouth. "Home. California. I don't know. Anywhere away from me." He laughed as he lit the cigarette, then coughed a couple of times, closing his eyes. "Had enough of my shit, I guess."

Outside, Rina beeped the horn, and Dave glanced behind him, pushing the kitchen door open to glance out the front window at her.

"Um . . . did she say anything?" I asked him. "I mean. . ."

"Nope," he said, shaking his head. Then he smiled, kind of grimly, and flicked his ash into the sink. "It's been coming a while, I guess. I just didn't think she'd really go, you know?" He rubbed one hand over his head, his hair springing up underneath his palm. "I just—I didn't think she'd really go." And then he laughed, like it was funny, but he wouldn't look at me.

All this time, Corinna had been the only one who just took me as I was, not caring about whether I wore primary colors, or stuck with cheerleading, or spent too much time with Rogerson. And now, she was gone.

Rina beeped the horn again, longer this time. She hated to wait.

"So," Dave said, "you wanna smoke a bowl or something?" And then he smiled at me, and I felt strange, as if it was suddenly wrong for me to be there.

"No," I said. "I mean, I have a friend waiting for me."

"Tell her to come in," he said.

"No, I should go." I took a step forward and he didn't move, so I dodged around him, knocking my hipbone against the handle of the stove. I could smell him—like sweat and sleep—and I was suddenly disgusted with both of us.

"Come back later," he called out as the kitchen door swung shut behind me. "I'll be here. Okay?"

I walked quickly through the living room, hitting the screen door hard with the palm of my hand. But just as I started to step out on the porch, I saw something sitting on the little table in a small glass dish where Corinna always kept her keys.

The bracelets. They were all there, stacked neatly, glinting in the small square of sunlight coming through the window above them, like a treasure, shining and waiting for me to find them.

I wasn't sure what I was thinking as I scooped them out of the dish, then slid them, one by one, onto my own wrist. I watched as they fell down my arm: clink, clink, clink, a sound I knew so well. I stepped onto the porch, wondering where Corinna was, and how she could leave them behind. But as I watched them catch the light on my own wrist, making her music, I knew the truth was that at home, or California, or anywhere in between, even Corinna couldn't help me now.

The first thing Rina did when we got to the lake house was put on her bikini and pop open a beer. We sat out on the front porch, overlooking the water, where she slathered Bain du Soleil all over her until she stank of coconut, and I sat in my dress—and jacket—chain-smoking, the cordless phone in my lap. I still couldn't get ahold of Rogerson, and I was starting to panic. If he showed up at Dave's and found out I'd been with Rina, and didn't tell him—no. I couldn't even think about it.

"Will you put that thing down, for God's sakes?" Rina snapped at me after I'd been dialing for a solid ten minutes, reaching over with one slippery hand to grab the phone away from me and dropping it onto the deck beside her chair, completely out of my reach. "Honestly, I have never seen anyone so co-dependent in my life. Why don't you go put on your suit, have a beer, and relax?"

"I'm fine like this." I stretched my legs out to make my point, easing the hem of my dress over the fading bruise on my upper thigh. The truth was I was sweating under my jacket: It was unbearably hot. I turned my attention to the lake, where I could see someone waterskiing, the motor humming as a girl on skis cut a swath back and forth across the water.

"Caitlin." She lifted up her sunglasses and looked at me. "What is the *matter* with you?"

"Nothing," I said. "Why?"

She kept her eyes on me, as if daring me to tell her, like I'd told her a million other secrets in this same place the summer before: my crush on Billy Bostwick, lifeguard at the community pool. That I secretly liked liver as a child. That I'd stolen Cass's pearl earrings, the ones she thought she'd lost at school. But this was too much for me to tell Rina. Even if I really wanted to.

"You're just not yourself," she said softly. "You haven't been in a long time."

I leaned back in my chair, closing my eyes, and reached my arm up to my face, letting Corinna's bracelets fall down my arm. I could still hear that motorboat, humming past, the girl on skis laughing as she cut across the waves. "I'm fine," I said.

"It's like he's done something to you," she said, and I squeezed my eyes shut tighter behind my sunglasses. "Like he's changed something in you. Hurt you or something."

I opened my eyes and looked at her, my best friend, her face worried as she waited for me to respond. I hated to treat her this way. But her face, slowly, was replaced in my mind with a flash of Rogerson driving, looking for me, his face changing and eyes growing darker, angry, the way they looked right before impact. It was like the mean lady on her bicycle in *The Wizard of Oz,* the music building as she raced to find Dorothy: You knew she was coming, you just didn't know when.

"Caitlin," Rina said softly. "Please. You can tell me anything. You *know* that."

But I couldn't. Rogerson was somewhere, on his way, looking for me. I could feel it, the way Boo always said she could feel rain coming in her bad elbow. I just *knew.*

I took a deep breath and sat up, grabbing my cigarettes. "I need to use the phone," I blurted out, reaching over her to grab it. My hand brushed against her skin, damp and sticky and warm, as I started inside the house, pushing the sliding glass door open. When I looked back she was lying flat on her chair, one arm thrown across her face, having given up on me.

I called Rogerson at every number I knew, standing under those rows of stuffed fish. They stared back at me, bug-eyed and scared, as the phone rang on and on, endless, with nobody home.

It was late afternoon and I was *long* ready to go when Jeff showed up. He snuck around the side of the house, crept soundlessly behind our chairs, and expertly dropped an ice cube on the small of Rina's already pink back, scaring the crap out of both of us.

"*Jeff!*" Rina squealed, sitting up quickly and slapping her top—which she'd untied to avoid strap marks—against her ample chest. "Jesus, you almost gave me a heart attack, you jerk."

"Lighten up," he said easily, sliding a hand around her leg as he sat down next to her. He waggled his fingers at me and did his signature move, flipping his hair out of his face with a snap of his neck.

I could see myself reflected back—anxious, angry, glancing at my watch one more time—in his sunglasses.

"Rina," I said, for at least the twentieth time, "I really need to go." I'd been pressing her for what seemed like forever, while she kept drinking beers and waving me off.

"What's your rush?" Jeff said. "I brought some steaks, invited over some of the fellas. Thought we'd have us a little cookout."

"Umm, that sounds good," Rina murmured, rolling over onto her stomach again. "Who'd you invite?"

"Ed and Barrett," he said. "Oh, and Scott from the store."

"I can't stay," I told him. "Rina was just about to take me home, actually."

"I told you, I can't drive home right now," she said in an irritated voice, scooping some more pimento cheese out of my mother's Tupperware container onto a cracker and popping it into her mouth. "I have to sober up first."

"Rina," I said, feeling panic rising in me, higher and higher, even as I tried to squash it down. I'd been circling like this madly for over an hour, like an animal about to gnaw its own leg off to get free. "I told my mother I'd be home by six-thirty, remember?"

"She doesn't care," Rina said easily, as Jeff rubbed her leg, taking a sip of her beer. "She won't even notice if you're late. Have some dinner and then we'll go."

I lowered my voice. "Rina. I have to go right now. Okay?"

"Caitlin, relax," she said. "God, have a beer or something." To Jeff she added, "She's been like this, like, all afternoon."

Jeff looked at me, flipped his hair again, and I wanted to kill both of them.

"You promised you'd drive me home," I said to Rina, and I could feel my throat getting tight. "You *promised.*"

"Look, give me the phone," she said, grabbing it sloppily from where it was lying on the deck between us. "I'll call Rogerson and explain everything. What's his number? Oh wait, I think I know—"

"No," I said, yanking the phone out of her slippery hand. I could only imagine how Rogerson would react to hearing where I was from *her.* "Please, just take me home. It'll only take a second. Okay?"

"What is the matter with you?" she said angrily. "God, you'd think it was *killing* you to be here with me or something." And then she looked at Jeff, raising her eyebrows in a can-you-believe-this kind of way.

For two hours I'd felt myself stretching tighter and tighter, like a rubber band pulled to the point of snapping. And now, I could feel the smaller, weaker parts of myself beginning to fray, tiny bits giving way before the big break.

Out on the lake the sun was hitting right by the dock, glittering across the water like diamonds.

"Fine," I said, standing up. "I'll get there myself." I walked off the porch, across the scrubby pine yard and out onto the road, which snaked ahead of me over a long bridge, around a bend and miles and miles into town. But I didn't care. Just walking would get me that much closer, give me the forward motion to feel that I could somehow fix this.

"Caitlin," I heard Rina calling out behind me, her voice sun-baked and drunk. "Don't be ridiculous. Come back here!"

But I was already hitting my stride, sandal straps rubbing my feet and Corinna's bracelets clinking, playing her theme music, with every step I took.

I must have walked about a mile when a car pulled up behind me and beeped, quickly, three times. I walked closer to the edge of the road, eyes straight ahead, willing them to pass, but they didn't. Instead, the car rolled closer, slowing down to stop right beside me. It was Jeff.

"Would have been here sooner," he explained, flipping his hair as I fastened my seat belt. "But Miss Rina threw a little fit about me leaving her. You understand."

"Yeah," I said, as he hit the gas and we sped toward town, his big convertible sucking up the road beneath us. "I do."

We might have talked on the way home: I don't really remember. My mind was already working my defense, figuring the play, setting the pick and the run and shoot. As we got closer to town, the pine trees and flat fields giving way to asphalt and strip malls, I could feel the dread that had been building in me all afternoon finally fill me up. And by the time we got to my house, every muscle in my body was tight and I could hear my heart beating. I had a crazy thought to tell Jeff to just keep going, gunning past what was waiting for me, driving on and on to someplace safe. But I knew Rogerson would find me. He always did.

There were cars parked all up and down the street for the party, but I could see Rogerson right in front of the walk. The BMW was right by the mailbox, windows up, engine off.

"You know," Jeff said in his slow drawl as he pulled into Boo and Stewart's driveway to turn around, "Rina was just a little tipsy is all. You shouldn't hold it against her."

"I don't," I said, opening my door before he'd even come to a full stop. The sight of Rogerson waiting for me, just like all those times at the turnaround, filled me with a fear that clenched hard in my chest, like a fist closing over something tightly. "Thanks for the ride, Jeff."

"Looks like quite a party," he said, nodding at my parents' backyard, where I could see the tent—still standing—all lit up, with people milling around beneath it. Someone was playing the piano, tinkling and sweet, and it was slowly getting dark. The perfect Fool's night.

"Yeah," I said, already backing away from the car. "It always is."

The grass was wet on my feet as I ran across it, with Jeff yelling good-bye behind me. My house was all lit up to my right, and I knew that inside it smelled like potpourri, all those dolls arranged in their intimate groups.

Rogerson's car was dark as I came up on it, with that eerie green glow from the dash lights coming from inside. I opened the passenger door and got in, shutting it quietly behind me. He didn't say anything.

I turned to face him, ready with my explanation, the defense I'd drawn out in the long walk and ride home: *I tried to call you, I couldn't get here, I'm sorry.*

But I didn't even get a word out before he turned, with the face I'd never captured on film—wrenched and angry—and slapped me across the face.

It was hard enough to push me back against my door, which hadn't shut completely and so fell open just a bit. I reached out behind me to try and grab the handle, but he was already coming at me again.

"Where the hell have you *been?*" he said, moving so close that his breath was in my face, hot and smoky-smelling. He grabbed me by the front of my dress, yanking me even closer to him, the fabric bunching in his fist, bulging through his fingers. "I have been waiting for you for an *hour.*"

"Rina," I said quickly, gasping, "Rina invited me to the lake, I tried to call you—"

"What the fuck are you talking about?" he screamed, and then pushed me away from him, hard, so that I fell back against the door again and this time it swung open fully, making a loud, scraping noise against the sidewalk. I felt myself tumbling backward, losing balance even before I hit the pavement, my elbows grinding as I tried to catch myself. My face still stung, my dress bunched up at my chest, and then he was suddenly out of the car, standing over me.

"Get up," he said, and behind me I could hear the party, the piano, now with voices singing along. "*Get up!*"

"Rogerson," I said as I struggled to my feet. "Please—"

"Get up!" he yelled, and grabbed me by the arm, yanking me toward him. I tried to duck my head, to turn away, but he was too fast for me. I saw his fist coming and it hit me right over my left eye, sending a flurry of stars and colors across my vision. I slid down, out of his grasp, onto the grass: It was wet and slimy against my bare skin.

I lifted my head and he was standing over me, breathing hard. I knew I should get up before someone saw us but somehow I couldn't move, like those voices—all those voices—were suddenly shaking me awake, pulling me to the surface. It was the first time he'd done it out in the open, not inside the car or a room, and the vastness of everything, fresh air and space, made me pull myself tighter, smaller.

"Goddammit, Caitlin," he said, glancing at the house, then back at me. "*Get up right now.*"

I tried to roll away from him onto my side, in the hopes of getting to my feet, but everything hurt all at once: my face, my fingers, the back of my head, my eye, my arms, my skin itself. Each place he'd ever struck me, like old war wounds on rainy days.

He nudged me with his toe, in the small of my back. "Come on," he said quietly. And I remembered the first time he'd said it, when all this had started, standing by that open door: *Come on.*

"No," I said into the grass, trying to tuck every bit of me in and hide, to sink into the cracks of the sidewalk beneath me.

"Get up," he said again, a bit louder, and now the nudge was hard, more like a kick. I rolled a bit, curling tighter, and closed my eyes. Out in the tent, the song went on to the rousing finish, then a burst of laughter and applause.

"Get up, Caitlin," he said, and I closed my eyes as tight as I could, clenching my teeth, thinking of anything else. Corinna, standing on a cliff in California with the blue, blue water stretched out ahead of her, with even Mexico in sight. Cass in New York, sitting in her window with a million lights spread out behind her. And then, finally me, left behind again. And look what I had become.

I jammed my hand in my jacket pocket, bracing myself for the next hit, and felt something. Something grainy and small, sticking to the tips of my fingers: the sand from Commons Park.

Oh, Cass, I thought. *I miss you so, so much.*

"Caitlin," Rogerson said, and I snapped back to reality as he reached down and yanked at my jacket, trying to pull me up with it. But I just shook it off, letting it slide over my arms and away from me, keeping the sand in my hand. My bare skin was cool, exposed under the streetlight with the white of the dress and the green ivy almost glowing.

I was tired. Worn thin, my springs broken, spokes shattered. I felt old and brittle. I braced myself, waiting for the next kick, the next punch. I didn't care if it was the last thing I ever felt.

"Caitlin," Rogerson said again, and I felt him draw his foot back, readying. "I told you to—"

And that was as far as he got before I heard it. The thumping of footsteps, running up the lawn toward me: It seemed like I could hear it through the grass, like leaning your ear to a railroad track and feeling the train coming, miles away. As the noise got closer I could hear ragged breaths, and then a voice.

It was my mother.

"*Stop it!*" she said, her tone steady and loud. "You stop that *right now.*"

"I didn't—" Rogerson said. And in the distance, suddenly, I could hear sirens. Rogerson stepped back from me: He heard them, too.

"Get away from her," my mother said, crouching down beside me. "You lousy *bastard.* Caitlin. Caitlin, can you hear me?"

"No," I said. "Wait—"

I could feel her smoothing my hair off my face, her own chest heaving against my shoulders. Then, suddenly, she said, "Oh, my God, Caitlin. Oh, my God."

I turned to her, but she wasn't looking at my face. Her mouth was open, horrified, as her eyes traveled over my arms, shoulders, back, and legs. Under the white of the streetlight, my skin was ghostly pale, and each bruise, old and new, seemed dark and black against it. There were so many of them.

Rogerson was backing away now, even as my mother wrapped her arms around me, so gently, sobbing as she tried to find a spot that wasn't hurt. The sirens were coming closer, and I could see blue lights moving across the trees.

The front door slammed and I could hear voices gathering, getting closer. The piano music had stopped. It seemed like *everything* had stopped.

"Margaret?" I heard Boo call out. "What's going on?"

"What's happening out here?" I heard my father say, his voice choppy as he ran through the grass. "Caitlin? Are you all right?"

"It's over now," my mother said, still crying softly as she rocked me back and forth, smoothing my hair. "It's okay, honey. I'm here. It's okay."

"What happened?" my father said, but no one answered him. The police car pulled up and I heard a door slam, a voice garbled and hissing over the radio inside.

I looked up, trying to find Rogerson, but it seemed like the dark had somehow sucked him up and he'd disappeared. I could hear everything that was going on around me: the murmuring of the Fool's Party guests, my father talking to the policeman, Rogerson complaining angrily as the cuffs clicked shut. I could hear the streetlight buzzing and Boo crying onto Stewart's shoulder when she saw the bruises on my skin, the way she whimpered again and again, *I should have known. I should have known.*

And all the while my mother was crouching over me, her voice steady, rocking me back and forth like she had the day Cass had cut my eye, saying everything would be all right. I couldn't even tell her I was sorry.

I was worn out, broken: He had taken almost everything. But he had been all I'd had, all this time. And when the police led him away, I pulled out of the hands of all these loved ones, sobbing, screaming, everything hurting, to try and make him stay.

Me

CHAPTER THIRTEEN

"Caitlin."

I rolled across my pillow, turning away from the broad green hills outside my window. My roommate, Ginger, the bulimic, was standing in the doorway of our room. She had on overalls, her hair in braids, a pencil tucked behind her ear.

"Yeah?" I said.

"You have another visitor," she said, cocking her head toward the other end of the hallway. "Lucky girl."

I got up off the bed, grabbing my sweatjacket off the chair of my desk. As I shrugged it on, Ginger jumped onto her own bed, pulling a rolled-up crossword puzzle magazine out of her back pocket. She slid the pencil out from behind her ear, licked its tip, and flipped a few pages in the magazine until she found her current challenge.

I pulled my hair up in my hands as I started out of our room, up the hallway that was flanked with huge, double-glassed, floor-to-ceiling windows. It was so bright at midday I imagined it must be like what people see in near-death experiences, that long, bright walk that takes you right to God. Here, however, you opened the door at the end to find the visitors' room, where the real world was allowed to peek in every Sunday and Wednesday from three to five.

I'd been at Evergreen Care Center since the day after the Fool's Party. What had happened was a blur, punctuated by flashes of horrific moments: Rogerson's face so dark, yelling at me. My mother, sobbing, as she carefully turned my arms and legs, examining the bruises. And finally, my own screaming, terrible shame as I pulled away from everyone, trying to hold on to the one person who had hurt me the most.

Once the police had taken Rogerson away, my father had carried me inside, where I sat balled up in a kitchen chair, clutching my knees and rocking back and forth. My parents and Boo and Stewart conferred in the other room, made phone calls, and tried to figure out what had happened. Later, I'd find out that it was Mrs. Merchant, from the Ladies Auxiliary, who'd glanced out the front window and seen us. She'd told my mother, then called the police, which effectively broke up the party. All that night, the tent stood empty outside, with pounds of tempeh salad and shelled shrimp rotting away. It was all still there, crackers fanned out on pretty party dishes, punch bowl half-full, surrounded by abandoned glasses and crumpled napkins, when I left the next day.

Rogerson's car was there, too, parked right where he'd left it. Later, someone would come to pick it up. Maybe Dave. But the sight of it, sitting there, scared me all night long, as if he was still sitting in it, waiting for me so that we could replay that night again and again, like a movie where you can't even tell the end from the beginning.

I'd heard of Evergreen Care Center before. Cass and I had always made fun of the stupid ads they ran on TV, featuring some dragged-out woman with a limp perm and big, painted-on circles under her eyes, downing vodka and sobbing uncontrollably. *We can't heal you at Evergreen,* the very somber voiceover said. *But we can help you to heal yourself.* It had become our own running joke, applicable to almost anything.

"Hey, Cass," I'd say, "hand me that toothpaste."

"Caitlin," she'd say, her voice dark and serious. "I can't hand you the toothpaste. But I *can* help you hand the toothpaste to yourself."

Which she would then do, passing it off to me with a pseudo-nurturing squeeze of my hand.

Ha, ha. It didn't seem quite so funny now.

Technically, I was admitted for drugs. This was because my mother had found a small bag of pot and my bowl in my jacket pocket, both of them coated with Commons Park sand. But everyone knew the bruises, Rogerson, what I had let happen to me—was the other reason I was here.

I wasn't able to tell my parents anything in that first twenty-four hours. I couldn't say I was sorry, or explain how I'd let this happen. I just sat in my room while my mother packed up my things, my knees pulled up tight and close to my chest. We left for Evergreen early in the morning, in the rain, and none of us spoke the entire way.

I suddenly realized, in that silent car ride, how long it had been since any of us had mentioned Cass out loud. It was like I'd finally done something to overshadow her completely, but not in the way I wanted to.

We met with the administrator, who checked me in and then took us to my room. My mother made my bed and put away my clothes while my father stood by the window, watching the rain, his hand in his pockets. Then it was time for them to leave.

"I'll be back on Wednesday," my mother told me, pulling me close to her chest. She was still handling me so gingerly, as if I was a piece of china already cracked and a fingertip's weight could break me completely. "I'll bring your blue sweater and some nice shams for this bed. Okay?"

I nodded. My father hugged me and kissed the top of my head, saying, "Hang in there, kiddo. You're a good girl."

I stood in my doorway as they left, my mother dabbing at her eyes and looking back every few steps, as if she wasn't quite sure she could leave without me. When the main door clicked shut behind them, I went back and sat on my bed. Then I started crying. I didn't stop for two days.

I cried in my room and through lunch. During group, individual, and specialized therapy. During crafts and personal time. I cried the entire time I was making huge amounts of potato salad in the kitchen for my chore work, and then I cried all night long under a huge, yellow moon that seemed to take up most of my window. I cried out everything I'd kept in since that summer day Cass had left, becoming a huge, drippy, snotty mess, a tissue permanently balled in my hand, my eyes so puffy I could hardly see.

I cried for Rogerson, and for Cass, and for myself. I cried because I was ashamed and I knew I could never face all of the people from the Fool's Party. I cried because I'd fought with Rina and never had a chance to apologize, and I cried because I was homesick and missed my parents more than I had ever thought possible. I cried because I missed Rogerson, even though I knew that was crazy, and I cried because Corinna was gone, probably all the way to California, and I'd never told her what a good friend she'd been to me. But mostly, I cried because my life had been going full speed for so long and now it had just stopped, like running right into a big brick wall, knocking the wind and the fight right out of me. And I didn't know if I ever even wanted to get up and start breathing again.

Evergreen was bearable. There was a certain peace to it, being so secluded, my day broken up into tiny manageable pieces. I didn't think about getting through the week, or what would happen the next day: I just concentrated on making it through chore detail, or crafts class, or another therapy session. It was easier to take the days in tiny swallows, rather than biting everything off at once. I wasn't sure yet how much I could keep down.

Ginger, who moved in with me after being attacked by her kleptomaniac roommate for using her nail file, said that the thing she hated most about Evergreen was all the talking.

"Group therapy, individual, specialized," she complained to me one day as she tackled another crossword puzzle—her vice—and ignored the tray of food sitting in front of her on the table between us. "I am so sick of myself, I cannot even tell you. It's like I'm some episode of the *Brady Bunch* I've been forced to watch eight hundred times. There's nothing *new* there."

But Ginger had been at Evergreen for almost a year, and she still had to divide her food into tiny little piles—a hierarchy I didn't quite understand involving color and consistency—as well as be monitored so that she did not purge after each meal. As for me, I kind of liked all the talking, at least after the first session.

My doctor, Dr. Marshall, was a short, round woman with wildly frizzy hair who kind of reminded me of Boo. She wore running shoes and jeans and kept a bowlful of Jolly Ranchers on the table in her office. That first day, I ate six of them, one right after the other, and didn't say a word. She sat and watched me. I thought of Cass, that solemn look: *At Evergreen, we can't make you eat Jolly Ranchers. But we can help you to eat them yourself.*

"Just start somewhere," Dr. Marshall had said to me as I ground a banana-pineapple one to bits between my teeth. "It doesn't have to be at the beginning." She'd pulled her legs up, Indian-style, letting the legal pad she'd been holding drop to the floor.

"I thought everything always had to start at the beginning," I said.

"Not in this room," she said easily. "Go ahead, Caitlin. Just tell me one thing. It gets easier, I promise. The first thing you say is always the hardest."

I looked down at my hands, stained mildly red from the particularly sticky watermelon Rancher. "Okay," I said, reaching forward to take another one out of the bowl, just in case. She was already sitting back in her chair, readying herself for whatever glimpse I would give her into the mess I'd become. "What was the name of Pygmalion's sister?"

She blinked, twice, obviously surprised. "Ummm," she said, keeping her eyes on me. "I don't know."

"Rogerson did," I told her. "Rogerson knew everything."

During my second week at Evergreen, my mother brought me my dream journal. She didn't know what it was, or even that Cass had given it to me. She'd just found it when she went to turn my mattress during spring cleaning, with all of my photographs tucked into it. I didn't ask if she'd read it, and she didn't offer if she had or not. After she left, I spread the pictures across the bed in front of me.

I soon realized that the ones of Rogerson—as well as the only one of us together—were missing. I could just see her carefully slipping them out, maybe ripping them to shreds, burning them in the grill among the briquettes. I couldn't really blame her; it was the only way left to protect me. But all the rest were there: Boo with her Buddha; Corinna and Mingus on the porch; Rina and her cigarette; my father watching the last-second shot. And finally, at the bottom of the stack, was one I'd forgotten. It was the last picture I'd taken, and it was of me.

We'd been assigned a self-portrait for our final project in photography: They were to be displayed by our names at the Arts Center exhibit, a way of matching our work to ourselves. I'd taken mine the week before the Fool's Party, in my bedroom. I was standing in front of the mirror, the camera held at my stomach, shooting up to catch my reflection. In the picture you can see my few certificates and pictures circling the mirror, and a slant of light coming through the window behind me. I am wearing a white short-sleeved T-shirt and barely, just barely, you can make out a gray, thumb-shaped spot at the base of my neck. I have my head kind of cocked to the side, and I'm not smiling. In fact, there is no expression at all on my face, just a kind of dead, stoned flatness.

I sat on my bed at Evergreen and looked at that picture for a long, long time. I hated the girl I saw there, and she didn't even care, didn't know, just staring out, oblivious. She'd spent her whole life wanting to be someone else, something else, and it had gotten her nowhere. I wanted to reach through that mirror and shake her, wake her up. But it was too late now.

So I ripped the picture, one long gash crossing her face. Then again, and again, tearing the pieces down until they grew smaller and smaller, tiny bits like the stones of a crazy mosaic. My hands were shaking as I brushed them all up, like tossed confetti, into my hand. I went to throw them in the trash can, but just as I was about to open my hand and let them fall like confetti, something stopped me.

I emptied the pieces of the picture into a small bag, then curled it shut and put it carefully in the front drawer of my desk. Then I went and lay down on my bed, closing my eyes and trying to clear my mind. But still, all I could think about was that girl, torn into tiny fragments, with nothing to do but sit and wait to be made whole again.

If there was one thing that set me apart from everyone else at Evergreen, it wasn't that I'd had a drug problem, or family issues, or that my boyfriend had beaten me. These things were a dime a dozen here, and everyone wore their neurosis like a badge, each carrying a certain weight, the way a particular brand of sweater or jeans had in junior high. There were some with it easier, and many with it worse.

What set me apart, though, were my visitors.

From the first Wednesday I was there until the day I left, someone came to see me each visitor's day. I found out later that this was unique, as well as a source of envy among a lot of the girls on my floor. But my mother, the queen of organization, drew up a schedule, dividing up days just as she had always allotted chores for PTA drives or Junior League functions. Between herself, my father, Boo and Stewart, and Rina, each Wednesday and Sunday, someone was always in the solarium waiting for me.

For the first week, it was my mother. It was hard at first. The minute she saw me she smiled, took a deep breath, and then opened her mouth to talk nonstop for almost twenty minutes, words flowing out of her as if they were the only thing keeping her afloat, a life preserver of inane details and incidents from the last week. She told me about a new doll she'd ordered, how my father had wrenched his shoulder reaching for something in the backseat of the car, how she'd found a perfectly lovely recipe for vanilla custard in *Southern Living*. She did not take a single breath while doing this. Finally, when she sputtered to a stop, the sudden silence hung between us, sucking up the last of her words like a black hole absorbing light.

We both felt it.

"Oh, Caitlin," she said suddenly, sliding one shaking hand over mine. "I just . . . I just don't know how I can ever tell you how sorry I am."

"Sorry?" I said. "For what, Mom?"

She looked at me, eyes widening. "For not protecting you," she said. All this time I'd been the one with everything to hide, everything to be ashamed of. It hadn't even occurred to me that someone else might think to take the blame.

She squeezed my hand, tightly. "I should have known what was happening," she said. "I should have known just by *looking* at you."

Maybe I should have agreed with her. Blamed her, even, for being so caught up in Cass's leaving that she'd allowed me to become invisible. But I'd had my chances to reach out to her as well, chances I'd passed up again and again. The night of the ceremony, when I'd come home with my face swollen and blamed it on an elbow. Or when I "slipped" on the icy walk. And even on that last day, when she'd tried to pull my jacket off of me.

But of course *now* it was simple to trace back and find so many places each of us could have done better. But after my two-day crying jag, I just wasn't interested in blaming anyone else. I needed my family and friends now, and sometimes, calling a draw seemed like the way to finally let it rest.

It got easier after that. We talked a little more each time, but it came slowly. Mostly, we walked, following the long footpaths that crisscrossed the Evergreen complex. We'd move slowly with her arm linked tightly in mine, winding around trees and benches, through the parking lot, circling the fountain, and back again. Sometimes, we didn't talk at all. But every once in a while she'd say something completely random out loud, as if she'd been carrying on a conversation in her head the whole time, that I was just now able to hear.

"I remember when I was pregnant with you," she said one day as we crossed the little footbridge, "and your sister would come up to me at the same time every day, while I was making dinner, and just put her ear against my stomach. She said you talked to her, that she was the only one who could hear you."

Or, as we sat by the fountain: "The night you fell off that pyramid, Caitlin . . . I didn't think anything could ever scare me that much again." She looked down at the water, gurgling beside us. "But I was wrong, of course."

I didn't know what to say to these things, and I was learning with Dr. Marshall that I didn't necessarily have to have an answer. So I'd just put my head on her shoulder, leaning against my mother, who would hold me like she did when I was a small child, rocking me back and forth. It had been so long since someone had touched me and I hadn't wanted to flinch.

As time went on, we talked about less important things. We traded stupid family anecdotes, like the time when Cass almost burned down the house with her Easy-Bake Oven, or when my father drank a huge glass of clam juice, thinking it was lemonade. We laughed ourselves silly, taking back our shared past gently, piece by piece.

My mother always came on Sunday, but Wednesdays were my wild card. It was kind of like a game: I never knew exactly who to expect at the end of that long, brightly lit hallway. I just pulled open the door and scanned the people waiting on the shiny vinyl couches and slippery easy chairs, flipping through out-of-date magazines, until I saw a face I recognized.

If it was my father, he always brought the book with him. He'd brought it the first day he came, when he'd stopped at Wal-Mart to pick up a new pack of socks my mother had forgotten to bring me the week before. The book was called *100 Fun Card Games* and had been hanging by the register, with a pack of cards shrink-wrapped to it. My father was not the impulsive type, but I figured he'd been nervous about coming to see me, about what we would say to each other. Games would make it easier.

After he'd hugged me, and I'd sat down on the couch beside him and received my socks, he slid the book across the cushion to me. "If you're not interested, that's completely fine," he said. "I just thought it might be fun."

CRAZY EIGHTS! HEARTS! CUTTHROAT! SIX DIFFERENT KINDS OF SOLITAIRE! the book proclaimed excitedly on the back cover, and then, in small letters, FUN FOR THE WHOLE FAMILY!

I looked up at my father, knowing how helpless he must feel, not being in control of this—my—situation. He'd done all the Dad stuff so far: making the arrangements, dealing with the insurance company, explaining to the D.A. that no, I wouldn't be available to testify against Rogerson when his court date came up. He was the ultimate facilitator, but this emotional thing, with the two of us one-on-one, was new to him.

"Sounds great," I said to him, ripping open the pack and handing him the book. "Let's start with the first one."

So we did. Each day he came to visit I'd find him waiting for me at one of the small tables by the window, the book beside him, cards shuffled. We had started with Crazy Eights, worked through Spit and War, and had just begun Gin Rummy. We were O'Korens, of course, so we kept score and played for points as well as pride. But sometimes, I'd look up from my cards and find him watching me with an expression of such sadness on his face that it almost broke my heart.

The first day Boo came, she brought a stack of my photographs and a bagful of vegan carob-chip cookies, which I ate as she regaled me with stories from our photography class exhibition at the Arts Center.

"Your mother won a special award," she told me, "because everyone had a head in her pictures. We all applauded."

"I can't believe I missed it," I said. During my two-day weeping binge, I'd even cried about that: I'd worked so hard for that exhibition. During the last few weeks with Rogerson, it was the one thing that had kept me going. Now, no one would ever get to see all the hard work I'd done.

She brushed cookie crumbs off her hands. "I brought you something else, too," she said, digging into her huge giraffe-printed bag to pull out something wrapped in bright blue cloth, placing it gingerly in my lap. "No pressure," she said. "Just if you get inspired."

I knew even before I was done unwrapping the cloth that it was my camera. She'd polished it, replaced my ratty lens cap, and included five rolls of film. Everything I needed.

"I don't know," I said. Seeing my camera made the past six months come rushing back: the solace I'd sought in the darkroom. Corinna smiling at me as I took shot after shot on the front porch. Rogerson glowering against that gray sky. And that picture that I'd shredded, its ripped pieces still sitting in my desk drawer.

"No pressure," she said again. "Just wait and see."

Stewart and Rina came to visit me also. Stewart told me stories about his wild days and always brought me something wonderful to eat: fresh mangoes, Fakin' Bacon and scrambled tofu, still warm.

The first time Rina came to visit me, I walked into the solarium to find her sitting on a folding chair, nervously swinging one crossed leg across the other. She was in cutoff jeans and a tank top, attracting the wistful stares of Robert, the depressive, and Alan, who had a little problem with fires, who were playing Parcheesi a few tables over.

"Hey," she said as I came over, sitting down beside her.

"Hey."

She swallowed, hard, then blurted out, "I understand if you hate me. I almost didn't even come here today."

"Rina," I said. "Why would I hate you?"

She looked at me. "I didn't know that's why you wanted to leave that night at the lake. If I'd known—"

"No one knew," I said. Again, this was easier. Another draw. "It's nobody's fault."

"Like hell. We all know whose fault it is." She shook her head, angry now: Rina loved a cause. "That bastard. If he shows his face anywhere near me, I swear to God I'll . . ."

I took a deep breath. There was still some small part of me that missed Rogerson, as crazy as that was. "Let's not talk about him, okay?" I said. When she glanced at me I added, "I mean, I do a lot of that in here already. You know?"

She sighed, still huffy, and nodded her head. "Okay. Fine. What do you want to talk about?"

I pulled my legs up underneath me. "Anything. Gossip. Dirt. Fill me in."

She grinned, raising her eyebrows. "Cheerleading or general?"

"Both."

"Okay," she said, dropping her purse, kicking off her sandals, and getting comfortable. My best friend, Rina. I hadn't even realized how much I'd missed her. "Listen to *this*."

Some days were good. I'd make a decent lanyard in crafts, perfect the mayonnaise-relish ratio for the potato salad in the group kitchen, beat my father at Rummy, and sleep thickly through the night and wake up feeling rested, changed, like things were actually getting better.

But other days I thought about Rogerson, wondering where he was or what he was doing. I kept the necklace he'd given me in its box, buried in my bottom drawer. It was the one thing I had left of him, and sometimes I'd just pull it out and hold it, sliding it through my fingers. I wondered if he ever thought of me, and hated the pang I felt when I told myself he didn't.

I wouldn't blame my parents, or Rina. I was even getting that much closer to not blaming myself. So it should have been easy to finally lift that heaviest of weights and place it squarely where it belonged, on Rogerson. But this, even on the good days, was hard.

After all that had happened, how could I miss him? But I did. I did.

Chapter Fourteen

I'd been at Evergreen less than a month when my mother brought me a pile of mail from home. A flier about the SATs, a stack of homework assignments from school, a catalog from a cheerleading supply company, trying to sell me barrettes with my school colors. And, at the bottom, two letters. One from Corinna, one from Cass.

"She's been worried about you," my mother said as I turned the envelope, addressed in Cass's clean script, in my hand. "I don't know who the other one is from."

I waited until she was gone before I went to that bright hallway, sat down with my back to one of the windows, and opened Corinna's letter first. I'd never seen her handwriting before, the letters small and curly, like a child's hand. She'd written in purple ink, on hotel stationery: The Red Rambler Inn, Tucson, Arizona.

Dear Caitlin,

By now, I guess you know that I decided to make my wild escape from both Applebee's and David. It was easier than I thought it would be. Between the power always getting turned off and our constant diet of Ramen noodles, things were getting less and less romantic. I do miss him, though. I've thought about him a lot on this long drive, and about you too. I hope you don't think I'm a bad friend for not telling you I was go-

ing. I just didn't want to leave you with a bunch of questions to answer.

You were a good friend to me, Caitlin. Without the good times we had I don't think I would have even made it to the spring.

My little car is still holding up, although things got a bit touch and go there in Tennessee. I've still got my eye on California, but Arizona and New Mexico have been interesting. There's something peaceful here, like that time of night at home in the spring and summer, when the days get long and it seems like it's twilite forever. It's like that all the time, here. I know you understand what I mean.

When I get to California I'm going to have my picture taken standing on some big cliff, with the ocean behind me. I'll send one to you.

I miss you a lot, and I hope you're not mad at me. When I land someplace for good, I'll send an address.

With much love, always,

Corinna

I folded the letter carefully, sliding it into its envelope. I could just see her trucking along in the Bug, nursing it through radiator problems and its popping muffler, with California in her sights. I was still wearing her bracelets: They were the one thing I'd had on Fool's night that I wanted to keep, and I never took them off, not even in the shower. Whenever I missed her, all I had to do was lift my hand and listen as they fell.

Cass's letter was harder. I didn't open it up that day, or the next. It sat on my desk, all by itself, and when I was alone in the room I made my bed over and over again, or straightened my sock drawer, glancing at it every few seconds. It was the first thing I saw when I walked into the room, and more than once I almost just ripped it into pieces.

"What are you afraid of?" Dr. Marshall asked me as I chewed Jolly Ranchers and glowered out the window. "What do you think she'll say?"

"I don't know," I said, and this was the truth. "Probably the same thing everyone's said: That what happened to me was somehow her fault, that she feels responsible."

"Would that be bad?"

I grabbed another Rancher, ripping off the plastic wrapper. "Yes. Because I'm tired of that. Everyone can stop feeling guilty now, okay? It's not *helping* me."

Dr. Marshall considered this, studying her hands.

"But what bugs me most," I added, "is what she's probably thinking."

"Which is . . ." Dr. Marshall said, sticking her pen behind her ear, ". . . what?"

I pulled my knees up to my chest—defensive stance, as they called it in group. "It's just that I've always been the weaker one, the less talented. The perennial second-place also-ran. The more likely to screw up. And now, with this, I've, like, totally proved it. To her, and to everyone."

"Caitlin," she said, taking her own Rancher out of the bowl and laying it on the arm of her chair, "we've discussed quite a bit that being a victim does not make you weak."

"I know," I said. This, too, though, was hard to learn.

"And from what you've told me about your sister, she doesn't sound like the kind of person who would judge you that way."

"Of course not," I snapped. "She doesn't judge anyone. She doesn't do anything wrong. She's perfect in every way."

Dr. Marshall raised her eyebrows, then picked up the Rancher on her chair and unwrapped it, not saying anything. The crinkling of plastic seemed to go on forever, with neither of us talking.

"Perfect people," she finally said, "live in picket-fenced houses with golden retrievers and beautiful children. They always smell like fresh flowers and never step in dog doo, or bounce checks, or cry."

I rolled my eyes at her, cracking my Rancher in my mouth.

"They also," she went on, "don't run away with no explanation. They don't leave their families with questions that aren't answered, and make their parents worry, and leave their younger sister to try and hold everything together."

I swallowed, hard, and looked out the window again.

"Your sister's not perfect, Caitlin. In fact, I'm willing to bet that if you take time to think about it, you might find you have more in common right now than you ever thought possible."

Since our first session, Dr. Marshall had been trying to convince me that things weren't my fault. That Cass leaving had led me scrambling to fill her place for my parents, which was impossible because I was me, not her, so instead I'd tried to be everything she *wasn't,* which led me right to Rogerson. She'd told me it was all right to be mad at Cass. That it didn't make me a bad sister any more than her leaving—and leaving me to deal with her absence—made her one.

So now I thought about Cass, and all the reasons she might have had to do what *she* did. Maybe they were the same ones that Corinna had as she stood by the highway in Tennessee, coaxing her little Bug to take her that much closer to the West Coast. Dreams, and plans, and a stark desire to change your life, all on your own. I wanted that too, but I didn't want to have to run away to do it.

After my session, I went back to my room, where Ginger was just leaving for crafts class. We'd done macaroni mosaics the week before, and were just about to jump full-throttle into clay sculpting. Ginger had been through this before, and had two lumpy, lopsided ashtrays she kept on her part of the windowsill to show for it.

"You coming?" she asked me. "I heard we can make bird feeders this year. Big rehab fun!"

"I'll be there in a minute," I told her. "Save me a seat, okay?"

She nodded, shutting the door behind her, and I went to my desk and picked up Cass's letter, feeling its small weight in my hand. Then I put it back on the desk. Picked it up again.

Stupid, I thought. *It's Cass, Caitlin. Just open it.*

The letter was folded neatly, and fell into my hand when I ripped the envelope open. Cass's careful script filled line after line, my name written big at the very top of the page.

Caitlin,

I don't even know where to start this letter. But if there's one thing I've learned in the last few months, it's that sometimes you just have to close your eyes and jump. So here goes.

I haven't been really proud of myself this year, with everything that's happened. But I don't regret leaving, or making the choice I did. Maybe you'll never understand this, but in a way it was a relief to know when I walked out that door that I was letting everyone down. I'd spent so much of my life working hard to make Mom and Dad happy, to be what everyone thought I should be. Coming here was like starting from scratch, and scary as it is sometimes, I like it.

I've been thinking a lot the last few days about that time when we were kids and I cut your face with that stupid shovel. Remember? I think you know I always cringe when I look at that scar over your eyebrow, blaming myself for something I can't change. It's funny. I don't even remember doing it.

Do you remember how Stewart and Boo took care of us that time that Aunt Liz died? (You might not—you were only about four or five.) I remember Mom had bought us a bunch of new toys to keep us out of their hair: a Play-Doh factory, books, puzzles, new Barbies for each of us. I was running around playing with everything at once, ripping open boxes and half-assembling puzzles before losing interest and moving on to the next thing. I remember that Stewart was exhausted, trying to keep up with me, and finally—I remember this so well, it's like it is burned in my mind—he sighed, so tired, and glanced over at you, so I did too. And there you were, sitting quietly on the rug with your Barbie in your lap, quietly concentrating on reading a book. You were just so still, and focused, and I remember that was the first time I envied you that, too.

You used to tell me—jokingly—that you hated me for being "perfect." But it wasn't easy, Caitlin, to always have Mom and Dad's expectations weighing so heavily. You were always able to make your choices based on you and what you wanted, nothing else. And as this summer ended, I realized that Yale was the last place I'd be able to do that. Up here, away from everyone's notions, I can be whatever I want. And that's crucial to me now.

I've been crying off and on ever since I heard what happened to you. From that day at Boo and Stewart's to right now, you've always been able to make your own choices: some good, some bad. But they're yours. And during this time we've been apart, it's you I've thought of when I'm at my weakest, and you who have pulled me through.

Please write me back if—or when—you're ready. And always remember how much your crazy sister loves you.

Cass

I read the letter three times before I folded it and stuck it in my desk drawer. Then I reached over it, farther back, my fingers exploring until they pulled out the tiny plastic bag where I'd put the pieces of my own picture after I'd ripped it up. I shut the drawer, and dumped the bag out onto the smooth surface of my desk.

It was strange, but I didn't remember that day at Stewart's. It's funny how someone's perception of you can be formed without you even knowing it. All along, my sister had been able to make out her vision of my present, and future. I only wished she'd once turned my head and made me see it as well.

The ripped pieces of the photograph were small, but I could still catch a bit of my skin here, or a slice of background, there. I spent a few minutes turning them all right side up, like the way you start a jigsaw puzzle, getting everything in order. Then I picked out a corner piece, smoothing its edges, and taped it carefully to the back cardboard cover of one of Ginger's discarded crossword books.

I can be whatever I want, and that's crucial to me now. I found another corner piece, this one the opposite diagonal, fastening it the same way.

It's you I've thought of when I'm at my weakest, and you who have pulled me through. The third corner was the biggest piece yet, almost an inch long.

Remember how much your crazy sister loves you. I found the last corner, taping it in place, then sat back and looked at my work. Four edges, like the face of a picture frame waiting to be filled in. I scooped the rest of the pieces back into the bag. I'd do the rest of the puzzle bit by bit, day by day. I'd take my time, being patient, and watch the images as they came into being right before my eyes.

Dr. Marshall said I shouldn't expect to forget anything about Rogerson, and in a lot of ways I didn't want to. At night, when I dreamed, it was his face I saw more than any other. Sometimes he was just out on the fringes of some complicated dream, leaning against the BMW, like he'd waited for me outside of cheerleading practice all those afternoons. Other times it was only him, his face right up close to mine, angry and red, ready to lash out at any second. Those were the dreams I woke up from sweating, the covers tangled around my legs, my hair damp and sticking to the back of my neck, panicked at not recognizing the room around me. Ginger was always sleeping soundly in the next bed, breathing through her nose in tiny gasps, and I'd close my eyes and concentrate on that sound until I fell back asleep.

But, strangely, the worst dreams I had about Rogerson were the ones he wasn't in at all. Instead, I was always trying to get someplace to meet him, with so many obstacles thrown in my way. Sometimes they made sense, like pushing through body after body in the hallway, running for the turnaround. Other times it was more surreal: my legs just wouldn't work, there was some long, involved sub-dream involving a baby who wasn't really a baby, or I had to make sandwiches but couldn't find any bread. They would have been funny, these dreams, except for the ongoing, steady sense of panic that I felt, knowing he was waiting for me. It built like a fist closing around my neck and I'd shake myself awake, heart beating, only to doze back off and pick up in the same place, again.

Dr. Marshall said this was a way for me to work out my issues with Rogerson, to fight through them even as I did the same thing in her office over endless Jolly Ranchers. And I had told her everything: about the trivia, and the drugs. About how he'd taken me away from that party, how sometimes still I felt this tiny soaring of my heart, so misplaced, when I thought of him.

"It's not a switch you can just flip off," Dr. Marshall had told me once. "If you didn't love him, this never would have happened. But you did. And accepting that love—and everything that followed it—is part of letting it go."

I was trying.

I knew, also, I had to accept that girl in the picture who I was slowly piecing together each day. The girl with the stoned eyes, and the fading and fresh bruises, who had kept silent, drowning, by choice. It hurt me to even think of her. But she was part of me, as big a part as what I'd been before her and what I was now trying to become. I wasn't trying to be the girl I'd been with Rogerson, or even the girl before that. I was thinking further back, to the one who sat on Stewart's rug, so focused, who was able to just be alone, at peace, and still.

There were so many places in my time with Rogerson that I wished I could go back to, hitting the stop button at just one moment to stop everything that came after. I had so many If Onlys: If Only I'd stayed with Mike Evans, or If Only I hadn't been allowed to leave with Rogerson on that first date, or If Only I'd told my parents, or anyone, the first time he hit me. But each place I thought to stop meant missing something that came later, like Corinna, all my photographs, even this time at Evergreen that was helping me find that bit of peace again. I needed it all, in the end, to make my own story find its finish.

Sometimes, I only reached as far back as that day so recently when we'd sat at McDonald's. The sky had been so blue, the breeze mild, and I could remember perfectly how I'd looked at him and wondered if, in another life, things might have been all right in the end.

Rogerson, I'd called out, to ask him what an eon was—a billion years. He'd lifted his head up, feeling that breeze too, and smiled at me.

Rogerson. I sometimes still called it out, late at night, even though I knew he couldn't answer me.

Finally I was making some real progress. With every Jolly Rancher–filled trip to Dr. Marshall's, every stupid craft project I completed (one lopsided ashtray, a passable bird feeder, two lanyards, and an impressive bead necklace), and each visitors' day, I added another piece to both of the girls I was rebuilding.

I tried to write Cass back several times, but I just couldn't figure out where to start. I pulled out my dream journal and reread all I'd written there to her, when the words came easy. And I crumpled up page after page of notebook paper before finally giving up altogether. Maybe I just wasn't ready to tell that story, even to her, since I didn't know yet how it ended.

I'd finally loaded my camera and tentatively taken a few pictures, just objects and still lifes, no faces yet. Boo developed them for me at the Arts Center and brought them to me when she visited. We'd sit in the good, bright light of the solarium, critiquing technique and squinting over contact sheets. I liked the solidness of objects: the cracked concrete inside the scoop of the fountain, the bright hallway leading up to a flat black door, the blurry view of the trees through the square blocks of thick glass bordering the cafeteria.

My mother and I took longer walks, talking about everything. My childhood, hers, how much we missed Cass and how her leaving changed both of us, for good. I began to see her more as a person, a woman, not just the queen of bake sales and lemon puffs. And when I was finally ready to take a picture of a face, it was hers I chose, sitting on the green grass on a blanket where we'd just finished a picnic of grapes and chocolate chips. She had her legs crossed, shoes off, her hair blowing in the mild near-summer wind, and she was laughing, her head thrown back, eyes squinting shut, one hand blurry as it moved up to cover her mouth.

My father and I had worked our way through a vicious round of Rummy and now were into Hearts, for which we recruited two guys from my floor—a former heroin addict and an obsessive-compulsive, who played for cigarettes while we played for money. My father and I, as a team, were practically unbeatable. I took his picture, too, his brow furrowed intently as he contemplated his cards, with the obsessive-compulsive blurred in the back frame, a cigarette curling smoke out of his hand. The last game in the book was Five Card Draw, but I hoped I'd be home before we got to it.

And finally, when Rina came, I got to just be a high school girl again, forgetting the hospital and therapy and all the talking I was constantly doing about My Issues. She brought *Cosmo* and bags of chocolate and a tiny radio she smuggled in and kept turned down low. We'd go outside to the grass and spread a blanket, then give ourselves manicures while she caught me up on all the gossip about cheerleading and school and Jeff (who was on again, at least until her newest interest—a foreign exchange student/basketball standout named Helmut—began to heat up).

She'd heard a little bit about Rogerson, here and there. His lawyer had brokered a deal for the charges against him for hitting me, so he was spending the weekends in jail and doing a lot of community service at the animal shelter, cleaning out cages. Apparently he was staying with Dave and Mingus at the little yellow house and keeping a low profile. She'd bumped into him at the Quik Zip one night and he'd brushed right past, not even looking her in the eye.

I knew I might see him again, but Dr. Marshall kept telling me that I was safe, and would be safe. Even after I left Evergreen I'd have what she called "a system of checks and balances"—group therapy once a week and therapy with my parents as well as without them, for at least the next year—to make sure I didn't get in over my head again. This was reassuring, but the thought of starting over for real was a little scary, still. The fall before, everyone at school had talked about Cass. Now it would be me. And it wouldn't be easy. But I had my family, my checks and balances. And what I'd been through already had been much, much worse.

Sometimes I thought about what would happen when I finally did see Rogerson. Did I think he would hit me? No. I'd slipped too far from him now. But I imagined all kinds of possibilities: We bumped into each other at the Quik Zip, at a party, or just passed on the street. In some of these scenarios, he was angry with me, or so nice that I felt my strength wavering, if only slightly. In others, he passed right by me, as if I didn't exist and never had, and that hurt the most. But I made myself see it, again and again, so I'd be prepared. No matter what happened.

I'd spent so many months feeling like I was underwater, half in dreamland with those mermaids, hearing all the voices from up above. And since I'd been at Evergreen I felt like I'd been swimming so hard, the water growing warmer and warmer the closer I got to the top. I wasn't there yet, but now I could see the surface, rippling just beyond my fingers.

And every time I got scared, I pulled out that picture I was still assembling and took a long look at it. The top half was almost done, with the bottom filled in here and there: you could see the dark of my hair, one eye, a bit of nose, the shape of my neck. And when it was done, I planned to hang it, patchworked and pieced together, on my wall at home. I'd put it with every other one I'd collected, including that girl, finally, with all the faces of the people I loved.

Chapter Fifteen

"Caitlin?" my mother asked, turning around in front of my stripped bed and hoisting my bag over my shoulder.

I was looking out the window, over the fountain, taking in the tiny square of the world that had been my view for the last few months. "Yes?"

"Are you ready to go?"

"Almost," I said. I had just about everything I needed. My lopsided ashtray, my bird feeder, and all my pictures: me and Ginger, Dr. Marshall with a mouthful of Jolly Ranchers, and the one I'd pieced together, the crazy mosaic, stuck in my dream journal which I held against my chest. "I'll meet you outside."

She smiled, nodding, and went out the door. I could hear her heels clacking down that long hallway, into the light, as I slipped my camera out of the bag on my shoulder and popped off the lens cap.

The sun was streaming in the window, bright, as I stepped up to my mirror and lifted the camera to my face, adjusting the focus until I could see myself clearly. I looked so different from the day I'd arrived. I'd gained weight, my hair was longer, my skin clear. I was wearing a red, short-sleeved T-shirt and my arms were tan from all those outside walks, clean and unbruised, like any other girl's.

I lowered the camera to my waist, tilting it upward. Then I put my finger on the shutter, swallowed, and smiled at the girl in the mirror. She smiled back, her head cocked to the side, and I knew she understood it all: trivia, time, our shared sandbox history, Cass, cheerleading, Rogerson, everything. So I kept my eyes on hers, steady, as I pressed down on the button, catching this final face for my collection. Click.

Boo and Stewart had invited us over for a dinner to celebrate my first night home, so at twilight my parents and I walked across the damp grass and over the small hill separating our yards to their backyard. Inside the sliding glass door, the kitchen and living room were dark.

I stopped and peered in, then raised one hand to knock. But my father, from over my shoulder, said, "Go on in."

I slid the door open and stepped inside, immediately recognizing the smells: Boo's damp ferns, the faint odor of turpentine, sandalwood incense still hanging in the air. Ahead of me the kitchen was totally empty, with shapes I couldn't quite make out on the walls.

"Hello?" I called out, as I moved into the living room, stepping closer to one wall where I could just barely see something hanging. As I leaned in closer, squinting, I saw it was a photograph.

It was, in fact, one of mine. The first one, of the old woman in the supermarket, eyes closed as she breathed in that cold, cold air. It had been enlarged and hung square on the wall, the first in a long line of identical frames.

"What is this?" I said, and suddenly the lights clicked, making me squint.

"Surprise!" a chorus of voices chanted, and I turned around to see everyone—my mother, father, Boo and Stewart, Rina—all standing in the kitchen, smiling and clapping their hands.

"I hope you don't mind," Boo said, walking over and putting her arm around my waist. "But I knew how sad you were to miss the exhibition. And these pictures—they deserve to be seen, Caitlin. They're wonderful."

I turned around, looking back at the living room, where my pictures lined the walls, each one framed, each one perfect. All my faces, all my objects. All of my world, laid out for everyone to see.

I turned back to my family, standing together, watching me as their own faces stared back at them. And I closed my eyes, just for a second, and felt myself swimming, harder, pulling myself up to the surface so close above.

Caitlin! they'd yelled at me as I ran across the gym at the first pep rally, before everything began.

Caitlin, Rogerson had said when we met at the car wash, that cold night under the stars.

Caitlin, Corinna had giggled to me a thousand times as we sat on her couch, watching game shows.

Caitlin, my mother had whispered that night on the sidewalk, cradling me under the streetlight.

Caitlin, I'd said aloud as I placed the last piece of my picture together, recognizing the face I saw there.

They were the voices I'd heard all year as I fell deeper, tangled with mermaids at the cool bottom of the ocean. But it was my own voice, or close to it, that I heard next.

"Caitlin?"

I was still swimming up, higher and higher, pulled by the sound. But I wouldn't drown. I could already see the sky, iridescent and just beyond the water above me. And farther on, much farther, was dreamland. But for now, I wanted only to stay between them, floating on all that blue at last.

"Caitlin?"

I opened my eyes just as my mother moved aside, one hand covering her mouth, and my sister Cass stepped forward. I would have known that face anywhere.

"Caitlin," she said again, and she stepped toward me, her eyes already moving to find my scar and claim it. I didn't know what to say to her just yet, but I knew I had a story to tell now, that was mine, hers, and ours. But for that one instant, I concentrated on reaching the surface, feeling the water break across my face as I burst through it into the air to finally breathe on my own.